LINES OF DECEPTION

Lines of Deception

Book Four of
the Kaspar Brothers Series

Steve Anderson

OPEN ROAD

INTEGRATED MEDIA
NEW YORK

ISBN: 978-1-5040-8613-4

Published in 2024 by Open Road Integrated Media, Inc.
180 Maiden Lane
New York, NY 10038
www.openroadmedia.com

LINES OF DECEPTION

MUNICH
Tuesday, May 17, 1949
12:01 a.m.

Max Kaspar learned about his brother, Harry, from the little man who brought him the severed ear. The nasty fellow even had the gall to bring it to the Kuckoo Nightclub, keeping it in a small purple box on his table along the wall.

Up on the club's small stage, Max had just finished belting out a recent jump blues hit from the States, "Good Rockin' Tonight," everybody clapping along. He flubbed a couple lines but his few fellow Germans had no idea and the Americans were too drunk to care.

The little man never clapped along. He'd just stared at Max. Max used to be fairly certain that a man watching like that was either a talent agent or a producer. But that was before Total War, before fire bombings, and concentration camps, stranded orphans, souls scarred for life. Before his own rehabilitation.

As the applause died, Max kept the man in a corner of his eye. Small head on narrow shoulders, an outdated curly greased mustache, and a frenzied glare like Peter Lorre, his eyes bulging, never blinking.

Max forced out a grin. "Thank you, folks, *meine Damen und Herren*," he said in that mix of English and German everyone used to please both occupier and occupied.

Then he pulled their young waitress Eva onto the stage.

Eva gasped. "Now, Herr Kaspar?" Between them, they embraced speaking their native German.

"You said you want a chance, my dear, so now's your shot," Max told her.

Eva beamed at him. Their four-piece band made anyone sound good since they had a hepcat GI playing drums and another on piano, a former Swing Kid from Cologne on the horn, and a steady old *Kabarett* veteran on bass. Eva's dimples and curves and sweet voice did the rest. She launched into a rousing version of "Slow Boat to China" festooned by her thick accent and the crowd cheered her on.

Not bad for a Tuesday. But Max was creating diversions. He'd needed to surveil the man, which meant throwing him off. He made for the bar. Then he disappeared into the kitchen and went down into the cellar, passing under the dance floor and tables above.

What could the little man want? He threatened to throw Max's shaky world spinning out of kilter. The day had started like any other here in Schwabing, that Munich quarter once home to pioneering artists, then to a small-handed, fatheaded blowhard named Adolf, and now to free-spending American occupiers. Max had peacetime, normalcy, a cozy routine. Fresh white bread from his American friends, toasted, with real butter and orange marmalade. Real coffee. He was finally forgetting what ersatz coffee tasted like, thank god or whoever was responsible. He'd arrived early at the club like usual, before noon, before anyone. Drank another real coffee. He went through the ledgers and checked the earnings stacked in the cellar safe, if only to confirm all truly was well and normal. Then he wandered the Kuckoo, his Kuckoo, wincing at the few dirty ashtrays and beer glasses left out from the previous night. He rolled up his sleeves, emptied the ashes and cleared the glasses, and wiped things down. His staff could do this, but a little chore always gave him something like peace of mind. A part of him was even hoping that Eva would arrive early and see him doing it. He went through his mail, finding the usual inquiries from bands and singers, and bills he had no problem paying now, at last. The occasional letter came from *Mutti* und *Vati* in America. But, still nothing from his brother, Harry, here in Europe. The void of letters, postcards, or even a surprise visit had been growing, swelling, prickling at him low in his gut. Just this morning, Max had gotten that creeping feeling he knew from combat: Things were all too quiet.

Down in the Kuckoo cellar, Max now felt a shudder, deep in his chest, and the normalcy dwindled as only a memory, a fog. An opened bottle of American rye stood atop the safe and he thought about taking a shot for courage, then decided he didn't need it. He needed to move.

He came back upstairs on the other side, behind their red curtain at the back of the stage. He eyed the little man closer from the shadows while Eva gave it all she had. The man was now watching the bar, craning his compact noodle for any sight of Max. That purple box stood in equal proportion to his short neat glass of Fernet, to his fresh pack of Chesterfields, to his sterling jeweled lighter, his gnarled knuckles revealing him to be older than his shiny face let on.

Why show off, Max thought, *when any secure communication would do?* This peacock was certainly not CIA. The Munich desk was more likely to send some new kid with a crew cut.

Eva was bowing now, the crowd whooping and stomping. As if sensing Max, the man slowly swiveled Max's way, still not blinking.

Max rushed out along the wall and sat down next to the man. They waited for the crowd to quiet, silent like two passengers aboard an airliner off to a rocky start.

"Good evening, Herr Kaspar," the man said in German, his accent as inscrutable as Max expected. "I enjoyed your routine."

"It's not a routine," Max blurted, sounding more annoyed than he'd wanted.

The man smirked, which released a sniffle. "You did not know all the words, yes? Tricky, keeping up with these Americans."

"What in the devil do you want?"

His waiter came over, Gerd. Max sent poor Gerd away with a snap of fingers.

The little man lost the smirk. He slid the small purple box over to Max.

It was larger than a ring box, smaller than for a necklace. Max pushed the box open with his index finger. He saw one human ear, lying on its side, with a neat cut and cleaned up.

"Harry Kaspar," the man said. "Perhaps he hears too much."

"My brother?" Max's head spun. Everything blurred and he shut his eyes a moment. "Just tell me what you want."

"Harry Kaspar is your brother, yes?"

The man had said *brother* like a curse word. Hot pressure filled Max's chest, and he wiped away the sweat instantly sopping his eyebrows. He grabbed the man by the collar. He could smell the man's toilet water, and possibly a bad tooth. "Why, you . . ." he roared.

"Now, now. Listen. You will find instructions with the ear, which I leave with you. You deliver the ransom soon? Perhaps the ear can be reattached, yes?"

Max had to assume it was Harry's ear. He realized he didn't know what his brother's ear looked like, not exactly, and the thought made his heart squeeze a little. He let go of the man.

"Why Harry?" he asked.

"I told you: He hears too much. But I suppose it could've been an eye—"

"Listen to me. You don't know who you're playing with. Harry's an American."

The man gave the slightest shrug. "Naturalized American. Unlike you. Still a lowly German . . ." He gave a *tsk-tsk* sound. "But with means now, I see."

Max's jaw clenched from loathing. "Who are you? I thought kidnappers were supposed to be anonymous."

The man pressed a hand to his chest. "Oh, we're better than kidnappers. And we're confident that you will comply. Because Harry told us that you would pay."

"He did? Why?"

The man smiled. "I don't think he wanted his embassy involved, and certainly not the Soviets."

"The Soviets? Hold on. Where did you come from anyway?"

The man gave another slight shrug. He nodded at the box. He scooped up his Chesterfields and lighter, stood, straightened his black crushed velvet blazer, blinked around the room, and left.

Harry smoked Chesterfields, Max recalled, and the thought stiffened his neck with worry. The ear box remained on the table. He pulled it closer, glanced around for privacy, and then opened it again. Tucked up into the lid was a note, typed on a small white square of paper:

Ransom: $1,000 or equivalent.

Come alone. No tricks.

9 Lessinggasse, Vienna

VIENNA
Wednesday, May 18
5:17 p.m.

As his train rolled into the grand old Austrian city, Max perched on the edge of his compartment seat. He hugged his leather bag and had a thermos slung on one shoulder. Early that morning—far too early for a showman—he'd removed nearly $1,000 worth of dollars and deutsche marks from the cellar safe of the Kuckoo and covered the remainder from his own stash. Before leaving, he'd quickly compared the severed ear in its box with the few photos he had of Harry. Ever since Harry had returned to Germany in 1945, mounting responsibility had aged Max's younger brother, sharpening the soft lines of his face. All that seriousness still offered a casual American confidence, though, especially in the sparkle of his eyes. Harry always seemed more American than German—he had emigrated with their parents to the US at an age young enough to sound American. Max's English, on the other hand, would always betray him if tested. And in a move both stupid and luckless, Max had returned to Nazi Germany right before the war. His brother Harry only returned in the harsh aftermath, as a US Army captain in the

8

occupation force. Harry had saved Max from descending into despair and made normalcy possible. With all his experience acting and singing, Max finally had decent prospects again. The Kuckoo was his lifeline. He was host, emcee, and manager and now owned a solid stake.

It had taken him four years to get to this point. The last thing he should want was to risk it all. But if he didn't find Harry, he might as well throw all that away.

The cold metal of the thermos against Max's ribs cooled the heat in his chest. Back at the Kuckoo he'd filled it with ice and put the severed ear inside after wrapping it in gauze. During the war he heard that certain body parts could last a couple days when stored correctly and could even be reattached. He had to try.

Inside the train compartment, his fellow travelers' open newspapers surrounded him, their oversized headlines looming. The Soviets had recently called off their blockade of Berlin, which could end the Berlin Airlift, yet the Western Allies had just approved the constitution for a new West German state. Dire crises averted, new ones already provoked. The atom bomb, germ warfare. This new Cold War could go hot at any time. Meanwhile the passageway was already jammed with passengers in grays and browns with pinched faces, their shoulders pressing against the glass as they maneuvered their exits. He'd wanted to be the first one off but had been too lost in thought about Harry.

Kidnappings happened too frequently on this desperate continent. But who would want to kidnap Harry, and why? A year ago, Harry had joined the American effort to fulfill the European Recovery Program—the Marshall Plan for short. Rebuild war-torn regions, remove trade barriers and modernize industry, facilitate business deals for everything from Coca-Cola to chain saws, all to prevent the spread of Communism. So maybe Harry ended up in a deal gone bad? No, his brother would never deal in black market goods. Harry might be six years younger, but he was the one who could only do right. He always thought he knew best what needed fixing. It was the whole world. If he could, Harry would spin the globe the other way, like one of those cartoon heroes the Americans liked so much. So had Harry crossed paths with someone who could only do wrong?

That creeping feeling Max got told him he had to act fast, on impulse. He'd had no time to alert the proper authorities, no time to have the ransom note's typeface checked, let alone the severed ear. Before leaving, though, he made sure to inform the CIA desk in Munich Old Town that he was going away for a few days, as was protocol. Luckily, they didn't ask questions. His colleagues at the Kuckoo would assume the usual—that he was working as an on-call translator for the Americans, his standard cover. Not even Eva and her lovely dimples knew. She'd been staying above the Kuckoo and caught him coming out that morning. The dear girl wanted to go along, wherever it was, but he asked her to help hold the fort at the club. He couldn't let himself get too close to an unspoiled creature like her. She had too much life ahead of her.

Max gazed out his compartment window at this former capital of the once grand Austro-Hungarian Empire. Hitler had annexed what was left and made it his willing vassal. Now Vienna was controlled by the victorious Allies—the Americans, British, French, and Soviet Union. The city presented yet another gray and jagged tableau of untold destruction and ruin, the mountains of rubble lingering in most every district. Children in rags and oversized caps waved at the passing train from atop mounds of debris, popping in and out of holes in roofs, and Max did not doubt for a second they would strip this train for all it was worth in food scraps and cigarette butts if they could get away with it. Something about that gave him hope, and he chuckled.

He kept his attire simple for the trip. He wore a blue suit of worsted wool with neat striping, collar bar, solid brown tie. Dull black hat. His papers posed no problems. As soon as denazification allowed it, Harry had made sure that Max received the "Temporary Travel Document for German Nationals" until the newly founded state of West Germany was permitted to issue passports. Harry's CIA friends, meanwhile, regularly supplied Max with the requisite permit stamps and an interzonal visa, and that morning the Munich desk had added a trip permit for this stretch.

The ransom bills were rolled into a shirt at the bottom of his leather bag, and no guards had checked it. His cover story, should he require it, was that he was off to Vienna to scout possible acts for the Kuckoo, which sometimes required cash enticement.

If the train would only get there. Max spotted a flash of gold on a passing building and took a deep breath. He felt for his hip flask, which he'd filled with a rich brown Sicilian vermouth. Took a sip. And why not? Harry used to claim that Max was more Austrian than German anyway—slightly decadent, didn't need to work too hard, not always on time, liked a certain flash in his wardrobe, yet always with a love of life. The memory made the vermouth burn going down because the truth was that the war had changed that carefree, pleasure-seeking fellow into something else. Last night in the Kuckoo he'd barked at that odd little extortionist, then threatened to rough him up and good. Before 1944 and Total War? His old self would've tried to wine and the dine that kidnapper into releasing Harry and probably would've succeeded. Max could only sigh at that, like he would about the frolics of a long-lost puppy dog.

The tracks clunked and thumped as they slowed, as if running right over all those who'd perished, again and again. Turning to the passageway, he found himself reflected in the compartment door glass—and told himself he'd regained at least some of the old prewar Max. His once soft and happy cheeks had indeed returned and his brow looked less heavy and his eyes less sunken. He was still only thirty-six after all.

Max felt the cold, oblong shape deep in his jacket pocket, weighing it in his hand. It was just a little *Klappmesser*, a pocket jackknife with a faux woodgrain wearing to a gloss and a dulled blade, the kind a Boy Scout would use to cut an apple. But it also didn't attract attention.

The people in the passageway started moving. Max shoved the compartment door open and joined the procession, his nostrils fighting the blend of hair tonics, stale wool, mothballs, body odors. *Those crooks just better give me Harry*, he thought, *and Harry better not pull anything stupid*. There was likely no way to put Harry's ear back on, he knew that deep down. But maybe it could help a doctor in the reconstruction?

He owed Harry that.

"I'm coming," he said under his breath.

The first thing Max did was buy a tourist map, with swirly, fanciful designs and colors attempting to make light of a city still occupied by four victorious nations. He exited the main station, strode up the broad Prinz-Eugen-Strasse, crossed the famed Ring streets, and entered the central old city, the one district of Vienna under rotating four-power control. Passing soldiers of the British, American, French, and Soviet armies, he realized how confusing and intricate Vienna's occupation truly was. A quilt knitted by a madman—how Viennese.

Seeing those drab olive-green Soviet Army uniforms again after so long had rattled him, he had to admit. He headed for the main street called the Graben. He spotted a *Kaffeehaus*, looked in the vast window, and found solace in the dark wood and gilded tiles, the marble tabletops and newspapers on sticks all around, the vaulted ceilings glowing from ornate Jugendstil light fixtures. Such warmth! Normalcy. He imagined himself ordering *Kaffee mit Schlag* and admiring the waiter's nasally Viennese German. But then Max turned away and saw a young man with no legs begging on the street, using an old board with roller skate wheels for transport, the man coughing, crying.

Max kept moving, he had to, his bag heavier now on his shoulders, his hard-soled shoes clopping on the cobblestones, and he seemed the only one on the streets.

Nine Lessinggasse was in the Soviet Sector, not far by tram, across the Danube Canal from Old Town. The street narrowed. He saw a long shadow approach, stretched by the lowering sun, and then it grew what seemed like two heads, and Max had a brief horrible vision of battlefield wounded dragging each other along before machine-gun fire tore them to shreds, and he squeezed his eyes shut to it. Sweat gathered in his armpits and ran hot down his ribs and stomach, filling every ripple of skin.

He backed into an arched doorway. He heard humming. The shadow was just a boy, strolling along, carrying a large stuffed teddy bear, the toy animal covered with grit and missing an ear. Of all the things . . . Max had to laugh bitterly at that, which made the boy start and run off whispering to his stuffed bear to "hurry, hurry, we must get back."

Max sighed. He shook his head and reached into his chest pocket for his Pall Malls.

Shapes came at him from both sides and crowded the doorway and clamped onto his wrists, leaning into him with muscle. He felt something at his back and it wasn't a door handle.

"Come with us," said a man in accented German.

VIENNA
6:33 p.m.

The two men set Max in the back seat of a long prewar sedan waiting in a side street. They placed a dark cloth over his eyes, drove for ten minutes through the city, walked him inside a building. Max was expecting a cold and windowless cell until he heard hallway floorboards creaking and got a faint aroma of potpourri. Then he felt a soft rug under his feet and too much warmth, got a whiff of burnt wood and ash. They removed the cloth and his hunch was confirmed—he stood in a Viennese-style salon room, the broad area rug oriental, the dark marble fireplace still showing embers, the burgundy drapes closed tight.

"Will someone tell me what's going on?" Max said in German from the tufted chaise lounge where the two men had sat him. The two wore nondescript gray overcoats and still had on their hats, their faces equally bland. "No reason for concern," one said in English—American style. They turned, left the room.

His skin felt tender from the warmth. He unbuttoned his jacket and thought about loosening his tie but remembered he wore that ridiculous collar bar. His heart was still racing so he did breathing exercises, using his diaphragm, then massaged and stretched his face and mouth, all like before a show. The two men hadn't bothered to ask him who he was, nor had they looked at his papers, he recalled. They had only taken his bag and the thermos, leaving his pocketknife.

He must have waited five, ten minutes.

A soft knock on the door.

"Come in," Max said in his best-sounding American English, and the door swung open.

In strode a tallish man with a balding head and pink skin and a loping stride.

Aubrey Slaipe.

His occasional CIA handler. Max straightened his shoulders.

Slaipe's lips pursed as if holding back a grin. Then again, Aubrey Slaipe was the only American Max couldn't actually picture grinning.

"Sit, sit," Slaipe said.

Max realized he had stood. He now knew Slaipe had him in a safe house, but he didn't know the game at hand—the "score," as Americans called it with their love of so many sports. So he just sat back down.

Only now did he remember Slaipe's prosthetic arm. It moved much better than he'd recalled, the hand covered in a fine leather glove.

He shook Slaipe's real hand. Slaipe moved to shed his light overcoat, using both arms, and Max fought the urge to help him. Slaipe folded it neatly on a chair at a table covered with doilies. He brought the other chair over to Max and sat facing him, their knees only a few inches apart.

What now? Max thought. Come alone, they'd said. No tricks. He needed to go and now.

"Munich desk alerted me," Slaipe said.

Max held up his hands. "To what?"

Slaipe smiled at that.

"I'm here looking for talent," Max added, "and some deals on liquor if possible. I checked in with the Munich desk as you know, and—"

"They said you were in quite the hurry."

"You had me followed."

Slaipe patted Max on the knee. "It's okay, Max. It's a fine performance, as always, but you can stop now."

Max sighed with relief.

"It's Harry's!" he blurted. He stood again.

"What is?"

"The ear, Mr. Slaipe, the severed ear. My thermos, your men have it."

"I see. All right, Max, let's start at the beginning. And please, sit back down."

Max sat and reported the whole story, from the moment that Peter Lorre pretender showed up in the Kuckoo Nightclub with that box. Slaipe sat upright the whole time, but something seemed to slump inside him, just a half inch of one shoulder, and his prosthetic arm hung at his side. Once Max was done, Slaipe's gaze wandered the ceiling as if Max were still telling the story. This lasted a good ten seconds.

Max wagged a finger. "You knew something was up with Harry? Of course you would."

Slaipe stood. After another few seconds, he said, "I need to check on this, I'll be right back. Would you like anything?"

"I lost my appetite," Max said, but blew air out his cheek. He might need sustenance for whatever may come. "How about goulash? Maybe potatoes, with caraway if you have any? A simple dish."

"I'll check," Slaipe said and pulled the door shut behind him.

Max shot up and paced the room, checking his watch, fiddling with his collar bar. He turned off the lights, went over to the window, and cracked the heavy drapes. He stared out at a nondescript cobbled lane, all the windows dim, the doorways embedded shadows. They'd said no tricks! He was wasting valuable time.

The problem was, he still had a debt to repay. Aubrey Slaipe's prosthetic arm was Max's fault. He and Slaipe first crossed paths during the war, in late 1944, the Battle of the Bulge. The SS had forced Max into a secret mission in which he had to impersonate an enemy American officer behind the US lines. Max fled the suicidal operation. But soon an American counterintelligence officer found him—Aubrey Slaipe. Then a Belgian Nazi intervened and shot Slaipe in the arm. And Max fled that scene as well, stupid and luckless as ever. Slaipe finally found Max again in 1946, right after Max had reunited with Harry in Munich.

Aubrey Slaipe could always revive the punishment that Max deserved as a supposed wartime enemy spy—the leverage was always there. Consequently, Max's lend-lease on life had required him to perform the odd job. His handler Slaipe directed him to do a timed drop or a pickup, signal a site, shadow a person, act as a go-between, wine and dine a certain gal or an older woman before introducing them to another handler. Not very often. None of it took Max away from his hard-fought normalcy. And these days it normally ran through the Munich desk—an anonymous phone call or a matchbook, coded letter, or postcard often doing the trick. But this was not Munich. This was Slaipe calling the shots.

Slaipe returned and didn't turn on lights or comment on the darkness.

"Quiet street," he said, joining Max at the cracked drapes. "We prefer you here than in some inn."

Max closed the drapes, turned, then checked the drapes again—he'd darkened so many rooms during wartime air raids that he still did this instinctively. He found his way back to the chaise in the dark. Slaipe paced the room. They were both so used to the dark. Maybe it was the light that scared them, Max thought.

Slaipe turned on the lamp, and he sat before Max, his eyes pinched in thought. "We think it may be his ear, but we can't be sure."

"So you did know about this?"

Slaipe didn't shake his head, but he didn't nod, either.

"Who has him?" Max said.

"That's what you're going to find out. We want to see where this goes. Who's behind it."

"*I* want to see where this goes. And bring Harry home," Max growled, a hint of the old adrenaline expanding his chest. "On my own. They said no tricks, I told you."

"That's correct."

"Harry would want it this way."

"I'm not so sure about that, but let's suppose so."

"What was Harry up to? Please, look at me. I have to know."

Slaipe shook his head, faintly. His eyes focused on Max, and they gleamed in a dull way that Max hadn't remembered. "I have something to tell you."

Max felt heavy, laden, as if he were wearing a suit of lead. The chaise actually creaked from it, and he held on to the edge in case it gave way.

"You've probably known it all along," Slaipe added. "You just didn't want to know."

"Tell me."

"Harry wanted to keep his work from you," Slaipe continued. "He didn't want you too involved. Wanted you to . . . recover.

Thus the odd jobs for you only. Never as an operative. I'd promised him that."

"Good lord," Max muttered. "Marshall Plan man, all those embassies, all that travel. It was just his cover."

He supposed he did know all along: Harry was an intelligence man.

He released a snort of disbelief. "So why would he send kidnappers to me? And why foot me the bill?"

"Harry was sticking to his cover. Keep it contained. Throw off the Soviets should they come sniffing around."

"There's that rotten word again: Soviets. What kind of operation was he on? Is he on?"

Slaipe held up a hand. "Max, listen. You're just his big brother, helping him. And for all we know, this truly *is* what it looks like. Happens all the time. Ransoms get paid far more here than they do back home."

"Great." Max shook off the lead suit, took a deep breath. "Can I go now?"

"What is your plan for Vienna?" Slaipe said.

"His ear, can it be reattached, rebuilt?"

Slaipe lowered his eyes, gave a slight shrug.

"I'll take that as a glass half full. So. Before I meet them? I normally would surveil the location tonight, then again tomorrow by daylight."

"Good. Just like we taught you."

"But I'm going to pay them a visit now instead," Max said.

"True to character—even better."

"Harry needs his ear."

"It's Leopoldstadt district, you know, you'll be in—"

"The Soviet Sector. I know." Max felt his mouth suddenly dry. "What if someone on the Soviet side is trailing us?"

"They're not. We think. Not yet."

Now Max's chest tightened, and he took a deep breath, then another.

"Relax," Slaipe said. "You're doing splendidly. Even that little knife of yours fits the character."

"Well, I don't plan on using it." It was true. He'd never used a knife on a human being.

His heartbeat had slowed. He didn't have much appetite for goulash now. He would just have toast and jam if they came asking, possibly a dark beer.

"Do I get the ear back?" he said.

"Of course," Slaipe said. "This should all look natural. Besides, who knows?" He lowered his eyes again, and it didn't escape Max that they'd landed on his prosthetic.

VIENNA
8:48 p.m.

Just north of Old Town, Max passed from the Alsergrund district in the US Sector into Leopoldstadt, an island between the Danube Canal and River. The Soviet Sector. In darkness. Still, Aubrey Slaipe had said that entering would be easy for him. An amusement park ride was easy, too, Max wanted to tell him, but you couldn't get off until outside levers let you, and when Max faced the two Soviet Army guards at the sector guardhouse, he got the nauseating feeling that he'd just strapped himself into a flying chain carousel. But they only waved him and his interzonal papers through with barely a glance.

Nine Lessinggasse was just beyond the east side of a vast park called the Augarten, where a massive concrete flak tower from the war loomed moonlit above the barren, blackened trees, a contender to the great pyramids in all the wrong ways, dwarfing all as if built by giants just landed from the stars. Hunched figures hurried along the park's many paths as if attempting to avoid its death ray.

Max didn't rush it. He checked window reflections for followers. If trailed, time was usually on your side, Slaipe once

22

counseled him. Take a moment to admire a store display. Stop in an arched doorway and light a cigarette. This put them off more than you, as they were the ones who could not be seen. Max had to admit that he had grown to like the role. Deception might be a sick and twisted stepchild to the stage, but it was still his child. All the thrills of performing came to life, yet with the threats and dangers greatly enhanced. One aspect was the opposite, though—the less flamboyant, the better in espionage.

It all fit Harry even better than him. Of course his younger brother was CIA. Of course Max had known somewhere in the far reaches of his reasoning. He only hoped that Harry didn't get burned in his devotion to America. Causes often turned on their heads and began to devour themselves if pursued too long and hard. Just ask the Germans, or the Russians.

As a rickety streetcar lumbered past, the moonlight dimmed in unison, as if that very train were pulling a cable to cloak the great orb in dark clouds for the night. Many nearby buildings were all but destroyed, full of holes, their windows blackened with fire. The top three floors of 9 Lessinggasse were as well, and Max could only make out part of the roof. But the ground floor had survived, the windows intact along the street.

Three Soviet Army privates passed, taking a bottle out for a walk. Max waited on the corner for them to pass. The address was a *Friseur*, a barbershop, all dark inside. He tried the door anyway, and to his surprise it opened, its bell jingling. The faint streetlamp glow let him see that the room wasn't in the best shape, some of the white wall and floor tiles chipped, the two mirrors blurry in spots.

Max started. He'd heard a crunch.

A man appeared from behind a curtain. He wore a white barber's smock.

"I'm looking for my brother, Harry," Max said in German, getting right to it since that little menace back in Munich had never given him a password.

The man just stared so Max added, "I was told he was here." He held up his leather bag. He clutched the thermos tight.

"This way," the man said.

They passed through the curtain and a room with more chipped tiles, a drain in the tiled floor, and the faint reek of ammonia, and Max wondered if the barber's used to be a butcher's. He didn't want to know. But he did wonder why they hadn't frisked him, let alone check his bag and thermos. He kept as much distance as he could, side-eyeing the darkness, his elbows out. The man led him into an inner courtyard ten degrees colder than outside, stopped him at a plain wooden door, then turned on his heels and left.

Max waited, the door opened. Another man in a smock waved him in quickly as if there were a sniper outside. Max rushed inside and found himself on a landing to a cellar. All was dim. He followed the man down old wood steps that turned and became stone steps so worn they were curved. The cellar was more like catacombs, with old stone columns and vaulted ceiling, all of it pocked and unfinished. It could've been the Middle Ages down here.

Two kerosene lamps on the floor were the only light. The smock man left Max at a modern metal table also reminiscent of a butcher's. The chairs were metal, too, and Max was surprised to find one warm. He wondered if it had been Harry. The smock man had left, back up the steps.

"Hello?" Max said to the dim room. After a while, he heard the creak of a door in the darkness and the shuffle of footsteps on crumbly stone floor.

A figure gained clarity in the shadows. The Peter Lorre pretender.

Max gritted his teeth. Harry had to be here or they wouldn't have made him come all this way. He reached for the thermos.

"Don't get any big ideas," the little man said, stiffening, those bulging eyes expanding.

"Says the one who didn't frisk me." Max stood.

"Sit down."

Max dropped back on his seat. "Now, look here. I'm just an actor. He's my brother. I have your money." He slammed the thermos on the table.

"*Were*," the man said.

"What? What are you trying to say?"

"You *were* an actor."

Max glared at the man half in shadow. But something was different about the fellow, he noticed. He wouldn't look at Max long, let alone stare, and he now blinked so much that Max would've suspected a tic. His face was pale. He kept his head turned, just so. And Max noticed that his farthest eye showed swelling at the temple and socket, puffy red and just now darkening from a widening bruise.

"Who roughed you up?" Max said.

"We do not want your money now," the man said.

"What?"

"Whoever you are."

"Come again?"

"The situation has changed."

"Wait, hold on. You bring me all this way? You could've done this in Munich, you were there, could've just brought Harry to the Kuckoo—"

"No. For me to come, yes. That makes more impact than, say, a letter, and it's faster. But, bringing your brother himself, over the border?" The man clucked his tongue, shook his head.

"Who the devil are you?" Max said.

The man glanced around as if someone were there. "We're smugglers, mostly, if you must know. Your brother was asking too many questions, about borders, crossings, about what we do. We thought his angle was moving black market goods, since he was presenting himself as a businessman. Marshall Plan, US Trade Council, et cetera. He was poking around certain routes. Austria, Czechoslovakia even. So we nabbed him. Turned him into a valuable commodity, yes? All we require is payment to release. But then? He tells us he has a certain brother, in Munich—"

"I'm sitting right here," Max said. "Harry wanted me to come? Here I am."

"Something wasn't right. Your brother was too calm. At first we thought maybe he was a cop, an investigator. There are certain routes we use, you see. Ratlines."

"Ratlines?"

"Escape routes. For people, not goods. Known to rats only. All manner of Nazis also use them, from Lithuania to Yugoslavia. It's how the Nazi rats get to Argentina and Brazil, England, America even. Usually helped along by Catholics, using their networks. The Vatican." Now the man smiled, his teeth all skinny yellows and browns, like a cob of corn going bad. "We also hear of Jewish assassin squads roaming Europe. Avengers. Ratlines being the best way to catch a rat."

Max leaned forward and tried a curled grin like a fellow smuggler or worse. "Hey, who cares? Right? I have your money. Give me my brother, we go. I need to get him to a hospital—"

The man held up his bony old hand. "Your brother is none of those people I speak of. He is certainly not who he says, a mere embassy official. We did not know this when we abducted him, as I said. Not even when I met you in Munich, just last night. But we should have known, yes? He was sticking his nose in too many places, here, elsewhere, asking too many questions."

Max lost the grin. He slapped the table. "Let him go. Now!"

The man only drummed fingers on the tabletop, his bulging eyes blinking in rhythm.

Max slumped. His suit felt like heavy lead again, pressing him into the chair. "Oh god. You're telling me Harry is not here? Is that it?"

"This is correct." The man swallowed, hard, which looked to give him pain in more than his face. "They took him."

"When? Who's they?"

"This morning." The man tugged at his collar. His fingers came away moist in the light, from sweat.

"Who's they?" Max repeated. The man didn't reply. Max added, "They threatened you?"

The man gave the slightest of nods, just a shift of shadow.

"Let's try this another way," Max said. "Where did they take Harry?"

"First things first." The man held up a hand.

As if on cue, a young woman with short black hair and a formfitting blue suit appeared and waited a few feet away. The man handed her the thermos from the table. She produced a small jar from the shadows, dropped the ear into the yellowish liquid inside, then turned on her tall heels and left.

"What are doing with that?"

"You fool," the man said. "Of course it was never his ear. We needed you to respond."

Max should've felt relief, but all he sensed were his fingers clawing up, and he stood and took a step around the table toward the man. "You bastards. That was thoroughly uncalled for."

"Not in this world," the man said, his eyes suddenly glossy.

And Max, to his surprise, fought a slight ache of empathy rising up his throat. Who knew what this man had seen? People that he loved, dead. Max wondered if the man had ever been an actor, too, once. In a less sick world, they might have formed a troupe together.

"Look, I ask you: Where did they take Harry?"

The man stared at Max, his eyes slightly wet. He said eventually, almost in a whisper, "They took him to Prague."

Max started. Prague was Czechoslovakia. Prague was behind the Iron Curtain.

The man only stared at the table, as if confirming the intimidating Other World on some invisible map.

"Last question," Max said. "Who took him?"

The man kept staring at the table, but now at its gnarled and dark edge.

"You want some of my money?" Max said, almost in a whisper too. "Would that help? You could tell me more."

The man only shook his head. After a while, he raised his head, slowly, robotically, his eyes leveling on Max's. "I have a message for you," he said as if reciting it. "You are to meet someone there. An East German. A Soviet official. His name is Hartmut Dietz."

VIENNA
10:29 p.m.

Max, his eyes wild and his blood pumping hot, rushed through a small interior courtyard and into Aubrey Slaipe's safe house, back inside the US Sector. He found Slaipe in the salon room with the chaise lounge.

"Those bastard smugglers tell me I'm supposed to meet Hartmut Dietz. You know Dietz, from Munich, he—"

"Stop. Stop, Max."

Slaipe wore an open collar for the first time Max had seen him, and his jacket and pants had wrinkles. Max had never seen the man rattled much, or at least ruffled, but this was close.

"Remember your training, as little as you've had," he told Max, his voice straining a little. "I need a full report."

Max caught his breath, walking the room. Slaipe waited it out, his chin high. Max reported. Harry had apparently been poking around the borderlands of Austria and Czechoslovakia. The smugglers used ratlines and didn't like him on their turf. But then they suddenly let Harry go, didn't even want the money. They wanted clear of the whole affair.

"Dietz, or Dietz's people, they took Harry. And now I'm supposed to go to Prague."

Max had expected Slaipe to at least twitch at mention of Prague. Slaipe only nodded.

"Has Harry made any contact with you?" Max said.

"No, he has not," Slaipe said.

Max stopped before him. "But Prague doesn't surprise you?"

"Prague," Slaipe said, "is Harry's current assignment. He's attached to the US Embassy."

"Ah. Oh. That's his current cover."

"He's economic affairs—which is now public affairs mostly since trade is all but dead behind the Iron Curtain. Still, one must try, I suppose."

"Can you confirm he's there now?"

"We're waiting for confirmation."

Max twitched. He started wringing his hands like a bad actor in a bad play. Prague wasn't good, not at all. Dietz was far worse. When he and Harry reunited in 1946, in Munich, Max had convinced Harry to help him rescue a group of Cossack refugees in hiding. The Soviets wanted to forcibly repatriate the poor refugees back to the Soviet Union, many of them women and children, the elderly. But Max's freelance operation also got his girlfriend, Irina, killed. A Munich cop with a Nazi past, Hartmut Dietz, had betrayed them. Then Dietz escaped to the Soviet East. Max had often wondered where Dietz lay in wait, mostly in his nightmares.

"How is this possible?" Max said. "Mr. Slaipe? Aubrey?" It might've been the first time he called Slaipe by his first name.

"Harry's presence, it made the Soviets take notice," was all Slaipe said.

"You know about us and Hartmut Dietz. So how does he fit? What could he want? What could he even make happen on his own? East Germans aren't exactly leading lights behind the Iron Curtain."

"You're correct. Dietz, he's just a proxy for the Russians. But they must know that Dietz knows you two, so they're letting him look into this Harry matter. A light job." Slaipe paused, holding his trusty old black pipe cupped in his hand, feeling its weight. "Still, we must think about endgames. I suppose there's the chance the Russians might think you could turn double. But they don't know you like I do."

"Dietz knows me. That doesn't make sense."

They heard someone go by out in the hallway, a door opening. Or was it closing? Then, a rare silence found them.

"Tell me all you know about Dietz," Max added.

"Yes, all right. You deserve to know. The East Germans don't have their own independent intelligence service yet, but we understand that Hartmut Dietz is one of those in line to play a role. Meanwhile it's the Soviet Ministry of State Security—the MGB, when it's not the Russians' MVD—Internal Affairs. You might call him a Nazi, but he never joined a single party—not until the SED, that is, the East German Socialist Unity Party. That goes a long way over there on the other side. When there's not a purge coming, that is."

"I'm going," Max said. "When do I leave?"

Slaipe nodded. "We'll authorize it. Fix your papers overnight."

"You want me to do something extra."

"No, just feel him out. Find out what they want. What Dietz wants. We have to trust our mistrust. That's the game."

Slaipe's shirt was now buttoned at the top, Max noticed, when it wasn't before, and his jacket and pants suddenly looked smoother. How had he buttoned his open collar with one hand? Max hadn't even noticed. He might be an actor, but Slaipe was ever the great illusionist.

Slaipe stood and went over to the window and ran fingers through his wispy ring of hair, pushing it back into neat position. He peeked out the crack in the drapes, and when he turned to Max the transformation was complete. He was the proud father attending a child's graduation.

"Well, we might as well have a drink while we wait for word. Just behind you."

Max turned to the wall just beyond the chaise. Dark wood shelving stocked with antique books and curios lined one half of the wall. Filling the other half were orderly cabinet doors arranged like a giant advent calendar, each with a little glass knob. Max tried a door but it wouldn't budge. Each had a small key lock, he realized.

"No, try three in, two down," Slaipe told him.

The door revealed a small bar complete with glassware. Max poured them brandies. They stood in the middle of the room, oddly facing the door as if awaiting a visitor.

"I was never going to be this before the war, you know," Slaipe said, adding a flourish of his unlit pipe.

"This?"

"What I do. I was to receive my PhD. In history." Slaipe added a low rumble of laughter.

"None of us were to be this, Mr. Slaipe. Look at me. At least you are living crucial current events, instead of me grappling with the past."

"Yes. Well put. This is what I tell myself. What I've told Harry on occasion. The United States has assumed the world stage, whether it wants it or not. It's all forward and into the future for us. So we must not foul things up like all the rest have."

Slaipe took his time with the first half of his brandy, swirling it, nodding along to it, but now he threw the rest back and waited for Max to do the same.

"Funny, I wish it was just kidnappers," Max said. "Wish it was just about Harry's ear." He took Slaipe's empty glass and didn't know where to put their glasses, so he set them back inside the little bar despite hating the thought of someone opening it to find dirty glasses.

A man knocked, cracked the door. Slaipe went over and listened to the man's whispers, nodding along. When Slaipe turned around, he looked the picture of grit and determination, his eyes hard marbles and his weak chin and soft cheeks all angles and iron.

"We just heard from Prague," he said. "The Czechs picked him up, it's the Soviets. Confirmed."

Max glared at all four walls of the room. A heat flushed his body that ended up in his fingertips, pulsing them, making them feel for the knife in his pocket. He should've gotten a better one, a switchblade maybe.

"Goddamn Hartmut Dietz," he said.

"You'll simply have to use your instincts, Max. And your patience, please. So quit caressing that knife in your pocket. That's better. There is obviously more to this."

PRAGUE
Thursday, May 19
5:02 p.m.

On a prominent corner just off the lower end of Wenceslas Square, Max stopped at a shop window to check the reflection for anyone tailing him. No one, he hoped. The new state-run store sign read PRAMEN, meaning "source"—the goods inside were uniformly lined and stacked like bullets and bombs, and the young attendants wore thin matching jackets with arcane insignia. Max couldn't tell what the goods were. The Czechoslovakian capital's main square itself was less a square than a boulevard running down a slope from the national museum, a giant slide, expelling him. Max felt his skin tingle. The blood in his thighs raced as if prompting him to flee. He'd just left the train station. Changed money, bought a cheap map. After he'd passed the statue of Saint Wenceslas atop his horse, he started noticing those tall banners of confident workers and scientists outnumbering the few ads and signs for private shops, and then he noticed variations on the word *Communist* among the Czech words he didn't know, and the hammers and sickles, and then it was the man of steel himself, Uncle Joe Stalin. And now Hartmut Dietz was one of them, no matter the short leash they must be keeping a German like him on.

The train today from Vienna to Prague had been bad enough, even though Max had a first-class compartment all to himself. Until the border. As the train sat, steaming, creaking, he had heard someone screaming, being pulled off the train. As he waited, he had tried recalling good thoughts. Slaipe was making sure that his ransom money was returned to Munich. And Eva would be there when he returned . . . Then two Czechoslovakian officers filled his cabin, bringing odors of well-oiled leather, newly greased gun metal, and strong cigarettes as two more men in overcoats planted themselves in the corridor. All eyeing him. Border control.

Max showed the papers Slaipe had provided—a three-day cultural visa complete with entry stamps. He was a glorified yet verifiable version of himself, the impresario Maximilian Kaspar, currently on a US Embassy–sanctioned foreign affairs assignment to facilitate international talent exchanges. But the two border guards never asked. They had only eyed his papers, each taking a turn, each taking their time, and handed them back. One, perhaps drunk, had then leaned over Max, sniffed at the air, and laughed. And the two had turned on their heels to move on, their gear jangling and crunching.

The intimidated smuggler in Vienna had given Max the address to meet Dietz and instructed him to make it there by 6:30 p.m. Max now crossed the river over the lovely and eerie Charles Bridge, with its grim, sooty statutes looking around for a god, any god, and if none were found, those statues looked like they were going to jump. Max tipped his hat to the last statue standing as he shuffled off the bridge along the cobblestones to a pension recommended by Slaipe, down to the left near the river, a nice street with small surrounding parks, the proprietors a middle-aged couple who looked so unassuming that he could only imagine what brave things they had done during the war, only to do it all over again.

Slaipe had admitted that he didn't like the idea of him going to Prague. The Czechoslovak Communists were solidifying power fast and hard after taking over in the coup of 1948, and the purges were well underway. The people hadn't been on edge like this since 1938.

"I'll be more forthright with you," Slaipe had whispered. "I'm afraid we've had plenty of false starts lately, far too many. Quite the inauspicious beginning for our Central Intelligence Agency, all over Eastern Europe. Plenty of mission failure. Snafus, your various fiascoes. We keep sending in locals who keep getting nabbed. So whatever this job was, it was different. Special. Harry wanted to run it himself, on the ground."

"And you really don't know what he was after?" Max had asked, one corner of his mouth smiling, but the other fighting impatience if not slight contempt. Slaipe wouldn't tell Max even if he did know. Max was too low on the totem pole, practically the part thrust into the ground.

And, right according to script, Slaipe had only shrugged.

At the pension, Max switched costumes in his room. Slaipe had given him a wardrobe change for his bag in case he needed to blend in. To replace his blue suit, he put on old light wool trousers and a charcoal-gray waist-length jacket with outside breast pockets like a military tunic. Ankle boots instead of his oxfords, and a brown leather flatcap. His only concessions to his usual flair were his collar bar and brown tie. He supposed he could use the collar bar as a weapon.

It started raining when he left. Looming atop the steep hill before him was Prague Castle, and just up the road was the US Embassy, in the former Schönborn Palace. "We have people in place," Slaipe had assured him, right after admitting their many failures.

The rain would not let up. It rolled off his cap, and he bought two newspapers to shield him on the way over, preferring to walk. The address was near the Old Jewish Cemetery, back over the river, this time on the Mánesův Bridge. He felt his pocket-knife in one pocket, then pulled out his pack of German Ernte 23 cigarettes and lit one, wishing he had Pall Malls. He expected to break out in cold sweats but only felt the adrenaline pumping through him. He laughed at the rain. He stomped out his butt, pressed on.

Near the Old Jewish Cemetery, the blocks were grander, more like Vienna. This was the former Jewish quarter, and Max wondered with a wince whether the very location he was to visit was free to use precisely because of what had happened during the war. Something about that made him feel for his pocket-knife again and again, his now moist hand almost sticking to it.

6:25 p.m. U Staré školy 113 was on a narrow lane carved through the corner of a larger block. Max knocked on the narrow double doors and practically hugged them to keep out of the rain, the ornate ironwork and embossing digging into his chest.

The door opened and he nearly fell in, catching himself, stomping off the rain as if this were his intention all along. A man in the darkened entry hall dragged him along by an elbow, and Max didn't fight it. The man turned him into a room and shut the door, leaving him alone. The room was spare but fine, with high decorative ceilings, polished parquet floors, and a marble fireplace. He saw a portrait of a woman in a flowing gown, and silver on a shiny buffet. One side of the room had a desk and the other side sleeping arrangements partitioned off by a screen with a modern geometric pattern. Max took a deep breath. He hung his jacket and hat on the coat stand. The office area had a comfortable-looking velvet sofa, again reminding him what had happened to the Jews here and so many places, a whole quarter of a town now repurposed not to mention the buildings' contents, the woman in the gown likely lost to history.

A door at the back of the room opened and two men in black leather jackets marched in, one pudgy, one wiry, both scowling at him in the way a man did when he'd had a nice long meal interrupted. They got close and Max smelled *pivo*. They didn't have to order him. He raised his arms and they frisked him. The wiry one found his pocketknife, showed the other one, and both smirked at it. It went into the wiry one's pocket.

Max could only bow his head. He told himself it would make someone's boy a nice gift.

Then a man strode in wearing a boring brown suit. His hair was cut shorter on the sides and he wore wire-framed glasses. And a feeling like hot metal shot through Max, but it wasn't the kind he wanted. It burned his stomach down low, melted his leg muscles, jabbed at his heart.

Here was Hartmut Dietz.

The hot metal settled in Max's chest and head, at a low boil. His fists had clenched up and he couldn't unclamp them.

"Herr Kaspar," Dietz said in German. "Please, sit down."

Max didn't move, couldn't. Dietz stared back at him, raising his broad face. He was close to Max's age. His jowls that used to hang had firmed up and his cheeks had filled out. He clearly wasn't half starving like he'd been in 1946.

"We should've just killed you back in Munich," Max said. It was like someone else saying it, like hearing a movie from another room.

"Please," Dietz repeated.

Max peered around for the sparest chair he could find, spotted a wooden one with no upholstery over by the desk. He dropped into it and faced the middle of the room, glaring at Dietz.

Dietz took a deep breath, nodded, and stared at the door he'd come through.

A woman walked in, or marched in rather, such was her strut. She wore a simple but well-tailored gray wool ensemble that didn't shift as she neared, like a suit of armor moving on wheels. Her hair was pulled back severely and parted even more severely down the middle, leaving a glowing white line. She exchanged words in Russian with Dietz, who then stood at another wooden chair. He and Max watched her go around the desk and sit. Dietz then scooted his chair closer to the desk, turned it to face her and Max equally, and sat. It reminded Max of a schoolboy summoned to the headmistress and threatened with expulsion. He even had his hands flat on his thighs as if ready to be struck. Another man entered in another drab brown suit and stood along the wall, out of the way. The Czechoslovakian version of Dietz, surely—in-country protocol had to be maintained, after all.

Max fought a sick grin. *Look at the kept men*, he thought, *the Soviet Russian overseers' puppets*. He said to the Russian woman, nodding at Dietz, "You do know that this man is a Nazi criminal, right?"

The woman's expression did not budge but, considering her manner, it hardly meant she hadn't understood his German.

"He was in the Wehrmacht Military Police," Max added. "On the Eastern Front—you know, what you call the Great Patriotic War? You might want to look into him."

"They know all about me," Dietz said. "I've been rehabilitated. It's all documented."

Max shot the woman in charge a sidelong glare but she still did not budge. Her demeanor delivered Max back to reality. There was so much he wanted to say to Dietz, most of it involving how he'd like to do him in for good, but he wasn't going to be able to explore such delights if he did not regain control. The Russians might not fully trust Dietz, either, he realized. Maybe he could exploit that.

"Why you?" Max said. "Why would the Soviets let you out from under your rock?"

Dietz's cheeks reddened, but he kept his voice steady. "My past involvement with you, of course. We discovered that Harry was using his so-called free time to probe the Czech frontier, first along the Austrian border, then the border to Soviet-occupied Germany. Monitoring trains, entering forests, looking for crossing routes. This was brought to my attention since I knew Harry. It's all in the reports."

"And you saw an angle," Max said. "Always getting ahead."

Dietz didn't respond.

Max looked to the woman. "I'm here about my brother. Where is he?"

Her chin lowered, subtly. She opened a drawer and slid a large envelope to Dietz. Their shorthand communication made Max realize they might know each other well, possibly real well. Dietz pulled out a document—a US passport of telltale green. He stood and handed it to Max.

"Special Passport," it read in gold on the cover. The "photograph of bearer" was Harry. His cover identity practically frowned at the camera. Same broad, freckly cheeks and those bangs wanting to curl. He didn't look older so much as angrier, like a movie still of the character actor who often played the baddie but was a swell fellow in real life.

"We obtained this from the kidnappers," Dietz said.

"When your people scared them off Harry."

No one responded. But Dietz's Czech counterpart nodded

sternly from his spot over at the wall, and Max briefly imagined the odd fellow with the bulging eyes kneaded into dough by those two in leather jackets.

"You might thank me," Dietz added.

"Thank you. And go fuck yourself. Now where is he?"

"Don't worry. He's doing fine. He's just a—what was it again—a trade representative?" Dietz added a chuckle. "Enjoying the countryside, he said. Sticking his nose where it doesn't belong, we said."

"Why did your people pick him up? For questioning?"

"We had questions, yes. It's my assignment. Now, it is true, he had been testing the softness of certain borderlands, but where is the crime? I see none." Dietz held up his palms.

"Why are you dragging me into this?" Max said.

"He's your brother. And he dragged you into this, not us—he told the kidnapper-smugglers about you, remember? Knowing you two, that means to me that he was trying to get out of his spot quietly. So he could continue whatever gambit he was playing."

"I never see him. I had no idea. Laugh all you want."

Dietz wasn't laughing. He wasn't quite frowning, either.

Max straightened in his seat even more. "I'm not leaving without my brother," he said to the Russian woman in German.

She looked to Dietz, one eyebrow raised.

"Just tell me what he was after here," Dietz said. "That's all you have to do."

Max held out his hands. "How should I know? I told you."

"Then, convince him to tell. And we let him go."

"You think he's going to tell me? You know Harry."

Dietz let a pause creep in. "You make a good point," he said. He added, louder, "Then again, he might even try passing you info . . ."

It continued like this, back and forth, Dietz pressing Max, Max pushing back. The Russian woman didn't interfere, though her chair creaked a little. Max knew he could be used as a weak link. They could use him as leverage against Harry. They could ask him to do jobs for them, all to have Harry released. They could simply torture Harry. And yet, after a few rounds of Max pleading his clear innocence, Dietz only sat back, stared at Max a moment, and released a long sigh. It felt fabricated to Max, unfinished and clunky, like a first table reading or one of those Soviet show trials. Dietz added a few words in Russian to the woman and to his wallflower Czech in brown. Each nodded.

They exited the room, leaving Dietz alone with Max.

Max tightened up inside. Dietz swiveled Max's way, leaned closer. Dietz snarled, but in a desperate way, like a man who couldn't believe he'd been finally arrested.

"Listen to me, we do not have much time," Dietz whispered in English, and with his heavy accent it sounded more like a hiss.

Max grunted a laugh. "Just what is this?"

"We must make certain they can't hear us," Dietz continued in English.

Max glanced around the room. He saw no two-way mirrors or obvious microphones.

"No listening devices," Dietz added.

Max nodded, thinking, *Go on, Dietz, get your little* Spiel *over with.*

"Harry isn't talking," Dietz said, practically spitting out his whispers, verbs tumbling into nouns. "I told them you would know something. I told them I could convince you. But I really needed you alone."

"For what? What do I know? I run a club in Munich. I came to pay a ransom, and that was in Vienna."

"I couldn't go to Vienna because of my status, as a . . . German, so I had a team bring Harry here to Prague. You see? I was the one who got you here. To offer a deal."

Dietz said it like he deserved a medal. Max grunted another laugh, but this one felt hot, like he wanted to vomit from deep down. "Oh, I know all about your deals—"

"Shut up." Dietz stood over Max, to make it look like he was putting the screws on him should his Soviet mistress come marching back in. The reek of stale cigarettes on his breath only confirmed his sick desperation.

"A rat like you," Max spat, "you have an ulterior motive. I can smell it. The last time you had one, my girlfriend ended up dead."

"Just listen. Before I tell you anything, I want assurances first."

Max stood. "Oh, so I'm on a job for you, is that it? How dare you!"

"Sit down. Please. If they come in . . ."

Max gave it a beat, just to make Dietz's double-dealing hot blood run cold. Then he sat, slowly. "Keep talking."

"I turn double. Work for your side."

Max released a howl of laughter. "Is this some new humor torture? It's killing me. Stop, stop before I split my sides."

"*Psst!*" Dietz sneered. "I'm doing you a favor. You can get ahead."

"Get ahead? How about I tell your Soviet mistress about this?"

Dietz smiled, all yellow teeth. "Svetlana? She'd never believe a man like you."

"Like I said: I see a rat."

"I turn double," Dietz repeated. "I prove myself. I'm proving myself right now, aren't I? And I can get Harry released."

"Can you?" A steel had filled Max. He was one with the seat and the floor and the centuries of earth below this old building. "Then what? By turning double, don't you mean triple agent?"

Dietz snickered. His teeth and eyes glistened from some unknown, faraway light. His mouth opened to speak.

They heard footsteps.

"*Verdammt noch mal*," Dietz muttered. "Too late, for now. Now it's plan B. I always have one."

Dietz stepped even closer to Max and shouted the usual threats in German, for show, his spittle brushing Max's cheek, neck. "Do you know what we'll do to Harry!? To you? We have methods! Just like the old days, eh? Maybe you won't like it too much . . ."

The Soviet Russian mistress and her goons strode back in. They watched for a moment from the middle of the room.

Max played along. He yanked down the corners of his mouth and, remembering past loves lost, felt his eyes go hot, and a tear ran down one cheek as his chin quivered. He wasn't sure why he was sticking to the script with this bastard, but he was. Maybe it really would get Harry released. Whatever happened, he told himself that it would put Dietz in a worse position, one that the two-faced murderer and war criminal finally deserved.

Dietz grabbed Max's right ear tight and twisted it, yanking it down.

Max let it burn, clenching his teeth. He didn't release a peep.

The woman barked at Dietz in Russian. He took a step back, and Max noted that Dietz had appreciated his performance, just the hint of a wink out of the woman's view.

The woman said something else to Dietz. He nodded along. He held up his hands.

When he spoke to Max again, his voice had lost any desperation. It was something like somber, as if he were a Munich cop again, telling a family member of a traffic death.

"Very well," Dietz said to Max. "We'll release your brother. First thing tomorrow. Officially, he's persona non grata according to diplomatic protocol. As long as you and he give me—give us—your word."

"Of what?"

"That he'll leave this country and never return to any other Soviet Socialist Republic. That includes Soviet East Germany."

Max felt his chest swell with warmth, and he fought a shameful urge to hug someone. He sat up straight. He couldn't help pressing a hand to his heart. "You have a deal."

The Soviet woman nodded, and Dietz hauled Max over to the front door himself. The door stuck a little, Dietz kicked it open. He glared at Max, his eyes wide and full of fire.

Max shuddered a moment but didn't let it show. "Say what you're going to say," he said.

"If Harry ever returns?" Dietz said. "If you come back? I am going to find you."

"Don't worry. You can have the Eastern Bloc."

Dietz snickered. "Just remember, I could have killed you any time. You and Harry. And I didn't. But if you come back? I still can."

Max stood tall, though his heels teetered on the door's awkwardly high threshold. "You won't see us ever again. I have a business to run, and Harry more important things than you."

"Oh, I think we will meet again," Dietz snarled. "I will find a way."

And he pushed Max out onto the cobblestones.

PRAGUE
Friday, May 20
5:37 a.m.

Max huddled with Aubrey Slaipe in the inner courtyard of a building a few side streets away from the Powder Tower. It separated Old and New Town Prague, a soot-stained turret of a gate from the 1400s that looked as if it had been separated from a gothic castle and plopped down here by a lazy giant with no sense of humor. Next to it stood the Municipal Hall, a splendid art nouveau structure that in contrast might have been lovingly cradled into place by a descending angel accompanied by harp-playing cherubs, its ornate facade an interplay of master ironwork and patinas and gilding. Max had always imagined himself performing there before reality darkened his daydreams long ago.

Yesterday evening, Max had wandered back from meeting Dietz, over the river and through the palatial gardens at the base of castle hill, listening to the aftermath of an evening full of showers, the downspouts trickling and the moss between cobblestones whispering, that smell in the air like street aromas reanimated. Shaking his head. Unable to get Dietz's desperate burning eyes out of his brain. Dietz was part of everything that had almost destroyed Germany and now was joining the effort to do it again in the East, it seemed. Was that all history was, just the same tragedies continuously doubling down? There was a time when his mood would've inspired Max to write or at least sing a sad tune about the state of things. But now, and to his sure demise, he only wanted to fix it. He hoped he was doing the right thing for Harry. Because Harry could not fail like he had. Max growled at the notion as he meandered side streets to reach his room.

He had found Aubrey Slaipe waiting inside. He'd given Slaipe Harry's Special Passport and reported in detail. Slaipe smiled. He even patted Max on the back.

"Whatever you did, it worked," Slaipe said. "The Soviets have already made contact. Harry's handover is now an international prisoner swap."

Max could piece together what had happened. Dietz, in his machinations, had convinced his Soviet mistress overseer and possible lover that he could get Harry to talk through his brother, Max. Dietz had only used this as a ruse, to appeal to Max in his own way. But Max had nothing to give either Dietz or the Soviets, so the Soviets went with plan B: the usual prisoner swap. It was probably all they were hoping for, anyway, since the Soviets only took Harry for another nosey parker trying to make his mark using an embassy cover. Yet a part of Max, deep and tight and searing inside his chest, wondered if he'd missed an opportunity despite Dietz's murderous and double-dealing ways. As if this were the start of something instead of the end.

He had reported Dietz's attempt at a deal, but Slaipe had shrugged it off. "Maybe in the future," he'd said. "But things are just too hot at the moment. The main thing is, Harry's going home."

"I just hope he's learned his lesson," Max had said, sounding like a big brother for once.

The Powder Tower and Municipal Hall overlooked a bend in the avenue that was part open square. The side streets led off every which way, but it was a relatively straight shot to the main train station just a few minutes away. Once handed over, Harry was to be put on a train for Munich. The Americans had agreed to it. They would both be back home in no time and Harry safe to recover. Max thought about the Kuckoo for the first time. They had another big weekend starting tonight. Maybe he could be back by opening even? He would let Eva sing again, as many tunes as she wanted. He was surprised to find himself missing her. Maybe he could treat her to a nice meal.

It was cold for May, especially inside this inner courtyard with its dewy cobblestones and the high walls of four surrounding stories. Slaipe, uncharacteristically, slumped against the wall in shadow just inside the entrance and had both his good arm and imitation one jammed deep into his overcoat pockets. He kept pulling out his pipe as if to light it, but then redeposited it, and Max began to wonder if he was signaling his men with it instead of simply showing some nervous tic that Max had never witnessed before. Prisoner swaps were routine enough, but things could always go awry.

"I have a family, you know," Slaipe said.

Max looked up, practically startled. Slaipe had never shared such intimate details and Max had never asked, assuming them off-limits. A warm café would have been so much nicer for such a fine moment. Max said, "You must miss them dearly."

Slaipe nodded. He produced the pipe and resubmerged it again. "Wife. A daughter. Your usual all-American story. House in New England. My girl is going to college. Every job was supposed to get me closer to home, yet every new one feels like the first stop on the long trip."

"I know what you mean," Max said. "My long trip has been departing for years."

Slaipe sniffed in acknowledgment. He checked his watch. He moved his pipe to the other pocket.

"Well, I suppose it could've been worse," Slaipe said, his voice now staccato, metallic. "Let's go."

5:56 a.m. Max was there to observe. Slaipe was there to hand their prisoner over. Slaipe and Max emerged from the courtyard passageway onto the sidewalk of Hybernská, the street leading straight toward the tower. The sun had just risen, but a low fog blurred all, and daylight only made it worse. They walked toward the tower, eyeing the arch at its base that once must have served as an important and intimidating passage.

"The tower arch," Slaipe told Max. "They'll hand Harry over there."

They reached the corner across from the gate. Slaipe looked one way, then the other, squinting through the low haze at the tall slablike buildings lining these streets like so many ravines, all the hundreds of windows only blurred black squares.

Max eyed the tall arch passing through the tower, up to ten yards deep, the gothic passageway dim. For a moment he imagined ancient gates dropping down from up inside, trapping Harry. Or Communist commandos lurking within like bats, lying in wait to rappel down.

He shook off his worry with a sigh and peeked at his watch: 6:00 a.m.

"Excellent work, Max, thank you," Slaipe said suddenly and showed him a half smile, though Max wasn't sure exactly which work Slaipe was referring to.

"You can thank me after," he said.

They crossed the intersecting streets, Slaipe stepping a little higher to avoid slipping on the dewy cobblestones and Max doing the same. Max spotted a silhouette on the opposite side of the arched passageway, then another man some feet behind. The front figure had Harry's dimensions, though he was wearing a hat.

Just then a light shined from somewhere, possibly a first ray of the sun breaking through the fog. Harry!

Light shined on all of one side of his face, and Max could practically make out the freckles. Heinrich! His little brother. He fought an urge to applaud.

Harry and his counterpart were walking their way—the other man was the Czech functionary from the Dietz meeting, Max now saw. Slaipe stopped, feet out like a gunslinger in a western and arms equally so, and Max figured it wasn't cockiness but protocol. The Czech functionary and Harry stopped. Max stopped.

Max heard a droning. An engine. What looked like a delivery truck came rumbling up the street, chugging and grinding. It halted.

"Stay here," Slaipe told Max.

A man exited the back of the truck in a rumpled suit, his hair hanging in his eyes. Their prisoner. Slaipe hadn't told Max what he'd done or what the Soviets wanted him back for and Max didn't dare. He just wanted Harry.

Slaipe hooked his good arm under the man's without missing a step and walked him into the arch. Harry came from the other side with his minder, each pair mimicking the other's measured steps, and it made Max think of a duel put on in reverse. Slaipe and the Czech minder stopped and let the swap proceed.

Their prisoner passed Harry and beyond, into the other

side, and Harry passed into the light on their side. Max stepped forward but someone said "stay here" again from the truck. This was all according to protocol. Max wouldn't be able to ride with Harry in case something went wrong. They were still in Communist Czechoslovakia, after all.

He watched from yards away. Slaipe gathered Harry and patted him on the back as they walked, and Harry gave Max a wink and Slaipe a thumbs-up. Then Harry climbed into the back of the truck, and Slaipe followed. The truck chugged off for a side street, Na Příkopě, the tires knocking at cobblestones, turned the corner, and disappeared in the fog.

Max knew the script from here. Harry would first be debriefed alone, and Max could see him in a few hours.

He glanced at the Powder Tower. All the players were gone and the arch was deserted, as if the swap had never happened. It was only then that Max realized no escort had been assigned to him, which meant no ride back in a warm sedan. He trudged back toward the embassy as if pulled by a heavy, heaving, slow-moving cable. To count the hours and minutes. He tried imagining a return to normalcy, a splendid meal and toasts all around to another disaster averted, but the fog wasn't even letting him imagine that. It only gave him a chill.

PRAGUE
10:41 a.m.

Four hours later, Max still waited in a stale but comfortable briefing room in the cellar below the US Embassy, only blocks from his pension. The former Schönborn Palace stood above them, at the base of a lovely hill. The CIA men had deposited him on a firm sofa, offered him coffee from the long conference desk. He had declined. Because he wasn't sticking around. But that was so long ago now. He felt like he was in a hospital waiting room, anticipating a surgery to end that was only supposed to last less than an hour. He'd asked all who entered, and anyone passing out in the hallway, but no one knew a thing. If he didn't find out something soon, he was going much farther than the hallway even though they'd told him to stay put. He did mention Aubrey Slaipe's name, which he wasn't supposed to, but it only drew blank stares.

Max paced the room, again. He'd drunk all the coffee in the pot they'd brought him after waving off their offer of food because he wasn't going to be there that long, and now he'd lost his appetite.

The door swung open. "Harry?" Max began.

But Aubrey Slaipe shuffled in.

"Where's Harry?"

Slaipe didn't reply. He lowered himself into the high-backed chair at the end of the table. Max watched in silence, hushed. Slaipe looked years older, his skin ashen in some spots and raw in others, his thin wisps of hair finding the indirect light of the room's sconces and standing lamps. Slaipe stared at the glossy tabletop a moment, then his eyes shot up at Max full of fire.

Max rushed over and sat at the chair nearest him. "What's the matter?"

"He's gone, Max."

Max kept shaking his head. "Gone? What? Gone how?"

Slaipe held up his prosthetic hand, then let it drop to the table with a thud. He gave a slight shrug. He said, avoiding Max's gaze, "I should have known."

"Known what?"

"He bolted, Max. Out into the cold. I'm sorry. I really am."

Max's leaden suit from Vienna was back again, weighing him down, pressing him into the chair so much it might crack. The fog from this morning was back, too, and he tried to blink it away, his eyes bulging.

One clear thought returned to him: *I will find you, Harry.*

"How could this happen?" he asked Slaipe.

Slaipe sighed. "He just walked out the door. No one expects that after a swap. I guess Harry figured on that."

"So there's no sign of him?" Max released a scornful chuckle.

"We haven't been able to locate him. It's not like he stepped out for a Danish. He's vanished, Max."

Both stared at the table for a good while.

"He must still be in the city," Max said. "What direction would he go?"

"Well, he's not skipping town to head west, is he?" Slaipe said. "He's gone solo, rogue, whatever you want to call it. Behind the

Iron Curtain. We have to assume that. We've informed the Russians and Czechs, and in no uncertain terms, that we had no idea what Harry did or is doing. We had to. What if they found out? He's a loose cannon. He's certainly not a spy now. In an operation, you don't want anyone to know you were there. You avoid a commotion, surprises, certainly violence, blood. In and out, like a burglar."

"But if no one knows where he is, then he's still a burglar? Isn't that right? And there hasn't been violence or blood, has there?"

Slaipe only grunted.

But something was stirring inside Max. There still had to be some way of finding Harry on his own. The old rush of operating solo himself returned to him, mightier and deeper than any performance on film or stage. He couldn't help feeling rejuvenated, more like a good premiere used to do. It was an addiction stronger than the theater—opium compared to champagne. He shot up from his chair, which only amplified his newfound warmth.

"Don't get any ideas," Slaipe told him. "You're going home on the next train. I told them that, too."

Max didn't respond. His mind was racing. Maybe he could hire someone. He knew a couple independent operators back in Munich. One drank steadily far too late in the bar and the other leapt under the nearest table when champagne popped, but he had to try something, someone.

He gave a fixed smile and his best American businessman posture. "But, look, Mr. Slaipe, let's talk this over sensibly. Now, I propose that we—"

Slaipe slapped at the desk. "No! I said no."

Max wasn't sure he'd ever heard Slaipe raise his voice.

Slaipe took a deep breath, started over. "You . . . you don't understand. It's now an international incident. Harry cannot be helped."

Max added a shrug of resignation and let himself deflate. He gazed around the room as if in a stupor, a man dazed by failure.

"You'll have a ticket, travel papers, all you need," Slaipe said.

I don't want your favors, Max thought. *I want Harry.*

"Very well," he told Slaipe. He added a sorrowful, fatalistic smile, his eyelids now drooping for emphasis. "But can't you tell me what he was really doing over here? His older brother would like to know."

"Stop acting. Don't even think about it. And don't give me that hangdog look."

"Surely you must know something, especially after what's happened."

"Well, I can't tell you anything. Of course I can't. Too much is compromised already." Slaipe paused, as if listening for anyone coming. "Though, all right, I can say that Harry was over here to rescue someone. An extraction. It had become his team's specialty ever since that independent job you two pulled for those refugees. But this was far more important."

"What could be more important than saving people?"

"I said don't give me that look. Every life is important, I know. But this, it concerns many lives. Far too many."

"Harry wanted it done right. He had to see it through."

"Yes. I told you. And now he's gone rogue."

"And you really don't know where he is?"

Slaipe ignored him.

"What about Harry's target?" Maybe he could track Harry to his target's location.

Slaipe only shook his head.

"Harry didn't have a choice," Max said. "He wasn't going back empty-handed. He couldn't rely on the CIA. Not after so many foul-ups lately, which you yourself mentioned."

Slaipe kept staring at the table, silent.

"Wait," Max said. "Did you help set this up?"

"No," Slaipe barked.

Max lowered his head, thinking things over. The fact remained that Harry did not tell the Russians anything. Dietz. And they didn't think this was any more than a standard busybody. So Harry, he still thought he had a chance. Harry still had a plan.

"It's time for you to go," Slaipe said. He stood. He put out a hand. "I'm sorry for this. I tried. Now, go back and enjoy Munich. Your money is already back there. We will be in touch."

"All right, Mr. Slaipe. All right. But please remember one thing: I let people lead me around once, in the war, because I had no choice. I'm not doing that ever again, not even in a cold war. You yourself should know that better than anyone."

"Point taken, Max. Now go home."

CZECHOSLOVAKIA, Bohemia
10:40 p.m.

Max rode a train heading west, destination Munich. In the dark. Aubrey Slaipe had provided him with first-class tickets again, another compartment all to himself, the seats plush. Comfy. Max had always liked that English word. But comfy was the last thing he wanted.

As he left Prague he had stared up at the city's many decorative buildings, some of them former palaces, and saw more of those tall Communist banners touting workers and scientists, mothers and fighters all striving in unison. Things had never been otherwise, the slogans proclaimed. Here was the one sole truth. But hadn't there once been some other eternal truth that those monarchical palaces had once proclaimed with their ornamental windows, and hadn't the fascists done the same with their intimidating poses and uniforms and flags and own banners cloaking those very same windows? Max winced now as he imagined a world where capitalism too eventually ran rampant and reckless, oligarchic and oppressive forever. An American future. It might take decades, if not the dawn of a new century, but the biggest profiteers of that system which Slaipe and Harry believed in so much would themselves turn to refabricating truth, all just to stay in power. And by then the people would never know any other truth. Sometimes he feared history and future truly were like a single train and it was barreling along in a tight circle, running along tall rocky cliffs, growing longer and longer with its weight, its feeble brakes unable to slow it. Eventually it would crash into itself, imploding forever.

He sat up straight, gazing out at the countryside passing as a dark blur while he considered Harry's whereabouts. His little brother could have vanished anywhere in Prague, a bridge, the river, train station, some inner courtyard, a tunnel, down a manhole under their feet, anywhere. That old city likely had more nooks and crannies and bolt-holes than Munich and Vienna combined, not to mention the shadows. And Harry had probably used one of those shrouded routes to flee the city itself by now.

Max shook his head at the thought. He still wondered if Aubrey Slaipe had played a role in Harry going rogue. Slaipe had said that Harry was planning to rescue someone, and the operation was far more important than any extraction that had come before, with far more lives at stake. If that were true, Slaipe would do what was needed. Slaipe had been the most capable and moral American Max had probably ever met. The competency of men like him was the only advantage the Americans had. If their country ever lost that edge, they were just as doomed as all the others. He thought of those banners and slogans again. All the high talk of freedom and better standards of living and some exceptional national destiny alone were never sustainable in the end—it had to be demonstrated in action. If not, the decay would prove unrelenting. It was the same old story from before Rome on down to the Third Reich and probably Great Britain . . .

Soon Max fell asleep, his head sinking into the comfy

headrest, alone in his compartment, while his past, his life, kept playing back to him like a film, but increasingly absurd, with locations changing at every street corner, from New York City to Hamburg, from the Russian Front and the Ardennes Forest, all the places he had faced failure and lost love and horrid carnage and death, all of it accumulating like this very train going twice and then three times normal speed as it headed into a tight bend, the tracks clacking and knocking as if ready to break apart right under him.

His eyes popped open. The compartment was all dark. Total darkness. He glanced out the window and could make out the dim lights of a faraway village just above a line of trees on the horizon, and above that, high in the sky, more stars than he'd seen since he'd been hiding out right after the war. The train was in open country, Bohemia, Western Czechoslovakia, what the new Communist government now called "border territory." But none of it was passing by. He wasn't moving.

The train had stopped? And the power was out, Max now realized. He listened in the dark and heard the muffled voices of others wondering in other compartments. Why had they halted? He listened for the bootsteps of Czechoslovak guards, or even the Russians.

He felt something in the dark, a presence. His heart started beating twice its rate, thumping now, and he peered forward but couldn't see the opposite bench, as the curtains on that side had been pulled. He hadn't pulled them. He tried to regulate his breathing, through his diaphragm, just like before a show but quietly, without gasping. He slid his fingers into his pocket for his lighter, slowly opened it with a clank.

"No light," a voice said from the dark in fluent native German. It was female. It sounded firm, determined, capable.

"Who are you? What's happening?"

"Just listen. Do you want to find him?"

She had to mean Harry. Who else could it be?

"Yes," Max said.

"It might get rough. Harry might not want our help. Can you accept that?"

"Oh, I know how to deal with Heinrich."

"That wasn't the question. We don't have much time."

"Yes."

"I am leaving, now. Are you coming?"

"What, off this train? Wait. You made the power go out. You made the train stop."

"Who else?" she said.

"Bravo!"

"Keep your voice down."

Max fell silent a moment. His eyes were adjusting. He could make out her silhouette, all in black with a shawl or a cap obscuring her face and head. Little black riding hood.

He had to think fast. He had to ask. "How did you find me here, on this very train?"

"Oh, you're not so hard to trail," she said, and he could hear her smile in her tone.

"I'm afraid you'll have to give me more than that," Max said, making sure his tone carried a smile too.

She chuckled a little, but her voice was hard again. "Let's just say that you and I, we have a common interest in finding Harry."

"More," Max said. "Remember, we don't have much time."

Now she fell silent. "Love. Retribution."

"More."

"Damn you, Kaspar," she grumbled. "Very well. Think of it this way: You do not believe the likes of Hartmut Dietz are going to give up on this, do you? And you know he will find out Harry's gone solo."

"There you go again—"

"People tip me off. Us. Allies. All right?"

They heard voices, in Czech.

She stood. "You don't want to go back to Munich. You could never live with yourself. Now come on."

"All right, yes," Max said.

"Follow me, at my back," she said. "Do what I do, don't improvise."

"Ah, we're stage directing, are we? Very well."

In seconds they were tiptoeing down the passageway. Footsteps came rushing their way. They darted into a compartment where the big and small silhouettes of a family stared at them. Someone whispered in Czech and she shot back in firm but kind German to be quiet, which did the trick. Max spotted a boy at his knee staring up at him and he held a finger to his mouth and the boy did the same, then smiled.

The footsteps were a man rushing by, just a conductor, likely trying to figure out what had happened to the power.

She tapped Max and they rushed out and along to the end of the car. She looked both ways, he looked both ways. She opened the door. She peeked her head out, Max did the same. In one direction they could make out the figure of a man out along the tracks, another train man, one hand on his hip, a rag hanging from his hand. Locomotive smoke and steam wafted by, tickling Max's nose.

The lights flashed, then came back on. People cheered modestly from inside the train and beams of compartment light appeared all down the track as myriad squares, some deformed by the curious still peering outside.

The train man outside shook his head and then stepped up into the next car down.

"Shouldn't we go?" Max said, tugging on her riding hood.

"Wait," she said, "and stop pulling."

The train lurched a foot, then started a slow roll.

"Now," she barked and she jumped down and Max followed, one foot sliding a little on train bedrock, but in seconds they were moving through tall grass hunched, she zigzagging, he copying her, until they reached a low rock wall they crawled over and hugged, watching the train chug away in rhythm with their panting, it seemed—a hauntingly lovely tune, Max thought.

Silence found them, their panting subsiding, his heart calming. The moonlight painted the countryside with pale grays and purples, and he could nearly make out her face, her high cheekbones and slightly dimpled chin. They could smell the damp grass, but also cowshit.

"Splendid out here," he blurted.

"Please, I need to listen," she added in a gentler whisper.

He waited it out. He watched her. She was peering around in a crouch, getting her bearings more than listening now, comparing horizon and ridges with vague possible landmarks and the angle of the tracks passing, checking it against the moon and stars repeatedly. She had been well trained, whoever she was. Max relaxed even more. He could trust her, for now. He wondered if she had food.

She let out a little sigh, and it sounded like her own relief. They were in the clear.

She faced him, leaning against the low wall, her eyes glinting at him from under her hood. "He doesn't like when you call him that, you know," she said in a warmer voice.

"What, Heinrich? No, I suppose not." Max added a bashful chuckle.

"Or Heino. Especially not Heino."

"Well, if he's going to call me Maxie . . . Wait, how do you know all this?"

She tried a chuckle. Her German was likely from the south, he could tell now, from near Munich even. "I'm guessing that he hasn't called you that in a long, long while."

"Yes, I suppose you're right."

They paused to look out together, scanning the dark and silent landscape once more.

"Who are you?" Max said eventually. "Why are you here?"

"Harry, he saved me once too," was all she said.

CZECHOSLOVAKIA, Bohemia
11:18 p.m.

They spotted a farmhouse, its pale stucco glowing from moonlight, a cluster of geometric beacons among the half timbers of the high gabled exterior.

"What are our roles?" Max asked the hooded woman as they approached the property using fences and bushes. She cocked her head at him. "Cover, I mean," he added. "Sorry, it's the old actor in me."

She snorted at that. "If anyone asks you, my name's Rosamunde. That's all you know."

The farmhouse stood next to a tall barn with only its gable half timbered and plastered, the main siding just tarred wood planks that remained submerged in the shadows of night. They stopped at a corner of the barn and peered across the dirt courtyard at the farmhouse, which had lights on. Someone was home. But who? Western Bohemia was the former Sudetenland, where everyone used to speak German. Based on the Allies' Potsdam Agreement of 1945, the Czechoslovakians' Beneš Decrees had started expelling the majority ethnic German population and the ruling Communists were making it stick. This farmhouse could be holding anyone from a Nazi on the run to Joe Stalin himself. Their best hope was to find a little old *Frau*, alone, without a country.

The hooded woman tugged at Max. They moved along the tar plank siding and crouched at the open doors of the barn, where she'd stop to listen, and the citified Max realized she was listening for any animals that could neigh or buck or charge. They heard nothing, only crickets outside. They smelled no farm animal dung, only the peppery, earthy reek of hay. Looking satisfied by that, she led him right into the barn, apparently able to see in the dark.

Five minutes later they were sitting on that hay, up in a loft that received a modicum of moonlight from a roof skylight. Sprawled out. Comfy.

Max should've been relaxed but he suddenly grew itchy and edgy and had to scratch at his neck, his forearms. He curled up. He was suddenly cold, in the dark, so dark. He was trapped in the Ardennes, in deadest winter. His heartbeat pounded hot in his ears, the tips of his fingers. He shot up. One leg started to bounce and he couldn't hold it down. He felt the urge to run out of here, they were trapped, see, surrounded—

She grabbed him by the collar and shook him. "You're all right. Listen to me. It's just the war. It comes back. I've seen it before, many suffer from it."

He wanted to tell her. It was the Eastern Front, then the Battle of the Bulge, then hiding out in ravines south of here with refugees who were walking dead if caught. But he knew better than to speak before he knew the score.

"All right, yes, thank you," he muttered. He tried to think, like he used to in situations like this, of something hopeful. Perhaps there was a trove of fine country eggs in this barn, a barrel of them, aspic and all. In that farmhouse might be a cheerful country daughter offering him homemade schnapps. *Fat chance*, came the response in his head. Why was normalcy always behind him or ahead of him, just out of grasp? He curled up again and pressed his head against his knees, his heart wanting to explode right out of his chest. He sometimes truly did miss the old Max, a fun-loving fellow who could appreciate even the shimmer of a horsefly perched on shit itself.

Soon a light came on. He raised his head. She had found a kerosene lamp and turned it on low. She pulled out a leather satchel from under her hooded garment and was going through it.

"You don't have a map in there?" he said.

She unfolded a worn and simple tourist map of Bohemia, surely just for show. It wouldn't get them far without more maps in her head.

"You know what you're doing," he added.

She slowly pulled her hood down. As he saw her lovely face, the prickly cords and barbwire constraining him inside loosened and fell away.

"You'll be better off now that you're getting this nasty feeling out of the way," she said. "You just haven't been on an operation for a long time."

"Also true."

"You asked what our roles are?" she said. "Me, I'm a refugee. Show me your papers."

He showed her his German temporary passport, three-day cultural visa, and travel permits. She groaned at them. "I suppose I should tell you to toss them," she told him, "but they'll have to do for now."

"What are you, an agent? Who do you work for? Did Aubrey Slaipe put you up to this?"

She grinned. "The Americans? Hardly."

"British? French? We can rule out the Soviets."

"We can rule them all out," she said. "We, my people, we have our own agenda. That's all I can tell you for now. What if someone caught us? The less you know, the better."

He had to know something. He studied her a moment. She had short dark hair with trim bangs. Her face, not the hair, looked somehow familiar to him. And he'd heard her voice somewhere. He cocked his head at her. "Say, have we met?"

Her head popped up, listening. A soft creak of boots, faint footsteps, from the farmhouse. They eyed each other to keep quiet. They had never heard a door open or close. The person might have sensed something and was sneaking over to inspect.

They slowly peered over the edge of the loft, careful not to crunch hay.

A shadow showed in the doorway below, with a grotesque distortion of a cap, hopefully one of a farmer and not a commissar. It said something in Czech, "*Je tam někdo?*" which Max guessed was "Who's there?"

He looked to her. She held up a hand like a squad leader. Max became as still as could be, just like offstage.

The person entered and switched on a flashlight, which revealed flashes of boots, leather belt, overalls, a worker's cap, a hard jaw. A man. The butt of a gun, slung on a shoulder. The man checked the empty stalls below, shining his light into each.

The man neared the ladder to the loft. Max looked to her once more. She held up her hand again and pointed at herself, then at the stairs. Max shook his head to tell her, *no, don't,* but before he could persuade her otherwise, she was up and striding toward the ladder and calling out "Hello, who is there, please?" in German and broken Czech.

She climbed down the ladder. The man shined the flashlight on her lean legs and curvy behind and kept it there.

She faced him. The man turned the flashlight to her face. The man smiled, grinned. Max could just see over the ledge from his spot. Her back was to him and he could barely make out their exchange. After a back-and-forth they settled on German, the man's German rusty at best and he spat it out as if someone had forced him to eat a bad apple.

Max crept closer to the ledge. He heard the man demand her name, which she gave in a low voice. The man ordered her again and she produced a thin booklet the size of a passport, with an upside-down red triangle on the cover. He shined his light on it.

Only now did Max notice the man wore a red star on his cap. He said something, she didn't respond. She turned away from his flashlight. The man pivoted and barked at her and lifted her hooded cape and shined his light on her body. Max saw pants, a sweater.

Max had crept to the very edge without realizing it. He felt at her bag for a weapon and his fingers ran over hard objects, but he couldn't tell what they were. He figured he could leap from here and land on the man, but what if he injured himself in the process? Would she still take him along? These thoughts flashed through his head in split seconds. His senses intensified, his muscles tensed. He could hear better, jump better.

"You come inside, with me," the man told her. "We drink. We sleep. Night."

"No," she said. She added a shake of her head.

Max grabbed onto the edge, swaying back and forth, eyeing the angles. He could land on the man's shoulders and start punching upon landing. He once leapt from a theater box onto stage, he could do this.

"You do it!" the man barked. His stuck the stem of his flashlight into his belt and pulled his rifle off his shoulders and barked again.

She showed him a blank face, like a mask.

"Inside!" he repeated in German. "You go. With me. Order!" He aimed his gun from his hip, feet planted far apart.

Max had his feet on the ledge, ready to leap.

She shook her head. To Max's surprise, she stepped closer to the man, the barrel nearly touching her.

A dark grimace spread across the man's face, and he shook his rifle to compel her.

Max leapt.

Right as he did, he sensed her lunge.

The flashlight beam shot around, hitting rafters, siding, hay and shadow.

Max landed where the man was supposed to be but only found hay-covered dirt, his knees and ankles buckling.

All went dark. He heard jangling, groaning.

He rolled and peered around and spotted silhouettes next to him, but they were conjoined and he shot back up on his toes, ready to pounce.

The flashlight came back on.

The man lay under her. She had one of his arms in a lock that made him moan. He stared up at her, his face ashen and his wide eyes bulging, spit jumping out the corners of his mouth. She tossed Max the flashlight with her other hand and he fumbled it and by the time he got it aimed back on them she somehow had a knife to the man's throat.

She released her lock, slowly, and he cautiously raised his arms, making him look like a snow angel.

"Is anyone else here?" she asked the man.

"No. Only me . . ."

She shook him.

"Owners sent away. West. Sudeten Germans. Maybe east. I don't know. Red Army take all, animals, machines. I caretaker, I—"

"*Psst*," she said to shut him up, then shook him again to seal the deal.

As he lay there suppressing a squeal, she said to Max, "Local Soviet ass-licker, every village has them. Probably just joined the Communist Party."

"Naturally. And was never, ever a Nazi. Just like back home."

She nodded at Max and then the rifle and Max scooped it up and stood, aiming the gun. It was a German model, a 98K like he'd avoided carrying during the war, and it felt grimy, almost greasy.

She stood and pulled the man up by his collar. He looked smaller down here and had to practically look up at Max, blinking with fear. Max could smell the liquor on him, sweet yet fiery like something homemade.

She pushed the man while swinging a foot at his ankles and he dropped, moaning again.

"I never told you to stand."

His face opened up. He shook his head.

"Do what I say."

He nodded. His eyes filled with wet. He clasped his hands together as if praying to her, ready to beg her.

"Do not exit this barn, understand?" she told the man. She repeated it in Czech.

He nodded. He nodded for Max.

"If you exit this barn," Max said, "our people outside will shoot you."

"You'll be dead before you can reach the house," she added.

"Yes, sir. Yes, ma'am."

She scowled at him. "It's *comrade* to you," she added, grabbed the flashlight from Max, clicked it off, and turned on her bootheel and headed for the barn door.

CZECHOSLOVAKIA, Bohemia
Night to day

She switched off the flashlight before they left the barn, and Max followed her back into the night. "Nice improvisation there at the end," she said over her shoulder, "despite my instructions."

"Thanks. It worked for the role."

As they marched along she fell silent, as if angry at the whole ordeal, and Max wondered if he had done something else wrong. After about a half mile, she held out a hand for the rifle. He handed it to her. She flung it down a hillside, deep into bushes.

"I wasn't tired anyway," Max said, shaking his head, which felt heavy now. He was becoming so drowsy he could have napped marching. He'd done it before. "You?"

"No, not me," she said. "I thought you would need the rest."

"You thought wrong," Max said, and smiled, and he rallied somehow and they marched much of the night, north along country roads lined with trees and skirted by fields, only hiding once or twice when engines sounded like military vehicles, but those proved only wartime vehicles repurposed. The sweetness of meadow flowers gave way to the peppery aroma of pines. Hills became steep at times, nearly mountains if not ravines, and the dense trees seemed to bend over them. This was one part of an operation Max could do without, as it reminded him too much of the Ardennes Forest again. At least it wasn't below freezing. The air had grown cooler, but their constant trudging warmed them. On one break, they drank water from a stream, their backs against a birch tree. He only saw her face at times like this, slight glimpses when the moonlight found it or when she dared a cigarette.

"You did well back there," she said. "You nearly had him." She added a smile, her teeth shining a bluish white from the moon and stars.

"Thank you. I'm just glad I didn't turn an ankle."

She let out a happy chuckle.

Max thought about how she had performed for that man in the barn, luring him in, her voice soft and lilting and innocent and sounding nothing like she had before.

And suddenly he was sure he knew her. His eyes expanded in awe, and his chest warmed with pride, but his brain didn't know if he should be grateful or terrified. He peered at her. Her eyebrows were thicker now than he remembered, and her hair much longer back then of course.

He flinched—she was peering back at him, too, in the dark, he now noticed. "What?" he said.

"You don't look that much like him," she said. "Like Harry. You're bigger, darker features, broader face. But there's an intensity there that you share."

"Now you sound like a casting director," Max said.

She held up a hand and opened her mouth to speak but inserted a cigarette instead.

They continued on, often following a river, and when they didn't she sometimes stopped to check a compass or the stars. She had them get some sleep, sitting up against secluded tree trunks in the dark. Most of the time Max only saw her back and her hood as they walked.

"Do you know where he is?" he asked her.

She ignored him.

"But you have a good idea?" he tried a little while later.

She halted a moment. "I have to do a couple jobs first. It's part of what I do. Along the way, I will find out more about Harry. All right? I can't tell you any more. Just trust me."

"All right. I just want to help my brother. I don't want him to fail, not like I did."

"I know," she said after a pause.

The sun came up, coloring the horizon with purples and oranges and the black treetop silhouettes with greens and emeralds, the daylight soon finding them along the road as if a blanket had been uncovered by the chirping birds. *Delightful*, Max thought even though his feet ached and his lower back kept tightening up. Luck finally caught up with them when they approached a village inn. The innkeepers, an elderly wife and husband, offered them food and refused payment, then made them drink from a tin mug of coffee. Max consumed it with both hands, his stomach warm and full from dried sausage, country egg, and rye bread, his spirits lifted by the strong *černá káva*. It renewed his faith in humanity, or at least in Czechs.

They pressed on, following a narrow river. On their first break in full daylight, as they sat on a log along the river, she pulled back her hood and Max observed her face in the sun for the first time. Her hair was even shorter than he'd thought in the dark and she'd made no attempt to style it. The thought occurred to him that she had been compelled to cut it, which he, from his stage and screen knowledge, attributed to various roles and ruses involving wigs. She offered him a cigarette. "Too early for me," he said, directing his face at the sparkling, rippling water. He stole looks at her. She wasn't wearing makeup, which made her look surprisingly plain by day. Her cheeks showed the faintest hint of pockmarks, from some bout of acne or pox in her youth that had never been revealed in any still or role or even newsreel. And the lines of her face were harder, her skin paler, nearly white blue, and he spotted a scar below one ear. Not even the sunshine reflecting off the stream could make it glow. She stared across the river, vacantly like he had done many times, like Harry had done, like so many who had seen violent death if not caused it.

Her eyes darted and she spotted him before he could look away, so he held the stare, adding a smile.

She yanked her cigarette. "What?"

"Nothing. Just observing." He looked away and spoke to the lovely current, finding the spots that were reflecting the birch trees.

"Harry told me about you," he said.

She nodded, one nod.

"This was after we were reunited in Munich, after the war," Max said. "Harry told me about you as a way to steel me, to give me hope."

She stared at the water, and the reflecting light finally softened her face, and her eyes.

"Harry had asked me, 'Did you know the actress Katarina Buchholz?' Well, not personally, I told him. I never had the luck or luxury of performing at your level. Or the skill to, I suspect. But who didn't know of you? German men had pinups of you in bunkers from Normandy to Stalingrad."

She rolled her eyes.

"No, it's true. I saw them myself. Russian Front, Western Front. You should never be ashamed of that."

She glared at him. "I'm not ashamed. It was just a former life, is all."

"I understand. Believe me, I do. Harry, he told me you were his partner in his first real test. May 1945. There he was, Captain Harry Kaspar of the US Military Government occupying defeated Germany, all wet behind the ears on his first post in far-flung rural Bavaria. The occupation of a town called Heimgau. Things were going very wrong there. He discovered major corruption among his fellow American occupiers. Plundering. Harry wouldn't put up with it. You helped him fight back, set things right." They were also lovers, Max knew.

"And Harry passed the test," she said. "He learned hard lessons. He set an example, for himself, for me. You cannot back down. You have to atone . . ." She let the words trail off.

"Harry told me you left Germany soon after, with a Jew you knew, a refugee partisan. Emil Wiesenberg. A good man." Originally from Munich, Emil had helped Harry and Katarina derail the corruption in Heimgau. "The two of you were living in Palestine, the last Harry had heard."

"Yes. We were on a kibbutz and in the Haganah together."

Harry had told Max that Katarina had needed more than what Harry and Heimgau could offer, and Harry couldn't argue. Emil deserved her just as much as he did.

"Not a bad tale," added the once famous actress known as Katarina Buchholz. "You should've written movie scripts."

"That's a young man's game, I'm afraid."

They shared a laugh.

"I'd heard of you, too, by the way," Katarina said.

Max waved away the notion. "Hogwash."

Katarina stared with sad eyes, leaving a pause where she might have added that she'd heard of him, early in the war.

He was the lover of that great young opera singer on the rise, Liselotte Auermann. She died in a Hamburg air raid.

"Emil died last year," she said. "Fighting in Palestine."

"The Arab-Israeli War."

"Was that the passport you showed that Czech? It was Israeli? I saw it in the barn, from that bastard's flashlight."

"No. I'm not Jewish. But . . ." Katarina pulled out the ID and showed it to him. The cover had a red triangle and the letters VVN, for the *Vereinigung der Verfolgten des Naziregimes*—the Union of Persecutees of the Nazi Regime. The photo inside was a humbler version of her, the name Rosamunde Klein. "It still works, for now, in a pinch. Though things are changing fast here in the East. Everyone's suspect. Even Holocaust victims."

"You were never in a concentration camp."

She didn't need to shake her head at that one.

"So it's your cover?"

She nodded again.

"But isn't the war back in Palestine? Your war."

"Our war is everywhere," Katarina said, then stood to go.

KARLOVY VARY
Saturday, May 21
Noon

Along the town streets, Max and Katarina Buchholz discovered a lost medley of Wilhelmine, Belle Époque, fin de siècle, and Jugendstil architecture, all born of the Austro-Hungarian Empire before orphaned by wars and expropriated as restitution. A daydream of a dream. They had walked high forest roads curving gently downhill until the dense leafy tree line gave way to promenades of compact adjoining city villas in pastel colors.

The street was clear and no vehicles could be heard. Max walked shoulder to shoulder with Katarina. They heard nothing apart from the breeze in garden hedges and a slight, faraway rush of water. No one was about, the town eerily noiseless for a weekend.

"Sadly quiet," Max said, adding a sigh for all the lost worlds. The legendary spa town of Carlsbad had been renamed Karlovy Vary. Carlsbad had been mostly ethnic German. Most of the town was forcibly expelled and their property confiscated. "It's like that farmhouse."

"Let's hope not," Katarina said.

"You need to tell me more," Max told her. "We've been heading north so far. I think. It's not as if I have a compass."

She gave him a wry smile over her shoulder that said, *Do you really need a compass for that? Poor boy.* She kept walking. They passed more bright Jugendstil facades. Max stopped contemplating them and fixed his gaze on her.

"Do you know where he is," he said, "or don't you?"

She sighed. "I will know," she said eventually, "but I need to do a job first."

"A job?"

"Here," was all she said, "in this very town."

Her face had hardened. After another couple minutes, she stepped to the side of the street and turned to him. She placed a hand each on his shoulders. "You know how sometimes we used to take those horrid roles so that we could do the roles that we loved?"

"And how! More so than you, I should think."

"Be that as it may. This is one of those roles. But they might even be able to tell me where Harry is, if we're lucky." She patted both his shoulders, then marched on.

Soon they sat in a corner of an empty café in the heart of Karlovy Vary, street by street the grandest small town Max had ever seen. Surrounding them were spas and churches and hotels and restaurants adorned with patinas and mansards, curly iron and gold and ornate stonework, plasters painted with more of those relaxing pastels, all miniature versions of Prague, Vienna, Paris, and Dresden before the bombings, if not Venice, complete with a surgically formed man-made canals and half plazas convenient for resting every few minutes. It was all peeling and cracking if one looked closely, but Max didn't care. For one brief moment it again became the majestic Central Europe of his prewar aspirations. He imagined the opera house, the theater, a cabaret, and he—

"Max, you still with me?" Katarina said.

"Oh, you can be sure of it, dear."

A skinny waiter who looked more like a farmhand had come out and spoke to them in Czech, in which Katarina ordered them coffees. She slipped a cigarette in her mouth, one of Max's Ernte 23s. They watched the street. It was just as empty as the café. A horse and cart carrying sacks passed once. A couple soldiers in Red Army–style uniforms did wander by, their caps pushed back, and Max pressed his shoulders to the shadows along the wall.

"I believe this is what Harry would call a 'ghost town,'" she said. "Ah, our coffee."

The waiter set down a battered tin tray—two mismatched cups, no saucers, and a tarnished old pot, all of it more like something they would've cobbled together at the front to somehow feel human again. There was a slip of paper underneath, right at Katarina's fingertips. She placed a hand on the tray and withdrew it and the note vanished. A female magician was always a lovely sight, and Max wondered if she'd learned sleight of hand for one of her films, perhaps that one where she played a Romani. He shook his head at bygone days one last time and poured them the coffee, expecting little better than ersatz, considering. There was no sugar or cream, either, but he'd stopped using both anyway. Katarina was watching him now with one corner of her mouth turned up, suddenly the young prewar actress from a small Bavarian town with aspirations all her own. So he opened his eyes at her with expectation, held an imaginary saucer in his other hand and set the cup on it, stirred in the notional sugar and fresh cream, his eyes lighting up, and then sipped. He was planning a spit take but that was too conspicuous. Her eyes had lit up too. He did his best hard swallow. Set down his cup and imaginary saucer. Then did his best comical death, arms splayed, legs straight out and feet up, tongue hanging out one side of his mouth.

He peeked out one of his shut eyes and saw her grinning, lovely so, just beaming.

"All right, you ham actor, that's enough," she said and gave him an exaggerated eye roll.

"Very well. It was a little too Chaplin." He sat up. "Don't you miss it, though, sometimes?"

"No."

"Listen, I have a little cabaret, in Munich; all right, not a true cabaret, but it's close enough if you ever wanted to branch out."

One of her eyebrows raised. "Do you?" she said.

"Do I what, dear?"

"Miss it."

"No, I guess not. Not as much."

"You know why?" she said. "That's because we're still doing it. Right here."

"Touché," Max said and took a real sip. The coffee wasn't horrible, and he appreciated the boost it gave him for whatever she had planned.

"What was on that note?" he whispered out the side of his mouth.

Katarina frowned at him, but with a little Chaplin in it too.

"Tell me something," he said, eyes on the street, listening. "How did you know?"

"Know?"

"Find out. About Harry being over here. About me. Was it through the Americans? British?"

"Not now," she said, sipping, watching. "I'm working."

"Does it have to do with refugees?" This reminded Max of Harry's other flame, after Katarina: Sabine Lieser. In Munich, Sabine had worked for UNRRA, the United Nations Relief and

Rehabilitation Administration, helping Displaced Persons. Through her network, Sabine had ways of getting people vital passports, safe passage, secure messages. "Plenty of refugees make it to Palestine—to Israel, I mean. Congratulations, by the way, for independence."

"Independence was a year ago, but thank you. And I'm not Israeli. I told you. I'll never deserve that, not as a German."

She'd said it in such a hard voice that Max fell silent.

But she soon placed her hand on his. She squeezed it. "Max. Max? Listen to me. I won't let anything happen to you. All right? Or me for that matter. And certainly not him."

"All right. Yes. Thank you. And I will not let anything happen to you."

"Deal. Now let's go. I have my job to do."

1:47 p.m. Katarina had ordered Max to wait for her at a grand spa in the middle of town. He was to stay put there for two hours, possibly three, and she would collect him when it was time to continue. He had objected, she'd insisted. For a moment, Max imagined what that wonderful spa would be like, as if in a movie script. A stout lady in a pristine white smock shows him around the facility. He has it all to himself, and he wanders in a white robe. He lounges on a chaise, drinks the thermal mineral water from the local springs. Soaks in a hot pool of the waters. Cut to him sipping Becherovka, the local herbal bitters. His body feels more relaxed than since possibly before the war.

But he never even went inside.

Something shifted, deep in his gut. That lever. It told him something was not right. Every actor and soldier had a version of the gut feeling whether they wanted it or not. It automatically made his blood rush, and his legs wanted to kick.

He checked the café he and Katarina had used this morning. It had closed.

He roamed the middle of town, choosing narrow side streets and pausing in doorways and before windows for safety. The afternoon had livened things up a bit. He eyed a few awed families and even heard a brass band in a park, but he mostly passed small groups of Czechs and possibly Russians in the ill-fitting suits of the political functionary.

And then he spotted a woman with long blonde hair and a lightweight overcoat that covered too much for this weather. She wore sunglasses. And she wore makeup now, her lips a shapely bright red. She had transformed her walk into a girlish strut, especially for this role.

Katarina.

Max followed, around corners, another alley, zigzagging through colonnades. She took her time, but was deliberate. She entered a small square. A café had two small tables outside, nothing fancy. Katarina sat on church steps across from the tables and lit up a cigarette.

The square was empty except for one of the outdoor tables. Three men hunkered around it, their broad torsos obscuring the tabletop. Two had suits on, but one wore an open-collared shirt with the sleeves rolled up and a flatcap pulled down to his eyes, and he sat facing out. He was the largest of the three, with a thick jaw.

Max eyed the square and still detected no one else, all the windows curtained or shuttered, all the other entrances and exits vacant.

Then the three stood and shook hands and the two in suits gave a hint of a click of heels to the biggest man in casual clothes, who stayed. He watched the two suits disappear down the next side street. He gestured for the waiter, who approached with some hesitation, took his order, and then darted back inside the café.

Max entered a far corner of the square, keeping to a wall as inconspicuously as he could, and stooped in a doorway, ostensibly to tie his shoe.

The blonde Katarina stood and strode across the square, letting her cigarette drop like an extinguished match, and approached the man at the table with her hands inside her pockets. He stared back, his legs far apart, as if ready to topple the table. The waiter came back outside and, seeing Katarina approaching, quickly backed up inside.

She stopped before the table, placed one foot against the table leg, and stood over the man. Max could only see from around Katarina's shoulder. She was saying something.

The man's jaw rose. It looked like a standoff.

Max wished he had some kind of weapon, even a lady's gun.

The man directed his large jaw around the square, peering around. He faced Katarina again and his mouth stretched wider, but Max couldn't tell if it was a smile or a sneer.

Katarina removed her foot from the table leg and planted her legs farther apart. The man stood and loomed even larger than he seemed sitting. Both nodded. The man took another look around the square. He came around the table to her, each side-eyeing the other. Katarina, her hands still in her pockets, removed her left hand and gestured for him to go first.

He laughed at that.

He struck her across the head and she fell back onto the table, skidding along with it.

The man ran, across the square. Max pulled back, around the corner. The man was coming his way. Max expected shouts or shots but heard nothing. The big man's footsteps sounded like a racehorse on the cobblestones, clomping, metallic, rushing closer.

Max planted one arm against the wall and cocked back one leg. As the man reached the corner, Max swung his leg out into the lane like a nasty fouling centerback. He heard a grunt, slipped and fell on his behind, and as he did, saw the man sliding along the cobblestones face-first, palms and chin scraping.

Max scrambled up, but his one leg stung like fire from the pain in his shin. The man scrambled up, too, and started off again, not even looking back. Max lunged at him. He couldn't quite reach the man with his hands so he jumped and kicked at him and the man went sliding forward again.

For a split second he stared back at Max, his chin blooded, his eyes white with incredulity. Max stared back from his seat on the stones, his head spinning. The man pulled himself up to a crouch and reached down for a pant leg, for something under his sock.

Right then two figures rushed into the lane from an alley. One punched the man, knocking him back down, and they dragged him off by the arms, shouting at him in German and a language Max didn't know.

Max stood clumsily, like a sleepy man rising from bed, his shin still throbbing, his rear end tender. He heard a car engine rev and echo off alley walls and speed off.

"I could have used that spa after this, not before," Max joked to soothe his pains. His rear end was cooperating, but his shin was sure to swell and bruise. If only he could've worn shin guards like a proper centerback.

They were back inside their café from earlier, Katarina sitting across from him. She had pulled off her blonde wig and the overcoat was gone, leaving her in a simple flowery summer dress with her short hair still mussed. The supposed waiter from earlier had brought her a cold washcloth, which she held to the side of her head. He'd also brought them cheap whiskey in cups, which was horrible but worked well enough given the circumstances.

"Luckily my hair should hide any swelling or bruises," she grumbled.

"Luckily your sunglasses got the worst of it," Max said. The man's blow had busted them.

She added a frown and a sip. "One of my last few souvenirs from my screen days. Now just another casualty."

"Don't forget that café table."

Both of them burst out chuckling, then grunted from their individual pains, then added a sip of rough whiskey. The cycle repeated itself.

"Why did he laugh at you?" Max said once they'd stopped smiling. "Right before he bolted."

"I told him we had men and guns pointing at him from every direction. That he was trapped, walled in. He took his chances anyway."

"What was he, a Nazi?"

She winked at him.

"He called your bluff," Max said.

"Yes. We don't have resources like that. Some actress I was. It was all we had. We were acting on a tip, had no time. I had no time to prepare."

"May I suggest a note? You might have approached him in that lovely dress instead of an overcoat."

Katarina sat up straight, her face hard. "Listen, you, I'm no honeypot! I don't take those kind of roles and I never have, I . . ." She winced from her pains, cutting short an apparent tirade.

Max held up hands like a contrite producer, suppressing a chuckle. "I meant nothing by it, my dear. I only suggested that because you clearly did not have a gun under that overcoat despite your excellent body language."

She lowered her cigarette. "You could tell? I worked on that so hard. I even used a pipe. All right, I could've used a gun, but I don't work that way. Going to the gun is for the movies or for psychopaths and only gets you into trouble."

Max placed a hand to his heart. "We really should have worked together. If only I had a talent agent worth his salt."

She added a smile, a delighted shrug. "But we are working together, dear. I told you. There is simply no audience."

Max held up a finger. "Or reviews! Thank god."

They laughed.

"In any case," she said, "I should thank you very much."

"What can I say? The second try worked like a charm, unlike that pratfall in the barn."

She held up her cup of whiskey, and she toasted him. "Now we can keep going."

"To get Harry?"

She batted eyelashes.

"When do we go?" he said.

She downed her whiskey, stood, and smoothed out the dress as if her aches and pains never existed. "Right now."

CZECHOSLOVAKIA, North Bohemia
10:22 p.m.

Max and Katarina hunkered down in a ravine, in the dark, in the middle of a wood. It might have been a lovely camping spot. They took their boots off, let their feet cool. They were miles from anyone, anywhere. After walking north from Karlovy Vary, they had hitched a ride in the bed of a delivery truck heading northwest. Katarina had proposed they take the small risk to give their bodies a break. But the road had jostled their tender muscles and bruises in the rickety old truck relentlessly, as if they were dough being kneaded by giant hands. After a couple hours of it, they had the driver drop them off in the next village, which they quickly exited, back on foot.

Now this secluded ravine gave Max more grim memories, of the bloody Ardennes and the treacherous Šumava forests, of fatally crossing deadly frontline borders, all while chased by cutthroat hunters. He and Katarina seemed safe enough here. They rested their backs against birch trunks and their rear ends on the soft undergrowth. But the truth was, they were hemmed in on all sides, by the thick low clouds that had set in above, by the ravine's high rock walls, by the dense tree line circling them, and by a fast nearby stream, and those were only the natural obstacles. His skin prickled all over as if from stinging nettles and his hands turned clammy. He wanted to run but had no chance, no way out. Didn't Katarina see that? He gaped at her in the dark but could barely make her out against the dark trunks.

"What's the matter?" Katarina said from her tree.

Max began to speak but it came out a sigh. He breathed deep, all diaphragm again.

"Breathe with your diaphragm," she said.

"I am!"

He spotted a glint of her teeth showing but couldn't tell if she was grimacing or smiling. "You'll be all right," she said. "I told you. Contemplating what's coming is the hard part. Once you're in the moment, in the role? You're fine. Look what you did for me back in Karlovy Vary. And before. You saved our operation."

"Why did you try putting me in that spa hotel? I should've been with you from the start."

"If the job had failed? You would've been in the clear. You wouldn't even know what happened. Don't worry—someone would've gotten you the message to clear out, I'm sure."

"Failed? As in you dead, or you arrested, what?"

"Perhaps both. Every mission is different."

"Mission?"

"I told you, there are certain roles we take on. Some even by contract . . ." Katarina stopped midsentence. She looked away.

"You have to tell me," Max said after a while. "Before we advance another inch. I have too much riding on this. No, not me. Harry does. It might well be his life at stake."

"You think I don't have a stake? I'm not some lady tourist here."

"That's just it. How could I know? You haven't told me."

More silence ensued. Something rustled high in the trees, a small woodland animal.

She was shaking her head. She released a long, low sigh. "Very well. How much do you want?"

"All you can. And thank you."

Katarina stared at him in the dark, the moonlight finding her eyes. "I wouldn't be here without Emil Wiesenberg. Without Israel. Emil's colleagues in the Haganah, then Israeli military intelligence, they had decided that I, as a German, and as an actress capable of becoming someone else, was of far better use back home. Throughout Europe. I've been hunting for some time now. Teams of capable, resolute Jews used to roam these countries, tracking down Nazi criminals they identified through various means. The teams had various names. Nakam. Gmul. The Avengers. It started inside a British unit called the Jewish Brigade, right after the war. But with the founding of the state of Israel, and the War of Independence especially, the thinking was that Jews currently can't be attracting any undue negative attention. Thus, a gentile. Blonde, if need be—" She caught her breath, clearly not accustomed to voicing the truth.

"And without makeup," Max said. "Define hunting."

"Abduction. Extraction. Assassination even," she said, staccato, punching right through the darkness to some other side. "Every role's different."

"So that man was a Nazi." Max recalled the mission in Karlovy Vary. They were good. They were smooth. He supposed they had to be. They knew from life or death. "Bravo, I say. That was Hebrew I heard? On that square. Your men."

"Maybe. It could've been Yiddish."

"Are you still working with a team? Are they near?"

"No. I'll rejoin them eventually." She added a sigh.

"You don't sound so thrilled."

"It's not the same since Emil died. But it has to be done. And at least I have time now, for you and Harry."

"So that job in Karlovy Vary? Which role was that?"

"My role, that time, was only abduction. The lure. The rest was up to others, wiser ones, those who deserve to judge. I'm just a soldier. My fight is making amends."

Max felt numb. He understood. He supposed it was one of the reasons that he'd returned to Germany after deserting the war, against all dire odds. He could have easily run, kept running. He might have ended up in Paris or New York even, under an assumed name. But that would've just made him another suspect Kraut on the lam, to most. He might've ended up using one of those ratlines that the smuggler-kidnapper had revealed—special escape routes, how the Nazi rats got to Argentina and Brazil, England, America even. Then again, the man had also mentioned Jewish assassin squads roaming Europe. Just thinking about the scenario made him press his back to the birch tree trunk.

"As I said, I did the Karlovy Vary job to get closer to Harry," Katarina said. "That meant taking chances, contacting those I would not normally, and vice versa. Exchanging information."

"You've heard of ratlines?

"Of course. It's where you catch the rats." She added a grim smile. "Most are so secret, we rarely find them. Some in the Vatican know things. But my sources are generally more respectable than that."

Max's eyebrows had raised. "There's only one person I know who operates in that realm—and who also knows Harry."

Katarina and Sabine Lieser had more than Harry in common, Max realized. All three had an interest in the myriad complicated movements of refugees, Displaced Persons, and, yes, suspects that crisscrossed Eastern and Western Europe and beyond. Sabine might pass Katarina tips about Nazis on the run. In return? Some might find an easier path to Palestine, then Israel. And the two women could exchange other sensitive information along the way, such as about Harry and his whereabouts. In his excitement, Max bounced on his rear, rustling leaves far up the tree trunk.

"Is that so?" Katarina said, but only after a telling pause.

"Sabine Lieser," Max said.

"Who?"

Max played along. "Harry knew her in Munich. Last I heard, Sabine had a big job with the UN. Still helping refugees, Displaced Persons. She's in Frankfurt, Berlin, you name it."

Katarina looked away again. Max thought he heard her growl softly in the dark.

"I was the one who left Harry," she said eventually. "I had things I had to do. To prove, I guess. As did Harry."

"Yes, certainly, I didn't mean—"

"No, it's all right. I'm not jealous. Neither is Sabine. There! I admit it. Yes, I know her. Women do become jealous, naturally, but we're also mothers. Friends. Humane. Unlike . . ." She left a pause where she might've pointed out that men nearly destroy the world every twenty years with their ridiculous childlike arrogance. "Good guess on your part. Calm yourself, Max. We're not working together directly, not usually—but her interests and those of my teams often share the same goals. This time, Sabine came to me—contacted me. She knew Harry was after something and had nowhere else to turn. She didn't trust the American CIA people, they've had too many failures, and Harry ditching Prague after the swap only proved it. Mr. Aubrey Slaipe is losing his special magic, I fear. You don't have to pretend, Max. I know you know the man."

Max nodded. "Does Aubrey Slaipe know about this, what you're doing?"

"No. He's in the dark. The truth is, we're now operating just as solo as Harry."

Max felt a lump in his throat and he tried to swallow it, but it ended up a hard ball in his stomach. "When I don't show up in Munich? Slaipe will suspect something."

Katarina only shrugged. "Harry had made contact," she said. "Right after he fled Prague."

"What? Why didn't you tell me? We have to get going. Where?" Max was already standing.

"Hold on. Sit down. Good. Thank you. And speak softer. Now, please listen. Harry, he'd contacted Sabine Lieser somehow. Going around regular channels. He had a wireless, a courier, pigeon, who knows."

Max's stomach felt warm now and it made him smile. "He's smart, that young Heino, smart as a whip."

"Don't call him that. In any case, he's gone quiet again. But I know where he was heading."

"Where?"

She made a *tsk-tsk* sound. "My god, you're as impatient as he is. You'll know soon."

"Do you know what Harry's after?"

"His mission? His target? No. And let's hope the Russians don't either."

Max closed his eyes and recalled the map of this part of Central Europe. They'd been heading northwest and were now well north of Prague. He considered this ravine, the streams and rivers, hills and mountains, the lack of population. They'd been skirting the northern border of Czechoslovakia and were now waiting for full darkness. It could only mean one thing.

The lump in his throat returned.

"I told you what I know," Katarina said. "Now I need you to do something for me."

They dug a small but deep hole with sticks and a flat rock. Max placed his Temporary Travel Document for German Nationals, cultural visa, permits, and train ticket in the hole. He stared down at them a moment, kneeling at the edge of the grassy hole as if burying a pet bird.

"We'll get you another," Katarina said.

He produced his lighter and lit the documents himself. He watched them burn beyond recognition. Then they scooped back in the dirt. They stomped on it. Katarina brushed herself off as if about to enter a nice office. Max did the same, with equal formality.

No turning back now. But Max supposed there never had been, from the moment he left the peace of Munich behind.

It wasn't far. They exited the ravine and tiptoed through a hundred yards of woods, then crouched at a clearing. They skirted that. They crossed through more woods for about five minutes, and Max continued to mimic Katarina's light footsteps and pauses. She crouched at a boulder, listening.

He crouched with her. "When do we cross over?" he whispered.

"We already did, five minutes ago. That clearing was a border strip. No-man's-land."

They crossed a road. Katarina pulled him down the embankment on the other side and they lay in the tall grass, tight to the ground. Max saw the horizon light up, and they heard an engine. Max buried his head in the grass. A jeep approached. It slowed near them, then stopped. The engine stalled, and someone laughed. Silence reigned. They waited it out. They heard a clunk and a spotlight beam bounced off the trees all around. It clunked off again and Max smelled tobacco now, but it was earthy and bitter and it took him back to his brief time on the Russian Front. Two men spoke, chuckling, and Max still expected to hear German, Border Police. The men spoke Russian. They got the engine running after a couple false starts, and the jeep moved on.

"Welcome to Soviet East Germany," Katarina whispered.

DRESDEN
Sunday, May 22
1:35 p.m.

The thoroughly battered and broken city brought all the old
chills back to Max. He and Katarina came in on the train.
They trudged over one of the dilapidated central bridges to the
Neustadt district. In every direction loomed what would have
looked like rocky desert from a western if it wasn't for the occasional charred church spire or crane poking at the gray sky. In
February of 1945, Allied bombers had transformed Dresden
into one vast, open-air incinerator. No one was safe from the
tall waves of flame, the asphyxiation, the buildings collapsing,
not even the children huddling in cellar bomb shelters. Max's
chest felt twenty pounds heavier just thinking about it.

After they'd entered East Germany in the middle of the
night, Katarina had led Max to a small town. There she located
a specific inn, and Max realized the owner was connected to
her cause. A man took Max's photo. In the morning, after a few
hours' sleep, Katarina gave Max his new papers. Like her—like
Rosamunde Klein—he now belonged to the VVN, the Union of
Persecutees of the Nazi Regime, his documents complete with

old and new travel stamps, permits. Her contact even threw in a few odd pieces to litter his pockets and wallet—a couple love letters, photos, receipts.

His cover name was Emil Wiesenberg. He didn't need to know much more than what was in his papers, Katarina had told him, because if the East Germans or, worse, the Soviets started grilling him, he was done for anyway—

"But that's his name," Max had said. "Your Emil."

"Yes." Her head had bowed a moment. "It's a little tribute."

"I'm honored," Max had said.

In the Neustadt district, Max and Katarina huddled in a corner pub that Katarina said would put them up for the night. They sat in the shadows yet could see outside, and every time Max saw a Russian soldier pass, usually smiling, often with a girl and never a weapon, it still made him want to press his back to the wall. He didn't even know any Russian phrases.

"Calm yourself," Katarina said. "You must calm yourself."

"All right, yes, you're right."

They had thin beers before them, neither drank them. The walls were wood planks but not some pastoral affectation, and Max figured they covered up original walls charred from the air raids. Another pair of Russian soldiers passed, laughing and smoking, but in tow were two long-faced German cops of the new People's Police, trudging along wearily and staring down and probably secretly scanning the ground for cigarette butts to sell. Max shuddered at the thought of goons threatening him with Siberia, then getting rehabilitated, then made to perform in horribly overly didactic productions throughout hopeless East Germany. What would his parents think in America? That thought made him grab his thin beer and gulp half of it down.

"I said calm yourself," Katarina said, but seeing his face made her gulp her beer too.

They sat in silence a moment. Neither commented on the smell of cooking grease mixed with the residue of smoke damage somewhere inside this building, both sour and peppery.

"What's our next move?" Max said.

"I can tell you now. All we have is a location. Supposedly Harry's safe house."

"Good. Wait: What's if it's a trap?"

"Everything might be a trap. Haven't you learned that?"

"I have a PhD in it." Max tried on a smile. He realized the beer wasn't that thin after all. He took another sip for courage. "Well then, let's go get ourselves out of our next trap."

Katarina took Max to meet her contact and had him keep watch outside. He positioned himself on the grounds of a blackened surviving church named after Luther, who surely was still spinning at high speed in his grave, while Katarina disappeared into a building with boards over smoke-blackened windows and no roof Max could spot. He sat on a blackened chunk of stone serving as a park bench and pretended to read the day's *Neues Deutschland*. A Russian jeep rolled by out on the street, the two soldiers riding in back sporting machine guns but looking bored if not asleep. Mostly it was the usual stern-faced locals making do or the occasional horse cart or shabby car spewing more smoke onto this already blackened town. Then a little girl offered to trade him a daisy for a cigarette. He gave her two Erntes and told her to keep the daisy.

Katarina returned and sat close to him. A streetcar clattered by, crammed with passengers, some riding outside clinging to it, women and children even.

"They surveilled the location for us," she said, using the rattling as cover.

"Where?"

"On foot, just twenty minutes from here. We have to act now. It's just you and me again. My people here won't risk it and I don't blame them."

"Does Harry know we're here, that we're coming?"

"We'll find out. He only makes contact when it's safe. Let's go."

She started strolling up the street, slightly uphill, adding a smile and a laugh, and so did Max, just like extras—but in a production they could not know.

4:29 p.m. The route remained steadily uphill, along streets both battered and relatively intact, some with now green trees and others with black trunks never to live again. Katarina kept a steady pace, taking a circuitous route as tactics demanded. To any unassuming passerby she was a keen shopper, checking all the windows, and she made sure to pass through a black market crowd. They kept climbing the street. A couple minutes later they approached what looked like the tree line of a forest—a narrow outcropping of the massive Dresden Heath woodland northeast of the city, Katarina told him. But she turned right, skirting the trees to enter a mostly unscathed district that over-looked the busted city, the river Elbe, and its bridges. They passed individual homes, some even resembling villas, now used by the Russians. Max tensed up and had to work to keep his stride looser.

Katarina stopped in a doorway on a steep street. A boy appeared and stepped into the doorway with them, and Max noticed he was much older up close.

"Still no activity," the man-boy said, sounding about ninety now. "The door's not locked. The rest of the building, unoccu-pied." Then he was gone before they could say thank you.

Each took a deep breath. They stepped out of the doorway.

"*Stoi!*" they heard. Russian. "*Stoi!*"

Both moved to step back inside the doorway but it was too late.

Two Soviet Army officers strode up the sidewalk toward them, their tall peaked caps catching sunlight, the insignia glistening. Was it a trap, the short pants man-boy?

Katarina smiled at the officers and pressed herself to the wall of the building to let them pass. Max did the same, keeping his distance. The two officers brought a cloud of harsh cigarette smoke and a stinging vapor of vodka. They stood between Max and Katarina. Max mulled his options. Confront them? Scream, make a diversion?

The officers spoke to Katarina in a mix of broken German and Russian, pointing and laughing, and Katarina did the same. Max caught none of it.

Then the two officers turned on their heels and marched off, right past Max, their faces practically matching the pale plaster of the wall. One of them side-eyed Max with the eyeballs of a spooked cat.

He looked to Katarina. She was leaning against the wall, eyes closed, mouth slightly open as if she were fighting nausea. He cradled her elbow and they moved on.

"What was that about?" he said.

"They wanted a female companion, for some officers' party—'handsomely compensated,'" she said, adding a roll of her eyes.

"What did you, how did you—"

"I told them their commandant wouldn't like that, seeing how I'm one of his mistresses."

"Good lord. The commandant of the SMAD, the whole Soviet Military Administration of Germany?"

"Huh, I guess so. I wouldn't even know the commandant's name."

Max held up a finger in praise. "That's an excellent improvisation."

"I told them you were MGB. Good thing they didn't address you."

Max's finger shot downward. He swallowed hard. "Good thing."

"There," she said. "Up ahead."

The street was lined with two- and three-story multifamily buildings and had more trees for cover and shadow. They slowed as they neared an intersection. The corner building had a decorative little gabled tower over the main entrance but a modest door down the side street.

"That side door goes to the cellar," Katarina said. "I'll speak. If it's the wrong house, I'll just say I'm looking for someone. Just make sure you have my back."

"Right."

It was still quiet, no one around. Max scanned windows, saw no one.

Katarina headed straight for the cellar door. She put on a smile and knocked, lightly, in a pattern Harry would surely recognize. No one answered. She pulled on the door handle. The door opened. She stepped inside.

Max stayed in the doorway and kept one eye on the street. They needed the light from the door because the stairs were dim. Katarina's footsteps moved deeper into the cellar.

"Come in, down here," Katarina whispered up the stairs.

Max pulled the door shut and went down the short stairway. He smelled bread, sausage. Only a single kerosene lamp lit the dim main room. He saw a plate on a table with food still on it— sure enough, dark bread and liverwurst, a few radishes. Harry loved liverwurst, to Max's dismay. A corner stove was still hot. Katarina opened the stove door and saw bright red embers. She closed the door, sniffed the air, and Max smelled it, too—a whiff of cigarette smoke.

"He's gone," Max said. "Again."

"Come on," she said and pushed through a hanging blanket and Max followed. They moved through the dark with their hands out in front of them, feeling along, and for a moment Max got a shudder in his spine from the thought that so many Dresdeners must have died like this. The ground beneath them shifted, like dirt, and a tang of mildew or worse filled his nose.

Daylight hit them. Katarina had pushed through another door and they ended up in the courtyard behind the building, the walls of similar buildings surrounding them. Max peered around for a witness, hopefully a child, but no signs of life appeared.

They pivoted around, on the spot, faced with too many directions.

"Shit," Katarina growled, "shit," and she stomped one foot.

DRESDEN
11:25 p.m.

Harry had bolted.

That meant Katarina was forced to implement her plan B, and now it was showtime.

Max bounded along through the night, raring to go like a racehorse finally released from the starting gate. He strode down the sidewalks and around corners of the Südvorstadt district and around another corner—and stopped. Looked around. It was dark, the streetlights out here. Katarina was gone. She'd been right behind him.

A shadow emerged from a passageway. Katarina. She pushed at his chest. "What are you doing? You don't even know where you're going," she snapped.

"You know, I think you're right," he said with a nervous chuckle. But he simply couldn't wait anymore. The delay had been excruciating. That evening they'd holed up in their safe room above the pub waiting for the night hours.

"You were going in a circle," Katarina told him, pulling back the hood of her cloak. Her contacts had also given her a tight black blouse and a bright red-and-black striped skirt with the lipstick to match. "Just stick to the script, our roles. We're Rosamunde and Emil, two former refugees on a rare night out."

"It's tough to do your looks justice, my dear, but I'll try," Max said. He'd gotten a black evening jacket. He produced a long, pale yellow silk handkerchief from the inside pocket, tied it around his neck, and stuffed the long end into his open collar, magically creating an ascot. He then smoothed the jacket, which truly needed a brushing if not dry cleaning. Then he pushed back his hair, pressed it down. "If I only had some hair tonic, more jewelry."

Her eyes turned white in the dark, from rolling.

A sign read NACHTKLUB KAZAK in red neon, but there was only a shiny black door on a corner and barely a hint of the thumping and hollering inside. The bouncer, a large Asiatic Soviet, didn't even blink at Max entering with the likes of Katarina, surely figuring him for her talent agent or press man if they even had such things in this other new Germany. They followed a long, neon-lit hallway and the noise started boxing their ears like an artillery barrage.

Five minutes later they were sharing a small table in one of the many alcoves along both sides of the main room. The crowd was a mix of young Russian officers, less-young Russians in suits, and a few ingratiating Germans who, Max tried telling himself, were not at all like the sort of fellow he was back in Munich, not to mention the waiters and waitresses who trudged around with heads down, as if trying to find their smiles they'd dropped somewhere on the floor, prompting Max to wonder if they were getting fed enough—he'd never let that happen in his joint. And yet the Kazak was indeed a loose doppelgänger of his Kuckoo Nightclub, he couldn't help realizing with a cringe—a doppelgänger standing on its head. The Russian music warbled and pounded and reveled and swooned, all jazzy guitars and accordions and feet stomping. Russian soldiers danced with each other and flung each other around, all elbows and knees. They grabbed women to dance, Germans most of them. Max smelled more drunkenness here than a week in the Kuckoo. Apparently they only had vodka and beer so Katarina ordered a bottle of the former with two shot glasses and a large glass each of the latter. One must fit in.

Katarina sat expressionless, back straight and chest out, her high cheekbones glowing in red light. Every passing *Fräulein* gave her the hard eye. Over a half hour passed. After midnight.

"Maybe he's not coming," Max said to her out one side of his mouth between sips of vodka and beer. She drank the same, telling him, through a puff of smoke, "He will. They assured me that he would."

A handsome Russian officer passed, halted and turned, and spoke in Russian to Katarina, and she responded with something in Russian that made the officer throw up his hands and continue on, but smiling. Somehow. Max didn't even want to know this time.

The next song pounded even louder and wilder and the Russians on the dance floor yanked Max into the crowd, egged on by the German women stomping to the beat, their hair flinging around. Max played along, keeping one eye on Katarina fighting a smile. He lost himself in it, shaking his head, twisting his hips, his bangs whipping at his forehead, letting the hot sweat flow. The song ended with a thump and half the crowd toppled over onto one another like dominoes, laughing and howling to cheers and applause.

Max returned to his table panting, practically giggling, still sweating. He plopped down next to Katarina with a happy sigh and patted at his neck with his ascot.

"He's here," she said.

Max could tell by the way she'd fixed her eyes on the band that their plan B man stood at the opposite end of the room. At the bar. Max sipped beer and she blew smoke for more cover and he scanned the bar, finding a man with dark features and a suit better fitting than most, with an insignia pin shining on his lapel. He had a cleft chin like Cary Grant and the brooding brow of Dana Andrews. Max knew the plan. The man wanted female company. Katarina's local contacts were providing her as *Kompensation*, for which the man would provide valuable information, believing Katarina to be simply the messenger as well as courtesan. Max would have to wait again, and he didn't like it, not one bit.

"I've already played this role," he said. "Last-minute savior."

"This time's different. He's a direct source. We don't want to spook him. We're too close for that."

The band went on break and the patrons chatted drunkenly, mingling in small groups.

"I'll take you over, introduce you," Max said. "Say I'm your, uh, matchmaker as it were."

"My pimp? No. I'll go alone, as planned." She gathered her cigarette case, lighter, and purse. Stood. Max rose to help her into her hooded cloak. Halfway down the long neon entrance hallway was a certain door, Katarina had told him. She would escort the man there.

"Be careful, my dear," Max said. "Harry needs you."

She batted eyelashes at him. "You need me. But, thank you."

Max sat and sipped and set out her drinks just so, as if she were returning any moment, then stole glances of Katarina approaching the man. They stepped away from the bar with barely a word. Neither of them so much as glanced at Max.

He sipped vodka, wanting to shake his head. It was like in a western, the saloon girl leading the mysterious stranger up the staircase. How long would this take? What if they were going for Harry right after this? He pushed the vodka away and snapped fingers and ordered coffee, a whole small pot.

1:00 a.m. The coffeepot was empty, its powers already waning. The Nachtklub Kazak was emptying out, too, most of the officers first, then the Russian suits, then the German men and girls now starting to trickle out, looking around for one last chance, one last thrill. They gave Max sad eyes or avoided his gaze, which had grown increasingly defiant. He suspected they were embarrassed for him, having been abandoned, so he used the shame as his cover.

The waiter came and whisked away the coffeepot and two cups. Max kept the sugar cubes in his pocket for who knew what, an impulse that was hard to break after all the postwar years of deprivation.

A muscle in his jaw twitched. *What if Plan B Man had certain perversions?* he thought—ones that left Katarina unable to fight back.

Or what if Hartmut Dietz suddenly appeared? The sick thought tumbled around inside Max's head. Stranger things had happened. This was Dietz's country now after all. Max's neck itched, and he tugged at the cuffs of his jacket.

He grabbed a half-empty shot glass of vodka off the neighboring table and planted it in front of him, to look natural. The remaining crowd sat around in slumped shapes or leaned against each other on the dance floor. A fiddler began playing a slow song and all sang and seemed to know the words except Max, all of them crooning along, even those with their eyes closed, and the fiddler was a revelation, telling a story with his fingers, and some began crying, and Max had to admit he felt his eyelids grow hot. Loves and lives and eras lost filled his head in a rush and he supposed the heads of those around him were just as haunted.

He had to do something. Katarina had told him: If it took too long, more than forty-five minutes, interrupt on a pretense.

Close enough. He threw back the vodka, stood and walked out, and pushed through the leather-lined door and down the neon hallway. A couple Russians in suits followed fast behind him. He halted, pretending to tie his ankle boot, his heart racing, the coffee giving him a hot sweat. But then a *Fräulein* joined the two and they all linked arms and skipped drunkenly onward and Max waited until they exited the front door. He stared at that certain other door, now looming before him, dark and nearly blending into the dim neon, no sign on it, clearly meant only for those who knew the spiel. He expected a bouncer behind the door. He instinctively felt for his old pocketknife or even a pistol but remembered he had nothing.

He opened the door. The hallway was just as dimly lit and as his eyes adjusted he made out a chair, possibly for a bouncer—in case of a VIP, he reckoned. He counted two, three, no, four doors up ahead. He tried the first handle, found it locked, stepped back. Someone shouted at him in Russian from the other side, then came muffled laughing. He took a deep breath. He stepped into the middle of the hallway, equidistant from all four doors, waited for full silence to return, and, using his diaphragm, announced, like a stern producer father figure, "Rosamunde."

He heard nothing. He tried again. "Rosamunde."

The door to his right eased open. Katarina poked her head out. Max rushed over, she pulled him inside, closed the door.

"What are you doing?" she whispered. "It's only been twenty minutes."

"They were giving me the eye downstairs," he lied, but his words faded.

The small room had little decoration apart from the washed-out, funereal wallpaper likely dating back to the Wilhelmine era. A dark wood table, two chairs. The one window was draped with an equally gloomy and dense curtain suitable only for an air-raid blackout. Katarina had returned to the iron-frame bed, standing over it like a mother in that western, concerned about a sick pioneer child, her arms crossed at her chest.

Max had expected clothes everywhere, booze, smoke, wild eyes, and possibly blood. The only aroma in the room was Katarina's gentle perfume.

Their Soviet intelligence contact sat hunched on the opposite side of the bed, facing away from them, face in his hands. His jacket was off, folded neatly on one chair.

Max heard the sobs. Katarina shot a glance at him. He kept quiet. The man was attempting to suck up the last of his sobbing fit.

Katarina floated over to Max. "It's the war," she whispered. Her face was puffy, her eyes red and wet. "He just wanted someone to talk to."

Max nodded. He had seen this so many times, and he supposed some had seen him the same way. The man had surely served at the front, had lost friends, family possibly. Seen things that came back more real than the actual event. For some, it returned stronger after a few years had passed. Men and women roamed Europe hounded by it, homeless, mindless, nerves all shot.

The man whipped around, spotted Max, and bolted over to him. "You have no idea," he blurted in decent German. "You American, British, what? You look Austrian."

Max remembered his ascot and nearly gasped a laugh. "I'm German," he said humbly.

The man snorted at him. "We lost millions upon millions,

all dead," he said, his eyes darting from Katarina to Max, back and forth. "So many more than even you, than all of you. That's why we do what we do. What we have to do." He choked back more tears and attempted to continue, but then his face opened up and he backed away. Max knew that look too. A ghost had seized him. It could've been anything. His first kill. A dead child, along the road. His trusted horse.

The intelligence man kept backing up, toward the bed, feeling the air like a blind man. On the table, Max saw, was a small open tin. He'd thought it was the man's cigarette case but now, as his eyes adjusted to the dim light, he realized it held a small syringe, a couple ampules.

The man slumped back on the bed, wheezing now.

Katarina's eyes fixed on Max, wide and alert. She had gotten what she'd wanted, her eyes told him. "Münchner Platz," she whispered.

"What?"

"Regional courthouse, used by the Gestapo. Interrogation, torture. Prisoner cells."

"Now it's the Soviets' turn," Max whispered back as she nodded. And he realized that, for this man, it might not be just the war but what his secret service was doing to people in those cells.

"I love my country," the man blurted between sobs, talking to the wall. "We are the only hope for the world, the only hope. So some actions, they become necessary . . ." He let the words fade, completing the argument in his head.

A jolt of adrenaline hit Max. He grabbed Katarina. "Harry, he's there?"

"Maybe. He doesn't recall anyone with the exact description of Harry, but they've just received a couple high-level prisoners there. Non-Germans—"

"Then let's go. Leave him."

* * *

1:39 a.m. They moved down the empty dark streets, pausing for the occasional faraway echo of shouting or laughter or roar of a jeep. They'd left the Soviet intelligence man to his demons after Katarina kissed him on the forehead. Münchner Platz wasn't far, she had told Max, but Max's rush of excitement had waned.

"How are we going to get past the guards?" he said.

Katarina didn't reply. She stopped and faced him, her shoulders trembling, her eyes wet again. Max pulled her over to a doorway. "What is it, dear?"

"Our contact, that Soviet intelligence man? He's Jewish. He thinks we're looking for Nazis. I went in there doing what I needed to do, Max. For Harry . . ." Her throat swelled, bobbed.

Max nodded. He stroked her shoulder. The work could put a strain even on a girl like her, even with women so much stronger than men. There were so many compromises to endure, so many little lies. Papers proclaiming herself, a once privileged German, a Persecutee of the Nazi Regime was just the start. And the Jewish intelligence man was likely not just reliving battles or interrogations but an SS officer with a gun to his head, or to his mother's head, not to mention the hangings, the ditches, the camps. Children's shoes and toys, piles of them. Max wiped at his own wet eyes.

"We have to try," Katarina said, her voice gaining strength. "Same way you always get past guards—with intimidation." She went over the details again. "We'll be there on behalf of our contact—from the Soviet MGB. To identify a prisoner. He's given me a pass, with orders, signed by a fake officer." She patted the pocket of her cloak. "But there's no promises, no clear way of getting Harry out. If he's even there. He could be at Bautzen Prison already."

It's madness, Max thought. They might as well lock themselves into their own cell. "We'll get him," was all he could say. His mouth felt dry, his throat sore. This was it. The big moment. His biggest role yet, possibly bigger than being forced to impersonate a US lieutenant behind American lines at the height of the bloody Battle of the Bulge. That could've gotten him killed and probably should have. But this could get Harry killed. He would never be able to explain it to his mother should he ever make it back to them in America. Sure, Harry had bolted, gone rogue. But it would be his fault Harry was captured, his fault that Harry was working clandestinely in an East Germany city ruled by Stalin. What was Harry thinking? What was he thinking? As he sometimes did before a major performance, he focused on a reward. He and Harry and two lovely women enjoying fine bubbly and an extravagant meal, a whole goose even, and they would all gather at the piano with brandies afterward for a few rousing tunes. He could do Broadway, Brecht, Piaf even, if you asked nicely . . .

Katarina shook him. "There's something else," she said. "Max, listen to me."

"What?"

"Hartmut Dietz is here."

Max let go of her. He stepped back. He felt his face slacken. The ghost had seized him.

"Our MGB contact has seen him," Katarina said. "Over at Soviet headquarters."

How did she know about Dietz?

"Max? I know it's a shock, but we have to."

He tightened his jaw. Squared his shoulders. "Of course, yes. But how do you . . . Does Dietz know we're here?"

"That remains to be seen."

"Fine," Max said. "Let's just do this."

They marched on. Max untied his ascot and stuffed it into a pocket. No disguises now. His expressions and manner and thespian chops would do all the work.

Dietz could go to hell.

The moon was out and the streetlamps on, and all was half-light, half-shadow, the cobblestones black-and-white checkerboards, whole buildings just movie set facades, doorways sliced down the middle like apples.

"It's not far now," Katarina said, the steel returning to her voice. "So let's go over it . . ."

"A Soviet MGB man sent us," Max said, "and we wave our VVN IDs around for good measure, play up the victims-of-fascism routine."

"That's right, and we have this pass. From there, once inside, we improvise. How about trying this—if we get sight of Harry, we point to him, say they've got the wrong man."

"We play up our outrage," Max said. "Maybe they don't know who he is yet. Maybe they set him free. We rely on a bureaucratic mix-up."

"Good, that's good."

"There's plenty to go wrong, lots of holes, but we'll just keep talking, keep it moving."

Max was saying what she needed to hear, but he was getting that sick feeling, low in his gut. Once an operation commenced, all laid plans got shredded, and any improvisation could mean life or death.

"Wait, hear that?" Katarina said.

It was the clip-clop of a horse cart.

Max nodded, and they stood against a dark wall.

The horse cart came around the corner. A scraggly donkey pulled the cart and one man rode atop a pile of sacks, his sagging reins an extension of his drooping shoulders and arms.

As the cart passed, *clip-clop, clip-clop*, Max thought he saw something move across the street, among the ruins of a villa. A silhouette faced them. Someone surveilling them?

The person shifted forward, into the moonlight, and the half-light brought him to life.

Harry. It was Harry.

DRESDEN
1:40 a.m.

"Max? Max!" Katarina pinched his rib.

"Ow. I know, I saw."

"Where did he go?"

They kept staring, peering.

But Harry was gone, leaving only shadows and piles of stones.

Max grabbed Katarina's hand and led her across the street and onto the villa's overgrown yard. A low iron fence poked above the tall grass. The street was silent, dark. Max searched for a fence gate but couldn't find it. Katarina hopped the fence and Max followed, navigating chunks of stone and beams, all of it scorched, the tall grass brushing at their shins, knees.

They approached the front door, but heaps of bricks and the remains of a fallen wall blocked it. Max wanted to shout Harry's name, they stopped to listen instead. In the distance, a dog barked. They heard nothing from inside. Some windows were boarded up, some not. Max led Katarina along the front to a blown-out corner window. He looked in and saw only jagged and shiny black shapes, and a sickeningly stale odor filled his nostrils. He pulled back, took in fresh air. Katarina led him around the side, past steps leading to nowhere, a balcony that had collapsed. They scrambled over debris like city kids raised on ruins, and Max grimaced with envy at his little brother navigating such a thorny labyrinth. The back of the villa had imploded, leaving more blackened rubble and debris.

Max and Katarina crouched in the backyard, peering around. The moonlight illuminated what was once a modest but charming classical garden. The contours of busted statues shined, and there was a toppled fountain. The hedges and grass were overgrown but the paths were clear. And Max remembered that saying in English about being "led up the garden path."

"Hey," Katarina whispered faintly.

Max followed her line of sight and saw what she saw. A new statue had appeared at the far end of the garden, or so it seemed. Then it vanished into the dark and Max and Katarina scrambled down the garden path, crouching and taking cover at hedges and statues, listening. "Careful," Katarina whispered but both kept going, maneuvering like a skilled fireteam clearing a bunker. The only thing missing was the weapons.

A narrower path led between more hedges and through to a garden shed that was a diminutive version of the villa, with the same stone and ironwork and a miniature mansard roof.

Max and Katarina were just shadows and silhouettes. They operated by watching the twinkles of each other's eyes.

They choreographed it. Katarina would watch the path for intruders or escapes and Max would enter. Max approached the entrance to the shed. It was the size of a closet door but ornate like the portal of a church. He automatically held out a hand as if holding a gun, and Katarina nodded at the ruse.

The handle squeaked. The door creaked open a crack.

Max squatted for cover, half behind a hedge. He glanced back at Katarina, who shrugged. Then the crack started expanding, the door opening.

A flame flashed inside with a clank. Max knew that clank—a Zippo lighter. Was it a signal? He tried to remember his Morse code and couldn't recall the slightest semaphore. The clank repeated. The flame glowed steady now. It lit up a face. Smiling.

Max rushed inside.

DRESDEN
Night

The flame went out. Max stood inside the pitch dark, pivoting around. "Harry? Shine a light, will you? I can't see."

"You're not alone," Harry said, his American English as metallic as ever, like a rusty saw.

It was Harry. It truly was.

"It's all right," Max told him in the dark, "she's with me. Keeping watch."

"She?"

"That's correct."

"Are we safe?"

"Yes. I promise." Max patted his pockets for his lighter but his fingers trembled and his heart swelled.

"How can I be sure?" Harry said from the blackness.

"Heinrich," Max shot back in German, "you fire up that Zippo right this moment."

Harry slowly turned on a kerosene lamp, just enough to glow.

"Don't call me that," Harry said in German, but he was smiling again, which widened his broad freckly cheeks even more and emphasized those bangs of his that always wanted to curl.

Max smiled. "Then don't call me Maxie."

"I didn't!"

"Not yet you haven't, Heino."

"Hey!"

They shared a brief laugh.

Max held out his arms. "Well? Let me see you."

Harry stepped forward. Max lunged and hugged his little brother and Harry took it as he always had, going a little limp, as if Max were about to lift him up and he didn't want Max to hurt himself with his buffoonery. Max let go of Harry and gave him a once-over, spotting even more premature gray in his hair and sideburns, a firmer edge to his rounded features, more darkness in his green eyes. His little brother's boyishness had faded, truly, and strangers just meeting him surely had no idea the boy had ever existed. Harry had seen too much, done too much.

"You look great," Max said. "I knew it was you once I heard that Yankee lighter."

"This ole thing? It's a Russian knockoff. Have to stay in character, am I right, master thespian?"

"Too true, Captain Kaspar, too true." Max still liked to call his brother by his last rank in the US Military Government. He wagged a finger at him. "Why didn't you tell me you were in this new CIA?"

"Why do you think? Supposing something, well, like our current situation happened?"

Neither laughed.

"Tell me what the devil is going on," Max said. "Tell me now."

Harry held his chin high. "What do you think is going on?"

"You're on a mission—one so important that you can't leave it to others. It fits your character, Harry, to a T."

"Very good. Which also means that I can't tell you what it is."

"You will," Max said.

Harry didn't reply. Max glanced around. The small room held a cot, a little table and cabinet, a small homemade metal stove with no controls—what Germans half lovingly called a *Brennhexe*, a "burning witch."

"Place is a loaner," Harry said. He eyed Max up and down. "You look swell, big brother. Put back on a few pounds finally, got that merry flush back."

Max nodded along, but he was now feeling all those pounds and his legs suddenly felt heavy, wearing, the adrenaline draining out of him again as he thought about the predicament they were in. He thought about sitting but didn't want to worry his brother.

"The last time we met like this," Harry said, "the shoe was on the other foot."

They were back in English now. Harry had always preferred it, despite any risk.

"Indeed," Max said. "So? Time to go. Let's get you out of here."

Harry showed him a curt smile. "Can't we even chat first? I have the place all night. Sit, for Christ's sake." He pushed back his bangs, and something about the resolve in his eyes finally forced Max onto a chair.

He told Harry about the severed ear con. "Those kidnappers, those bastards, they tricked me."

Harry fought a chuckle, but his face quickly darkened. "Well, I am sorry you had to go through that. Now, listen, I want you to know, when I sent those kidnappers your way, I really did just want you to pay the ransom. That was early in the game."

"Why me, if you want to keep me out of the game? You didn't even want me to know what you really do."

"What, did Aubrey Slaipe tell you that? All right, it's true that I wanted to keep you out of it, of course. But then, when those goddamn two-bit smugglers turned into would-be kidnappers, you suddenly became the only person I could keep in the know. I was hoping it would let me keep my cover. Thought I could stay on course. With your help, that ransom. I'm sorry. Best-laid plans and all."

"Don't worry about it. I'm honored."

"I would've paid you back."

"I know." Max stood. He pushed at Harry's shoulder. "And what's the big idea, hightailing it like that back there? We all could've been nabbed. Wait. You were tracking us, weren't you? How long? Since back at your first hideout? You could've gotten us killed!"

Harry shrugged. "What could I do? Look where we are. I wanted to see what would shake out, all right? Don't worry. I wouldn't let you dangle. I had a hideout for us, inside the Heath. Still do."

"The what?"

"The Dresden Heath. Huge forested area right above the city. Reach it by foot."

"I know what it is," Max said.

But Harry kept staring at him.

"Who's the dame?" Harry said finally. "Out there."

Max had forgotten all about Katarina. He took a deep breath. "Oh, right. Well, you're not going to believe this, little brother, but . . ."

The door was still cracked, and Katarina opened it all the way, filling the gap with her dark and curvy cloaked silhouette. She pulled off the hood and stepped into the doorway, squinting with one eye and biting her lower lip as if about to give a child an injection.

"Hello, Harry," she said.

Harry shot up, gazing at her. His was a look of naked awe that awed Max in turn.

"Hello, Kat," Harry said.

Katarina took a step inside, and she closed the door behind her without looking. Still they stared at each other, and might have been glaring. Max wanted to exit altogether now. He moved around the edge of the room and ended up sitting on the cot.

Harry and Katarina showed each other the slightest smiles, just curls at the edges of their mouths.

"Max, what the hell have you gotten us into here?" Harry said eventually.

"Me?"

"On second thought, don't answer that."

"Don't blame him, Harry," Katarina said. "Max was just looking after you. I might have prodded him a little."

They shook their heads at each other and their smiles widened. Max was suddenly the spectator at a vigorous tennis match, rapt from all the action.

"It's good to see you, Captain Kaspar," she said.

"You too," Harry said. "But it's not captain anymore."

"So I hear."

"Sit down, Max," Harry said out the side of his mouth, still watching her.

"I am sitting," Max said. "Why don't you two sit?"

"Right, yes." Katarina sat and gave him a look of thanks with now bright eyes, and only then did Harry sit back down, still staring at her, barely finding the edge of his chair. Max now watched with his hands clasped in anticipation, like the host of a child's birthday party. He didn't feel silly like this. It was rare to feel like he used to, so full of joy and wonder at the world and all its splendor, and he wanted them all to celebrate. If only they had champagne.

"Man, I was hoping you two would finally get to meet," Harry said to Max and Katarina.

"Me too. Not quite like this, though," she said and laughed, which made her cloak open, revealing her evening wear. Harry did a mock wolf whistle and Katarina slapped at his hand, which got them both laughing. But their laughs faded quickly and they exchanged hard glances that made them stand, and face each other, and share a long hug.

In her ear, Harry whispered, "Thank you for coming."

Meanwhile, Max's heart started racing. He stood. He bounced on his toes, rubbed his hands together at an imaginary escape map in his head. West Berlin wasn't far, the border of the American Zone of West Germany just as close, if not closer. "Well, like I was saying, let's get you out of here."

Harry only stared at him. "Hartmut Dietz is here," he said.

"I know," Max said. "We must leave. You have a route, I take it?"

Harry nodded. "I want to thank you for doing this, Max. Truly. Mom and Dad would be thanking you."

"And we won't ever tell them!" Max threw up his hands. "*Mutti* already has a weak heart. Well? All right, let's get going."

"Not yet," Harry said. "Sit back down. Let's have some joe first."

Harry cooked them coffee on the primitive stove. As they sipped it from tin canteen cups, Max told Harry about their journey so far, and about how Katarina had stepped in. He told Harry about the Nachtklub Kazak this very evening, thus Katarina's evening wear. Katarina let Max tell it. Max described his contact with Hartmut Dietz in Prague.

"He's got an angle," he said, "but he couldn't spit it out, not with his Soviet minders around."

"I got the same treatment from him," Harry said. "Oh, sure, he threatened to put on the screws, showing off for those Czechs in their leather coats. I was expecting to lose more than my ear, I can tell you. But nothing of the sort happened. He said he wanted to act as a double, but he didn't get a chance to take it further. And I wasn't about to let him, the rat bastard."

"Bravo," Max said.

Harry told Kat more about Dietz. She bit at her cheek. "Could this Dietz know that you're here?" she asked.

"I doubt it. But Dresden is the first logical stop inside East Germany after a trip to Prague. And the place to gather more intelligence. He now works for the Soviet MGB, and the East Germans' new agency."

Katarina nodded. "K5."

"You know what else Dietz told me?" Max said. "He said, 'I will find a way. We'll meet again.'"

Harry said, "Let me guess the rest: 'I could kill you any time.'"

"That's it. Same script."

"You can take the boy out of Nazi Germany, but you can't take Nazi Germany out of the boy."

Katarina nodded gravely at that.

They sat in silence a while. Sipping. Thinking.

"I wonder whose severed ear that was," Max muttered eventually, his shoulders drooping. "They store it in formaldehyde, just keep using it."

"Hey, buck up," Harry said.

"I'm all right." Max tried a grin.

They both smirked.

Soon Harry knocked on the table and announced that they all needed sleep if they were going anywhere. But there was only the cot. Max and Katarina would have to leave now if they wanted to get back to their safe house before daylight. "Otherwise," Harry said, "there's my cellar safe house, or even the Dresden Heath, though I don't recommend roughing it."

"We're not done," Max said. "What in the devil was that back in Prague? You gave us all the slip?"

"Yes. None of you can be involved. I had people I could work with, so I used them—outside of normal channels."

"For what? What was your mission?"

Harry, slowly, shook his head.

Max pointed at him. "We're not leaving you alone."

"We haven't talked about our next moves," Katarina added.

Harry stared at them staring at him. His head pulled back a little. He set down his coffee. "What, you two ganging up on me now?"

Max glanced at Katarina and could tell by her hardening cheeks that she was thinking the same thing. She might even be wanting to bash Harry's head in with her tin mug. They had come all this way, both of them, each in their own manner, and all to help Harry.

"What?" Harry repeated.

Max had always thought Harry would've been a terrible actor. He tried too hard.

"Goddamn you, Harry," he said. "You're not going back. Are you?"

DRESDEN
Monday, May 23
Night to day

"Let's just get some rest and we'll talk," Harry said, but Max and Katarina shook their heads at him. He was not their father. Neither was about to let Harry dodge them again.

"We are not leaving this garden shack," Max told Harry.

Harry released a long sigh, glaring at the glossy green door with its decorative iron strap hinges, at the arched stone ceiling complete with simulated ornate buttresses.

"In architecture," Max said, "they call a costly ornamental shed like this a 'folly.'"

They waited out the stalemate, Katarina in her chair with her cloak closed up tight, her arms folded on her chest, Max leaning forward on the cot with both hands planted on his hips.

"The Soviets, they don't know my current location," Harry said to kick things off.

Max snapped fingers and shot a look at Katarina that said, *I told you he wasn't going back.* She nodded back glumly.

Harry nearly laughed. "You two aren't my parents, you know."

"I could just imagine what they would say," Katarina said.

"Hey! That's not fair, Kat."

"I came all this way," Max said to Harry.

Harry sighed again. He looked to Katarina, who only shook her head again.

And Harry glared at the floor, all stone slabs. He was running out of room.

"All right, look," he said. "I told you, they still do not know I'm on a mission—they meaning the Russians. Not even that bastard Dietz. They could've gotten something out of me, sure. Brought out all their tricks, syringes, tools. I even broke down. I was crying, if you can believe it. It wasn't a put-on."

"Good, that's good," Max said, "it lends credibility," but Katarina waved at him to let Harry speak.

"Well, I was distraught," Harry said. "No sleep, banged up, especially after those extortionist smuggler bastards. And Dietz, he's capable of anything. But Dietz never really put on the screws, did he? He had his own angle. You saw it yourself. And his Soviet minders just wanted a swap."

Max could only nod at that.

"I threw them a bone," Harry continued, "feeding them a load of bull about snooping around the countryside seeking a new opportunity, the old reckless American cowboy bit. Then the swap. Then I bolted. I'm telling you, there's no way they can know where I'm now headed."

Max and Katarina stared at him for more. They were going to need additional exposition if this script was to be believable.

So Harry continued, summarizing what Aubrey Slaipe had told Max about early CIA operations either launching dead in the water or instantly getting exposed in-country. That was why Harry had gone on this mission himself. Solo. They couldn't keep compromising agents. So many were valuable locals, and they were losing more than they were recruiting. Harry simply could not be responsible for any more death.

"I have new information. The Soviets have moved my target. He's now up north," Harry told them. "But there's still time. My operation is the first in a good while that hasn't been found out. Understand? I'm going to see this mission to the end. And I can tell you that it's far too important not to."

Max and Katarina exchanged glances. *He*, Harry had said. His target was a man. It was the first real detail Harry had given them. At least he was opening up a little. At least they weren't about to blow up a dam, steal a nuclear bomb, assassinate Stalin.

A sudden thought seemed to jolt Harry. He turned to Max. "How is Aubrey Slaipe feeling?"

"He doesn't sound too happy with you."

"Can't blame him," Harry said. "And knowing Aubrey, I assume he told you to go straight home to Munich, probably put you on a direct train."

Max only nodded. He was suddenly finished with reunions. The room was lightening, the kerosene lamp dimming—the sun would be up soon.

"You're coming back with me," he told Harry.

Yet right as he said it, he knew there was no turning back. He should have demanded that Harry return. Pleaded, scolded. But he supposed he had committed to this as soon as he jumped off that darkened train with Katarina.

Harry's eyebrows raised. He reared up. He thrust out his arms. "Oh no you don't, Max. Don't even think about coming along. I'm not going to put you on the spot too. You've done enough already."

Max ignored him. He looked to Katarina. She was eyeing him, studying him, as if reading his mind. Max had expected her to put up more of a fight, but he supposed she had her own reasons for sticking with Harry instead of forcing him to return.

"And that goes for you, too, Kat," Harry said.

DRESDEN
9:17 a.m.

"How can I let you come with me if I don't even know the score myself?" Harry said to Max as they trudged along the trail through the Dresden Heath. Harry didn't look like Harry out in the open. His clothes were far from his usual neat and slightly elegant attire. He wore a surplus Red Army jacket, threadbare trousers, boots so scruffy that the brown dye had worn away in spots. His oversized newsboy cap obscured his hair and ears and face, his wire-framed glasses his eyes, and the scruffy, bushy disguise mustache he had applied with the deftness of a Hollywood makeup artist completed his camouflage. He could be anything from an out-of-work engineer to a former Socialist agitator once hounded by the Gestapo. And Max had felt a slight tug of envy. He, too, had wanted a better disguise, perhaps a beard, or thick glasses, and a stoop to his walk and powder to his cheeks to look paler.

"Why would either of you want to?" Harry added. "Huh? Especially you, Kat."

Neither Max nor Katarina replied, so Harry stopped in the middle of the trail to block their path. Again. Max and

Katarina had been tailing him like two kids following their dad to work despite his objection. It was full daylight now, the sun streaming through the birch trees and glowing the green leaves like jade coins, lighting up their right shoulders. They had caught a few hours' sleep in the destroyed villa's garden folly as daylight spread over the ruins and rooftops of Dresden. Harry had produced a couple bedrolls, calling his own bluff about the cot. In the morning they sat in their places, eyes bleary, knees to their chests. Max made them coffee and realized he'd never seen Harry so well matched with a girl, possibly not even with Sabine Lieser—their eyes kept locking on each other and wouldn't let go. Katarina softened, too. She told Harry about Emil Wiesenberg. The British, the "fucking English" in her words, had shot him in Jerusalem just days before Israel's independence. The incident was declared an accident—British troops had mistaken him for a rogue Arab bomb-thrower as they attempted to secure neighborhoods before their withdrawal. Harry fell silent a while, brooding about that.

Max and Katarina first made Harry come with them to their safe room above the pub, where they stashed their evening wear and grabbed their bags. They followed Harry to his own safe room, where he switched into his disguise and grabbed serviceable papers he'd gotten after escaping Prague. Then Harry had entered the Dresden Heath above the city, heading northeast, and Max and Katarina had simply kept following him. It was ludicrous for them to trail Harry like this, without an agreed plan, but Harry had to appreciate that it gave them extra eyes all around.

"We came to save you," Katarina told Harry in the middle of the trail. "So what's the difference?"

"Listen, doll, I'm not the old soft touch you first thought I was back in Heimgau, so don't go supposing you'll convince me otherwise."

"Do not call me doll."

As they bickered, Max frowned at the reddish-brown trail under his feet, at all the skinny birch trunks and sparse undergrowth surrounding them. He wasn't sure he wanted Katarina coming either. She had already done her part. Of course she wanted to help Harry. But he sensed that she had a particular agenda. He hated to suspect her, but there it was: Why would she double down on her winning gamble, and why would her organization let her?

Katarina huffed. Harry puffed.

"Please, you two," Max tried, but they ignored him.

"I made a promise," Katarina told Harry, "to Sabine Lieser."

A direct hit. Harry squeezed his eyes shut a moment.

Katarina frowned at Max for help, but Max only held out his hands.

Katarina stomped one foot and bounded two steps over to him. "You, too? What, because I'm a woman, is that it?" Max and Harry only exchanged startled glances, each unsure who was to take the brunt of this. "What is it with you men? Is there some lever that engages inside you? Is that where this stupidity comes from? *Ach, bitte.*" She wiped at air as if erasing them from a chalkboard. Then she marched off in the direction Harry had been heading.

They had only emboldened her. Harry showed Max a frightened grimace.

They continued hiking through the Dresden Heath, Max and Harry working to catch up with Katarina. She turned to face them, her hands on her hips. "What?"

"You don't even know where you're going," Harry said.

Her arms locked on her chest.

"Look, I'm sorry I called you doll. But I wouldn't blame you if you went your own way. I told you. You've done enough."

"And if something happened," Max said, "we would hate to be responsible—"

"Stop! Do I have to spell it out for you, boys?" Katarina scowled at both of them, giving each an equal five seconds. "Yes? No? I am the only one the other side doesn't know to look for. And I'm a woman, at that. Understand now? So stop biting the hand that feeds you."

Harry stared at her a moment. "Can't argue with logic," he grunted. Then he marched onward and took point, waving them to follow like the seasoned combat patrol lieutenant he'd probably always wanted to be.

BAUTZEN
2:48 p.m.

Simply seeing the name on the train station sign had disturbed them all. Bautzen. Even Katarina looked paler. Harry's lower lip hung a little, so Max could just imagine how he must have looked. He touched his cheek and it felt cold.

Bautzen meant internment. The Gestapo had a prison here during the war, part of the Gross-Rosen concentration camp network. The Soviets and their East German vassals had taken over from there. Halfway into the Dresden Heath, Harry had led them to the main road, where they had hitched a ride on a truck, then taken a local train from the next town. Now Harry, Max, and Katarina had just stepped off the train.

As they exited the station they kept their heads down, making no eye contact with passersby, barely looking around to confirm they had no tail. A few People's Police stood shoulder to shoulder outside, hands clamped on their new belt buckles, eyeing those leaving. They gave the gauntlet a wide berth, using a group of schoolchildren for cover. Their cover identities wouldn't pass intense scrutiny. Katarina and Max were still Rosamunde Klein and Emil Wiesenberg, card-carrying Persecutees of the Nazi

Regime, and Harry was a fellow they met traveling. His Soviet Zone of Occupation identity booklet, his SED—Socialist Unity Party—card, and a few other papers claimed him to be Stefan Breitner, a biological research assistant. Herr Breitner hoped to become a doctor one day, but Harry knew about as much about biology and medicine as the homicidal surgeon Max once played in a B-movie. Harry had managed to obtain the ID using a known helper agent in Dresden, a main reason he was there. The less they knew, the better. None of them spoke about the punishment for getting caught with forged documents behind the Iron Curtain, though the sentence would likely begin right here at Bautzen.

"What have you gotten us into?" Max quipped once they had cleared the station. Harry didn't respond. He took them to a café just outside the old city walls with a view of the winding Spree River and a round medieval tower. He had a quick coffee with them. He drank it mechanically, staring at the ancient embankments, his lip still hanging, trembling a little.

Max put a hand on his shoulder. "You all right, brother?"

Harry set down his coffee, again mechanically. "I'm not really a spy, not an agent, operative, whatever you care to call it. Got me? I direct agents. I don't have much on-the-ground experience. In-country. We've lost good people who had far more."

Katarina put a hand on his knee. "Sometimes it helps to share. What's your next move? You don't have to give me details."

"Gain information. From a contact, another helper agent. Pay a visit, use a code phrase. It's not far from here."

"Child's play. You'll be fine."

"Right, you're right." Harry took a deep breath and stood. He smoothed out his rumpled trousers and disguise mustache, then yanked down his big hat. He was careful to make warm eye contact with both of them. "I will be back, you hear me? If I'm not, my contact's been compromised like others. So clear out as soon as you can."

3:47 p.m. An hour had passed. Max and Katarina waited it out. They sipped coffee while sitting in a café corner with a view to the window—as usual, the bane of every agent's existence. The coffee reminded Max of the war—it was ersatz, likely chicory, and overboiled. The place had far fewer pastries than German cafés in the West. Katarina picked at a piece of *Mohnkuchen* and declared the poppy-seed filling surprisingly tasty and moist, but Max had no appetite. The few customers who came and went this late in the afternoon ignored them, as befitted strangers in a town like Bautzen. The odor of an astringent cleaning agent lingered. "Ammonia," Katarina said.

4:39 p.m. Almost two hours now. The train station–sized clock ticked away on the café wall and Max wanted to smash it. They got more coffee, brackish mineral water, a roll with ham, the ham off-color. Katarina took such hard swallows that her Adam's apple resembled a man's. The now late-afternoon sun shined on the two tables outside and Katarina released a little sigh.

Max concurred. It would have been nice to relax out in the sun. "If only you had your sunglasses—"

"Look, slowly," Katarina said under her breath.

Across the street, Harry appeared. He was smoking. He rarely smoked these days, but every operative did, as it allowed them to move their eyes around. He took his time, changing hands, looking both ways. He stood and faced the café and removed his hat. Finally—it was the signal to join him, the coast was clear.

Harry led them to the pub on the corner and it was another back table, facing out, a lager each and a shot of clear schnapps for Harry. Max and Katarina were breathing easier, yet Harry looked worse than when they'd stepped off the train. His bangs were wet with sweat. They gave him a moment. He wouldn't look at them. Katarina caressed the back of his shoulder. He downed the shot. He released a sigh.

"My target has been moved," he said. "Again."

Katarina nodded at the rough news.

"Where?" Max said.

"Farther. East of here."

Max slumped, and the hard wooden bench cut into him. No one spoke.

"I have something to admit," Max said. "Mr. Slaipe told me your target was an extraction."

"He told you that?" Harry growled. "You mean *is*. You said *was*."

"In any case. You need to get this man out, is that correct?"

Harry nodded.

"Any sign of this Hartmut Dietz?" Katarina said.

Harry shook his head. "But that doesn't mean anything."

They drank to the sad truth of that. Soon Harry had regained color again, and he seemed to have gained an inch in sitting height. Max knew that look on Harry. East or not, there truly was no turning back.

"It's time for more answers," Max told Harry.

"All right. Yes. Come on."

First they checked into a regular inn like any travelers, Herr Wiesenberg and Herr Breitner in one room and Frau Klein in her own, the elderly male innkeeper recording their IDs in a ledger but barely checking them. Dinner was downstairs at the inn. It was beef goulash, which Max had been craving on and off since Vienna, but it was greasy, as were the dumplings. And the elderberry soup, well, no color could look more like fresh blood. He pushed it over to Katarina and she slurped it down without speaking. They ate it all hastily. Afterward the three of them huddled in Katarina's room, which was unexpectedly larger than Max and Harry's, on a corner with a view of the street. The wood furnishings were carved in the rural fashion and had more frightening doilies, like so many spiderwebs, Max thought, so he concentrated on the bottle of rough local brandy Katarina set out in the middle of the small table. Max poured them all a glass while Harry stretched out on her bed American-style, all splayed limbs, which provoked embarrassed smiles between Harry and Katarina.

Harry cleared his throat. "All right, you two, question time. Knock yourself out."

"Are you still using your local helper agent?" Katarina asked.

"No. Probably thinks I'm gone already. As far as he knows, I am still operating solo."

"Bautzen is a prison—was your target here because of that?" Max asked. "They were keeping him there?"

"That's right," Harry said. "But this was a while ago."

"Did they move him to another prison?"

Harry shut his eyes a moment, his jaw grinding away. "No. That phase ended. Apparently it was only for the first few days, I'm hearing. Questioning. Vetting. He's been in open detention—a halfway house. But that was a while ago too."

"Could that mean, what, that the Russians somehow trust your target?" Katarina asked.

Harry shook his head at the mere suggestion. "Whatever is going on, it can't last long."

Katarina thought a moment, her eyes scanning the doily under the bottle as if the intricate lace were tarot cards.

"Does Dietz know about your target?" Max asked. Katarina nodded along.

"I don't know," Harry said. "I told you that."

"It's a very good question," Katarina said.

"Well, supposing he does happen to know the target exists? He wouldn't necessarily put the two together, me and said target. There are plenty of reasons for my being over here. I flew the coop, left the fold, went rogue. Remember? For all he knows, I'm looking to defect. At any rate, I highly doubt the Russians would have reason to inform a mere East German like Dietz, no matter his position, about a target as important as mine, and certainly not the whys and wherefores." Harry nodded at that, but gravely, like a doctor reading a damning medical chart.

They sat in silence a while. The dumplings weighed in Max's gut now, low and hard and yet unctuous. They heard a siren outside, far in the distance, and waited for it to fade. Harry was still sprawled on the bed, hanging one foot off the side. *An odd American trait*, Max thought—it wasn't so much calm under pressure as a spiteful casualness.

"Your extraction target, he knows secrets," Katarina said.

Harry didn't answer. His eyes said, *I can't comment.*

"Is he Nazi?" she asked.

"No, Kat. That's your angle, not mine. When I can help it."

Katarina leaned forward on the table. "Is he capable of creating secrets?"

Harry didn't speak at first. "Getting warmer," he said eventually.

"Ah, I see." Katarina retreated into her thoughts again, consulting the doily.

Max asked, "Is he American or German?"

Harry shot up and growled and paced the room. "Look, can we cut the parlor games here? The man knows certain things and can help create certain things that will make the last war look like, well, like a cakewalk. And that's just for the civilians. Goddamnit . . ." He stomped around until finding his glass and he downed it. Max was already holding out the bottle for him.

Harry looked at Katarina, and then at Max.

By "things," Harry meant weapons. None of them had to say it.

"It concerns a certain facility," Harry said. "All right? A clandestine facility. That's where we're heading next. I can't tell you any more. Not until we know the full score. What if someone caught you?"

Max glanced at Katarina. "I know, I know," he grumbled, "the less I know, the better."

GÖRLITZ
Tuesday, May 24
10:20 a.m.

Max, Harry, and Katarina stared at the remains of the Old Town Bridge, demolished by the Wehrmacht at the end of the war and never rebuilt, now just two small crumbling concrete abutments on either side of the Neisse River, a calm and leaden moat.

The Neisse River running through Görlitz was the new German-Polish border. The opposite side of town had been renamed Zgorzelec. It now belonged to the Soviet-controlled People's Republic of Poland.

They had taken the early local train east from Bautzen. The night before, Max had left Harry in Katarina's room, telling them good night as if their spending the night together had been the plan all along, and retired to the room meant for him and Harry. He could only imagine all they must have discussed, revisited, renewed. He worried they would not get enough sleep, but his last thoughts before he dozed off were accompanied by a smile. In the morning, Harry and Katarina had been all business again.

At their backs the spires of old churches both Protestant and Catholic loomed, their survival in Soviet East Germany now as uncertain as that of this once centuries-old bridge. Before them, across the river in Poland, stood more of the town. A tall blocky turret resembled a flak tower but was likely erected before any European had set foot in North America. The side of town across the river was all cut off now. They might as well have built a high concrete wall topped with barbed wire. An absurd idea, Max told himself—walls never lasted. But the Soviet Union had lost tens of millions during the war, civilians and soldiers. So they never wanted it to happen again. Max could understand. Katarina surely could.

Harry only shook his head in anger. He refused to decide on their next move in Görlitz until they reconnoitered the town, the river, the various routes. They had seen enough Soviet propaganda walking over from the train station and through Old Town and could see even more on the other side, slogans, banners, and billboards, promising a better life yet threatening all the same. It seemed to get under Harry's skin. He stomped back through Old Town, glaring around, not taking the usual precautions to remain inconspicuous and alert to tails. He even crossed an avenue in front of an oncoming streetcar and in view of a police jeep.

Max knew his brother: When surly, he was feeling desperate. Katarina knew him too. They were all walking separately again, to check for any tails, but once Harry turned onto an empty street she caught up with him and Max stayed at a safe distance, keeping watch. She had directed all this with eye contact only, like she had a radio transmitter in her head.

Next stop was the Stadtpark, just south of Old Town. They stood on a slope inside the trees flush with May leaves and surveyed the river below, no more than two hundred feet across, the water equally calm and nearly a mirror in the sun. They didn't dare get much closer. Below, a sign read STROLLING ALONG THE

NEISSE RIVER IS STRICTLY FORBIDDEN. To their right stood a rebuilt bridge with the generic title of Stadtbrücke. Soviet engineers had incorporated the former demolished bridge's stone abutments and positioned intricate wooden trusses to prop it all up. Another sign closer to the bridge read ATTENTION: BORDER! CLOSED TO TRAFFIC AND PEDESTRIANS.

They kept moving so as not to attract attention, down the slope, through the trees, back out onto the road leading to the bridge, stealing glances that they would piece together later like so many camera snapshots. The bridge border crossing presented the usual barricades. A guard hut like a pillbox with two narrow diagonal slots for windows; warning signs in three languages, German, Polish, Russian; spotlights at the ready; and flags, always flags. The look was oddly decorative. A large wooden gateway spanning the approach looked like the finish line to a great race, with bold red and white stripes, the gate itself topped with a gable for little more reason than to display more stripes, more red stars, more stark warnings in Cyrillic.

"Keep moving," Katarina said. She also appeared to have a map in her head because she now led them, Harry scowling, Max scanning the perimeters, back into town to a secluded arched passageway that kept them in shadow and lent them a view out two sides. The cold stone gave Max a chill, and it reeked like mold. Harry shoved his hands in his pockets, leaned his back against the stone, ground his jaw as if chewing gum.

"You're moping; quit moping," Katarina said.

"The hell I am," Harry said.

"Your target needs you," Max whispered.

"You bet he does." Harry kicked at an imaginary pebble. He took a peek out both sides of the arch.

"You need to tell us more," Max said. "You're going to anyway."

"Fine," Harry said in a low voice. "Our target, he's American as apple pie. Russians don't care. They grab an American citizen in broad daylight and force him to toil for Joe Stalin. All for what his brain can do. What he knows, up here. Even though they have their own great minds—some of them even, you got it, former Nazis the Russians had captured or smuggled out themselves. Because the big race is on. Because god knows we've nabbed our own great minds, and former Nazis in the bargain." He grimaced at Katarina. "Sorry, Kat, but it's true."

"I know, Harry, I know."

Max knew he probably wasn't supposed to hear what was a highly inconvenient American secret. "What does that mean?" he blurted.

Neither replied. "All those banners, all those promises," Harry grumbled instead. "Who would want a system like that? It's simply fascism turned on its head. Same result."

Then, all fell silent. They couldn't continue until Harry told them the next step. Where their target was. If they could get to him.

"Do you have an extraction route?" Katarina said.

Harry recoiled as if she'd just shoved him. "Of course I do."

"At least there's been no sign of Hartmut Dietz," Max said and immediately regretted it.

Harry snorted. "I tell you, Max, sometimes you sure got a way," he barked.

"Keep your voice down," Max growled.

"Says you. Why don't you can it?"

"You can it—"

"Hey," Katarina snapped at them, "hey." She eyed them both as if sizing up which of them should get their head bashed in first with her imaginary billy club. Max pulled back a little, because a person never knew. Harry only sighed.

"Sorry," Max said. "Likewise," Harry added.

"You're both right," Katarina said. "The prospect of this Dietz on our heels, it only complicates matters."

She placed a hand on Harry's shoulder. She was trying to look into his eyes, and finally found them. Harry gazed back at her, and at Max, and at the both of them.

"Supposing I do need you two," Harry said. "All the way. We go for broke."

"We stand with you, brother. I told you."

"But no mucking up," Harry said, and he added a sad smile.

"No mucking up," Max said.

Katarina nodded. She peeked out both sides. She gestured at them to follow her.

"Wait," Harry said. "Our target, sure, he's an American scientist. I'm here to extract him. As I said. He'll be happy to see us. But there's one hitch."

"A hitch, or what you call a snafu?" Katarina said.

"Both," Harry replied, his eyes wandering back toward the Neisse River. "Because he's over on the Polish side."

GÖRLITZ

11:59 a.m.

"That's not just the Polish side," Max said, his voice strained. "That's Soviet Poland. We might as well be entering the Soviet Union."

His lungs wanted to collapse and swell at the same time. He thought he might hyperventilate.

"Well, I only just found out myself," Harry said.

"Back in Bautzen. Right? But you didn't tell us!"

"Will you calm down? See, I told you you didn't want to know."

"I'm calm, I'm calm," Max panted. "But once we cross over, that's it—our passes and papers, no good."

"You think I don't know that?" Harry said. He wandered off, out through the arched passageway, which led into an abandoned interior courtyard. The other side of the block was heaps of rubble, with large wooden splinters and bent iron rods sticking out like so many bayonets and barbs, and Max and Katarina watched Harry stare at the jagged spiked scarps, thinking, pacing. He consulted the sky. He stared at his boots. He even stroked his disguise mustache.

145

"At least an East German like Dietz has no authority over there," Max offered to Katarina, who only nodded solemnly.

Harry marched back to them. He gathered them inside the deepest shadow of the archway. "So. The next step. I did not want to do this, but . . ." He wouldn't look at them again. He sighed. "I'll have to meet a new contact. A different group. But they might have a way."

"Where?" Katarina said. "Who are these people? Can we trust them?"

"Catholics," Harry only said. "I think. They're not far. But, this time, if I don't come back? It definitely means I've been had."

That afternoon, Max and Katarina did their best to stay out of sight, to act normal, blend in. In town was a Jewish cemetery, with a new monument to the Jews pulled from their homes and sent to yet another subcamp of the Gross-Rosen concentration camp network here. They visited it as might any Persecutee of the Nazi Regime. Katarina took her time, and Max gave her all she needed. He proposed they split up a while before rendez-vousing later with Harry.

Max strolled back into Old Town, the day and the buildings turning gray from high clouds. He ate a potato soup that was mostly flour. He rode the creaking, wooden, prewar streetcar. He had another ersatz coffee. He wanted a drink but didn't want to tempt fate.

He rode the streetcar again. This one passed the oblong plaza the Soviets had renamed Liberation Square, the space vast and open, with mowed grass and paths and a white fountain with statues around it, all of it dwarfing his streetcar squeaking and inching along. Figures passed through the park, the usual mix of mothers and elderly, the occasional man in long coat.

Max started. He spotted a man sitting at the fountain,

staring straight ahead, toward the direction the streetcar had just come.

Hartmut Dietz?

Max pressed his shoulder to the window, peering out. The streetcar was passing the man and turning away on a slight bend. Max looked to the driver, the other passengers. He couldn't force the car to stop or it would make a scene, possibly even alert the man at the fountain.

Was it Dietz? Max jerked around in his seat. The man was still staring ahead, in the direction behind Max now. He hadn't moved. His arms rested loosely on his legs, his hands hanging off his thighs.

It had to be Dietz. He wasn't wearing a hat like most other men. Those jowls, his face harder, sharper. One corner of his mouth was turned up—he was fighting a smile as the streetcar passed.

Max craned his head for the next stop. He jumped up and pushed by other passengers who groaned, pushed back even, an old woman shaking her head at him, another grumbling "Unverschämtheit." He kept elbowing his way through, kept eyeing the fountain, but the streetcar had passed for good and his view of Dietz was gone. He waited at the door, practically scowling at the driver for the next stop, shifting on one leg, then the other. If he only had his pocketknife! He should've obtained a blade somehow, any sharp object. It was the worst thing to have on him in a situation like this, but he didn't care now.

A couple blocks more, the stop. Jingling. Max jumped off. He made his way back toward Liberation Square, doing his best to eye his surroundings as much as his fast walk would allow. He noticed a short rod of iron at the foot of rubble and snatched it up and slid it into his pocket.

He rounded the square from the opposite side of the street, craning his head again, bounding in and out of doorways, arches, hardly caring anymore.

The fountain stood alone now. No one was there. Dietz was gone.

"Are you sure it was him?" Katarina said.

"It had to be," Max said.

Her face hardened. "Well, I'm sorry I missed him."

Max and Katarina had met at the rendezvous point, a dim alleyway beer garden on the edge of Görlitz Old Town. They huddled around the end of a long table, letting the breeze in the trees and other guests' cheery conversation cover their voices and all the cigarette smoke their faces. Max was late for the rendezvous as he'd taken longer, meandering routes to be sure he wasn't followed. He'd tossed the little iron rod long ago. He'd expected to find Katarina and Harry together, but Harry hadn't shown either. Max checked his watch again, an old flaxen-faced Emes, part of his disguise. It was 4:47 p.m.

Harry finally wandered into the beer garden like he was already drunk. His face loomed like a mask, white and tinged green. He looked like he might vomit. When he spotted them, he stopped in his tracks a moment, then rushed over.

"Who died?" he said. "You two look worse than me."

The waiter approached, saw their faces, backed off.

"Max, look at me, what?"

Max glanced up at him. "I saw Dietz. Here. It must be him."

Harry sighed, a long release like he'd been holding his breath.

The waiter passed again. Harry ordered a beer. "Did he see you? Were you tailed?"

"No. I don't think so, from what I could tell." Max reported the rest, in detail. He was on that streetcar, Dietz on the square, then Dietz vanished.

"We have to assume it's him," Harry said. "We have to move." He swallowed hard, clearing his throat. "We're going tonight, late. It's all worked out."

They nodded, in unison. When Harry's beer came they drank in silence, like along a chain, Harry, then Max, Katarina. A fly moved along the chain. It landed on the table and Harry flattened it with his palm. The muck was all over his hand. They had no napkin, so he scraped it off with his beer mat.

"Maybe," Katarina said, "we should stick around and locate Dietz. To be sure."

"No way, Kat. Nothing doing."

"You would have told us if you'd known that he was here, wouldn't you, Harry?"

"Of course I would have!"

"*Psst*, keep your voice down."

They drank slower but steadier, sipping, as if it were the last water on a long hike.

"At least this will get us clear of Dietz," Max said.

"Now that's the Max I know," Harry said, managing a smile. "Ever the optimist."

"What's the quote?" Max said: "The basis of optimism is sheer terror. Oscar Wilde."

"I'll drink to that." Harry toasted Max, but Katarina didn't join in. She was too busy keeping watch for them.

ZGORZELEC
Wednesday, May 25
7:15 a.m.

Soviet banners hung from old buildings, half ruins, and new construction alike. Giant placards of Joseph Stalin loomed, his twisted smile barely contained under his near-comic mustache. Posters on every kiosk, wall, and window proclaimed the clear and righteous merits of Communism and Socialism and Stalinism in Polish and Russian, complete with the hearty farmer, child-bearing wife, keen scientist.

Max and Katarina, led by Harry, continued up a main street lined with pleasant four-story adjoining buildings on both sides, all high gables and pastel plaster and decorative windows. It could have been a suburb of Munich, Vienna. But all the signs were in Polish now.

They had made the crossing during the night, just south of town, the river's current barely a whisper, the darkness so black Max couldn't tell if they had been surrounded by open fields or tree lines. In the dark he'd concluded they were crossing a strip of no-man's-land, then another stretch with barbed wire that Harry's contacts had likely breached for them. It had only taken minutes. They waited in a barn. A silhouette appeared. Harry whispered a password and the next thing they knew they were riding across in a dinghy. The silhouette passed them a small pack full of food and water and Polish zloty. Then, as instructed, they waited in a woodshed until full light. Harry had brooded the whole time. He again didn't seem to be able to look Max in the eye. Max hadn't seen his younger brother stare at the ground so much since the single time Max could remember when Harry had gotten poor marks in school. It had never happened again.

Harry stopped on the sidewalk to check window reflections, waiting up for them.

"I think we're all right," he said and led them on.

It wasn't just about getting caught and sentenced, jailed, or even a death penalty. Aubrey Slaipe had once told Max: *Once you enter Soviet territory, you are fair game to be compromised and nastily so.* It was the Russians' modus operandi, their way of life, practically their national industry. Besides having millions of unwitting masses, it was the one advantage they possessed.

"We have to play it safe," Katarina said, as if reading Max's mind again. "We have no idea who might've been using us, could be on to us. Come on. And pick your head up," she urged Harry under her breath and smiled to give him his cue. "Look at all the pretty trees."

They were pretty, lining the street now, leafy and bushy green, showing them the way. But to Max it was only another deep forest.

8:29 a.m. Harry's new contacts back in Görlitz had told him of a safe house—a safe room, to be exact, the half basement of a nondescript building sitting on a slight rise, accessed by a door on a quiet backstreet with few windows facing it. Harry had a key. He led them inside, found the light switch. The space was large, the layout open. No stairs or doors connected to the structure above, though Max wasn't sure that was a perquisite. He couldn't stop thinking about escape routes, like a worried child did at night in case the family house caught on fire. The light bulbs were dim, the one small window set in the door nearly dimmer. They peered around as if into a long unopened crypt. The floor was lumpy brown linoleum with a fading leaf pattern, the walls a dull plaster, the ceiling buttressed by coarse beams. Four simple beds stood in a row out in the open, reminding Max a little too much of a barracks, and the tarnished metal kitchenette shined from grease. There was a persistent smell like mothballs even though the place didn't have a wardrobe, oddly, just various hooks and hangers on one wall. Only the column-like green tile oven in the corner suggested comfortable shelter.

No one spoke much. Each knew the plan from here. Locate Harry's target, find a weak spot for extracting him, use Harry's route for getting the man and whatever secrets he had back home and as rapidly as possible. At least Katarina knew some Polish from the Jews in her teams, from refugees in Palestine. Anything helped.

"As you know, my contact in Bautzen revealed the location of the facility," Harry reported as they stood in the middle of the dim room. "I suggest we start there."

The site wasn't hard to find, only a few streets away. That afternoon and over the course of the next day, Thursday, they took turns casing the facility where Harry's scientist served the Soviet Union. Nearby streets with their mix of parks, residential blocks, storefronts, and streetcars provided good cover, though most buildings and stores were oddly empty and closed, which they attributed to the Soviets expelling the Germans across the river to Görlitz. Yet the place was camouflaged by existing in plain sight. It resembled a small factory and might have been one once. The complex, about the size of a couple soccer fields, consisted mostly of old redbrick buildings like every city or town had, producing anything from beer to rail coaches to packed meats. It had two tall smokestacks, which constantly released pale billows of what looked like steam, these evoking a range of memories, nightmares. Extinct old Germany, New York City, concentration camps. They could not get very close and could not linger. It had the sort of high security, cloaked as casual, that revealed something important was taking place inside. The gate and guardhouse looked routine, but a second gate loomed inside a courtyard. New fences lined the perimeter, snaking between the high trees that camouflaged more small guard towers like so many tree forts. The new buildings were utilitarian in nature—all metal huts and block houses, as were various spheres and silos and strange antennae. All the guards and the vehicles coming and going were Soviet. The civilians entering and leaving passed through slowly, solemnly, with their heads down even, many wearing coveralls. Harry, Max, and Katarina took turns watching over morning, lunch, and quitting time. Far fewer came or went at lunchtime, another indication of utmost security. The only way they would get into a place like that was as guinea pigs.

That evening they briefly shared findings in the safe house, huddled around the rectangular birch table by the kitchenette. Harry had just returned from his shift.

"I saw him," he announced with a distant stare of resolve.

"You could see inside?" Max asked.

"I didn't need to."

Katarina lowered her cigarette. "They don't keep him there?"

Harry shook his head. His hands on the table didn't shake and he kept it together pretty well, considering. It was quite the revelation. "The Russians, it appears, are letting him come and go on his own free will."

They had a shot at this. It should've been reason for celebration, but no one was smiling.

Harry described him: short, slight of stature, dark thinning hair, large nose, wire glasses.

"Does he have a tail?" Katarina asked.

"I didn't see one."

"That doesn't mean he doesn't," Max offered.

"Of course not. He has no close minders that I can see either," Harry said. "I didn't try getting too near, but I also didn't see him showing any papers coming or going. No one frisked him." He shook his head again. "He was one of the few who actually waved at the Russian guards. What does he think this is, the country fair?"

Their target wasn't a prisoner. It made things easier, but only in theory. They had a bottle of vodka. Max poured them each a glassful. They stared at the clear liquid before them.

"Tell us everything," Max said to Harry.

"Konstantinos 'Stanley' Samaras," Harry said finally, in a measured tone, as if he was reading out a phone number and had not just revealed the scientist's name. "He has a code name: Reiter. This was originally Operation Reiter. That team got nowhere. Then it was just me."

They nodded. It was a common surname but in German also meant "rider," "trooper," "cavalier." In plural it alluded to the Four Horsemen of the Apocalypse; and they themselves were four—counting code name Reiter.

"Since we're now sharing the whole truth, my dear brother," Max said. "What is that place? And, please, do not tell me it's about the nuclear bomb."

"I've heard of a hydrogen bomb," Katarina said.

Harry didn't answer at first. He took a drink, glaring at them from over the edge of his glass, then baring his teeth from the fire in the vodka. "What could be worse than that?"

Max and Katarina exchanged glances, but neither had an answer.

A fly had found its way in, buzzing around. Harry swatted at it and Max, in distraught wonder, imagined it the same fly as in the Görlitz beer garden.

"That fly," Katarina whispered. "Oh, my god. It's in the air."

"Bingo," Harry said, practically sneering with dread. "Biological warfare. What we're now calling germ warfare. Delivered through the air, or by insects, always silent, unseen. Which alone makes it a horror. It's secret death."

The next day, Friday, Max, Harry and Katarina again took turns casing the facility and the way Reiter arrived and left. It did not deviate. He simply walked in, walked out. On his morning shift, Max noticed Reiter had a confidence in his step in a way that only Americans managed, as if he were kicking pebbles from his path. He was the only man who did not keep his head down. In fact he had kept his chin up. That puzzled Max even more.

They convened in the safe house briefly that afternoon. Harry, as usual, frowned at the grim half-basement room as if someone had defecated in the corner. He truly hated the place.

"He have a family, this Reiter?" Max said.

"He did, yes," Harry said. "I can tell you now. What does it matter? He and his wife are separated. Apparently she couldn't take the lonely hours and lifestyle of a secret US scientist's wife, and who could blame her? Took the two young boys back home to the parents' and the word is she's meanwhile reunited with the high school sweetheart. With Reiter gone, I imagine the deal's all but sealed."

"Is he actually an American?" Katarina said.

"What, didn't you see him?" Harry said. "Oh, I get you. On account of the work you do. Is he a Nazi we'd first brought over or some such? His code name might make you think that, but, no. Like I said. US passport holder, born and raised. 'Stanley' Samaras. His parents are Greek immigrants, but their son is as American as the Model T. Favorite ballplayer? Stan the Man, of course."

"Could he be conning the Russians?" Max said.

"He has to be," Harry said. "He's stringing them along. Biding his time until we can get to him. It's a smart move."

"There could be something else going on," Max said.

"He's right," Katarina said.

Harry nodded along, slowly. "Reiter, being a scientist, is one smart egg. Bacteriologist by training, germ warfare specialist by trade. Separated as I say. Wife's new man is rich, to boot, and Reiter's two boys probably don't even remember him by this point—first thing rich lover did was probably buy them matching baseball gloves." Harry added a sigh. "So. Reiter, he was in the US Zone of Occupation of Austria, as part of a special project. Vienna. He disappeared. Abducted, we figure. Our people fouled up, another snafu. This was a good three months ago, mind you."

"Which was why you were snooping around."

"Yes."

"We need to discuss motivation," Max said. "Maybe there was coercion involved? Blackmail. Threats."

"Maybe," Harry said.

"I think I know," Katarina said.

"You do?"

"He has a girl."

"Who does?" Max said. "Reiter?" Harry added.

"Yes, and he seems quite smitten."

Harry cocked his head back. "And just how do you know this? Don't tell me it's woman's intuition."

"Not this time," Katarina said. She hesitated, biting her lower lip. "I . . . might have veered off the plan a little. I might have followed him home at lunch today."

"You what?"

"Well, it was my shift."

Harry lowered his forehead to the table and left it there like a schoolboy at naptime. He rolled his head around. "You coulda been tailed," he muttered, "you coulda been nabbed, and we wouldn't have been the wiser . . ."

"Well, I wasn't."

"We all coulda been!"

"But we weren't." She raised her chin, and to their surprise her eyes sparkled. "So just hear me out, you two. And just wait until you see it."

"See what?"

ZGORZELEC
Friday, May 27
5:25 p.m.

They were all going. They needed to follow Reiter all the way home after work, despite the risk. Then they would grab him. The girl was a wild card, but they had no choice.

On a corner a few streets from the facility, Max tied his shoe on the sidewalk to look for Harry and spotted him leaning against a tree on another corner, smoking, holding a newspaper. He glanced at Katarina down the street as he stood and she nodded, having already spotted Harry. Harry opened his newspaper a moment, closed it again.

The signal. Reiter aka Konstantinos "Stanley" Samaras strode up the street. He had on an open collar shirt with the sleeves rolled up, his jacket hanging off one arm, his hat tipped back. He very much reminded Max of a man strolling home from watching a baseball game in New York City. He could barely recall the teams—Yankees, Brooklyn Dodgers—but he'd seen such men enough times when he'd lived there in the late thirties. He had wondered at them and had been looking forward to one day growing as happy as them when they won their games.

Reiter passed Max and Katarina, reached the next intersection. He did not wait for the streetcar, luckily, as that would create complications. Reiter just kept strolling, and strolling, due east, a good five, then ten minutes, until the relatively grand neighborhoods became sparse streets of multifamily homes and the occasional modest villa. More buildings looked empty from all the Germans kicked out. Another ghost town. They kept their distance because of the lack of passersby for cover. Harry had caught up but kept to the other side of the street. A Soviet Army jeep sped by, and they stiffened for a moment, keeping their heads down.

"It's coming, wait for it," Katarina said under her breath.

They turned a corner.

All of a sudden, they were in Greece.

The old women wore black smocks and headscarves, the younger men and women a mix of civilian and military dress, repurposed Russian tunics and Anglo-American waistcoats mostly. Most people had dark hair. The men kept their hair combed slick and didn't frown as much as the Germans, Polish, Russians. Their expressions looked something like hopeful, or at least relieved.

"In some ways," Katarina told Max, "it reminds me of Palestine."

The signs and colors and smells confirmed what they saw. There were instructions, warnings, and information kiosks in white and blue and the Greek alphabet, and briny, crumbly cheese and green olives on sale, then smoky aromas of grilling meat, and Max even thought he smelled piney retsina wine as they passed a small outdoor market. The Greeks now filled the sidewalks, and the open spaces had tents and temporary huts for those not yet assigned a vacated building.

Reiter tipped his hat to the younger women and exchanged pleasantries with the old women resting on their canes. He popped into a shop, came right back out. A group of children ran up to him. He gave them candies, they ran off laughing, and he shouted after them happily in American-accented Greek.

At the next corner Reiter stopped again to chat with the Greek men his age who'd gathered to smoke. Max, Harry, and Katarina manned the opposite corner, using the crowd around a shop for cover, considering the items displayed outside the shop, linens, doilies, dry milk, and of course retsina. The three of them weren't the only non-Greeks, luckily. Yet people still eyed them warily, gave them a wider berth. Sure, these refugees had been allotted this street, this block, this shop, but nothing came for free. At least the Soviet Poles in uniform stood out. The three of them could have been anyone.

Harry nudged Max. They glanced at the building diagonally opposite, then consulted the reflections in the shop glass. The building was residential, with laundry drying from windows. Reiter skipped up the short steps, disappeared inside, and that was that.

Katarina showed them a nervous shrug. "What now?"

"We hunker down," Harry said.

6:01 p.m. Max and Harry holed up in a makeshift café a few storefronts down. Reiter's building had too many windows over the street for all of them to surveil in plain sight, so they were taking turns observing from the corner—they could just see Katarina there now if she needed to signal. The café also served as a dry cleaner's, which made for much coming and going, and the bustle helped cover them. They drank Greek coffee in small cups, strong, foam on top, grounds in the bottom. The flaky pastry dripped with honey, and Max couldn't stop licking his fingers as the smell of nuts and butter lingered. This took him back to New York City again and Harry also reminded him, smiling, that there was just such a place like this in Manchester, New Hampshire, where their parents had brought him up. Their father, Manfred, a baker, had admired Greek pastries while their mother, Elise, preferred American donuts, to their father's constant chagrin.

Everyone on the block had left them alone. Ironically, the residents likely took Max and Harry for Soviet minders.

"Greeks." Harry said. "Who woulda thought?"

"It makes sense," Max said. "Reiter's Greek American, so the Russians recognized this as a benefit to offer Reiter. To make him feel at home."

"That won't last long. This isn't exactly New Jersey. He'll be hugging and kissing us to take him home like I was his grand-pappy himself."

Max was certain of it, too. Maybe Reiter even had a plan for it. He was secretly playing along, to lull the Russians. Max had done the same during the war so he could desert that ridiculous mission the Waffen-SS had forced him into. A fellow could hope, in any case.

"My turn," Harry said. He stood and exited the café.

Soon Katarina came back and took Harry's seat, slightly out of breath.

"Take a moment. Have some of the coffee." Max snapped fingers for another *kafés* and a woman darted over and snatched up the ornate metal server pot with diagonal handle.

"Pretty decanter," Katarina said, staring into Harry's empty cup. "They must've brought them all the way with them. So many empty streets, buildings. These Greek refugees could move right in."

Some of the buildings might've been German-owned, but many had probably been Jewish or both. Before. Neither needed to mention it. It was a sad fact all over.

"I asked around, discreetly, read what I could understand," she continued. "Last year the Soviets started taking in refugees of the Greek Civil War—Communist partisans mostly. Thousands of them, most simply families. Children. Zgorzelec is a main haven. They're building a Greek school, and there's talk of a factory to give them work and even a retirement home."

Max directed a thumb at a poster on the wall. The imagery of broad-shouldered fighters marching while wearing the red star clearly commemorated Communists fighting for Greece. He began to say, "I bet you that—"

The café door swung open. It was Reiter himself.

Max and Katarina lowered their heads. Reiter aka Konstantinos "Stanley" Samaras had a bundle of laundry under an arm. He squeezed by their table as two elderly women shuffled out.

Reiter reached the counter. Max and Katarina took turns stealing glances. Up close he looked a little older than his thirty-five years, his face pinched like that of a person used to some persistent, low-level pain. There was a little of the nebbish to him as well, his shoulders narrow, his eyes darting. And yet he could smile big and wide. He greeted the counter lady in Greek and Max could hear his American accent loud and clear.

"Where the devil is Harry?" Max out the side of his mouth.

"He'll be all right," Katarina responded under her breath.

Max glanced out the window and, among the people going back and forth, their hair and eyes catching the last of the sunlight, he saw a young woman standing stock-still, arms folded, glancing around.

"That's her," Katarina said.

Reiter was happily protesting something at the counter, but the lady rebuked him with mock indignation, handed him a pastry wrapped in wax paper, and gestured toward the door. Reiter strode past them, back outside.

The young woman's face looked hard as she faced out, but when she whipped around to face Reiter it was a completely new expression, beaming, expectant.

"Don't be obvious," Katarina reminded Max. "We wait."

Reiter had the pastry behind his back. He handed it to his girl, adding a little bow, and she flushed. She wasn't exactly pretty, but her big brown eyes, clear olive skin, and rounded features clearly made the most of what they had. Then Reiter and his girl stepped in front of the setting sun and became only silhouettes, their features blurring. Katarina's coffee had come. Max put money on the table and she poured her coffee and threw back as much of the hot stuff as she could stand.

Reiter and his girl moved on, leaving only the oranges of lowering sun.

One of Max's legs bounced, raring to go. He had counted one minute in his head.

"Now," Katarina said.

They waved goodbye and said thanks in Polish and Greek and were out the door. Reiter and his gal were walking down the street, in the opposite direction.

Harry was coming their way from the corner. "No way to warn you," he said as he passed and kept tailing them.

Katarina and Max crossed the street, to tail separately on the opposite side.

They kept their distance. Reiter and his gal soon entered a small park, not landscaped, little more than a meadow lined with trees along a gravel street. She had a basket. She set out a blanket and pulled out a bottle of wine and items in wax paper. They had their backs to Max and Katarina and were facing the sun, to watch it set. Max and Katarina watched from one tree, and Harry watched from another. Others crossed through the park, on a packed dirt path that ran through it, an old man with a dog, two boys and an admonishing young mother, a stray balloon rising away from them. Harry walked the path through, to look normal. He then read his newspaper on a bench from the opposite side, facing away from the sun, in silhouette, observing Reiter and the girl, taking stock of the perimeter. They should always expect to detect a minder or at least a shadow. But all Max saw now were two stooped Catholic nuns passing, their combined ages nearly as old as the Holy Roman Empire itself.

Harry's newspaper closed, opened. Max listened, heard it. A two-door sedan was rolling up, tires crunching gravel, engine rumbling. It was a DKW, mostly dark as coal but with blood-red sides and regular Polish plates, white characters on black.

Katarina, on cue, planted her back against a tree trunk, thrust out one knee, and cocked her head sideways, smiling. Max plucked a flower from her feet and held it up, smiling back. It was clever improvisation as they had no time to hurry off without creating even more notice.

The sedan rolled to a stop along the trees, in line with Reiter and his date out in the meadow. The car reflected the sun lowering across the park, the windows now mirrors of dark orange, striped with the shadows of tree trunks. All they could make out inside were fragmented contours of shoulders, a head, maybe a hat or two. The car might as well have been sitting in the dark with its lights off.

"What now?" Max said.

"Wait. Keep smiling." Katarina threw in a laugh for show. "They're not trying to hide. On the contrary. I think they're letting Reiter know he's on a short leash."

"Good. Yes. All right."

After a couple minutes, Katarina gave Max the nod to move

on and they did so holding hands. The car stayed in place. Across the park, Harry had meanwhile walked off. Others were passing through the park, the nuns long gone.

The three of them regrouped within the trees at the far end of the park, behind a crumbling old wood shed that gave them a view of both the tailing sedan and Reiter's picnic.

That old feeling hit Max. His heart was racing, his legs wanting to kick. It was moments before the big show. He saw it in Katarina, too, and in Harry. They stared and scanned and didn't seem to blink, all their movements mechanical.

"We do it soon," Harry told them. "When the car leaves, we move in."

Max: "The sun's going down."

Katarina: "That's what they're waiting for."

"It's not for the sunset," Harry said. "Reiter needs to know that he's safe from a tail. Dark. No one watching. We make contact when he walks her home."

They would move out that night if possible, using Harry's escape route.

"Today is Friday," Katarina said.

"That could give us all weekend," Max said.

Harry: "Provided he has the weekend off."

Max: "What about the girl?"

Harry: "She stays. We tie her up if need be."

Katarina: "Agreed."

Max: "We could wait until tomorrow, until they're apart."

Harry and Katarina at once: "No."

Max nodded, mechanically too now. The longer they were here, even a day longer, the risks increased exponentially.

8:30 p.m. Over beyond the trees, the black-and-blood-colored DKW F8 sedan released smoke from its tailpipe and rolled off, its lights coming on. It disappeared. The trees around them had dimmed. The sun had lowered behind the trees, painting the few streaks of clouds pink. They had plenty of darkness now. They peered into the meadow and could see the silhouettes of Reiter and his girl packing things up, standing, their cigarettes glowing. Max thought he heard them laughing, though it could have been one of the many ravens now finding the treetops.

"He does seem to be making the most of his lot," he said.

"He's lulling them into complacency," Harry said. "He must be itching to get back. Safe. Free. Baseball season has started. Oh, he's good. The refugee Greeks are good cover. Locals are calling them gypsies, I heard, even giving them the stink eye, but Reiter knows the Russians want him pacified."

Max: "The girl could be a honeypot."

Harry: "All the more reason."

Max: "No violence, please."

Katarina: "I can handle her. Talk to her, threats only. Whatever the case may be. She wouldn't want her family hurt."

They nodded agreement. Just in case, Harry had a pipe that would do for a pistol barrel in the back.

Reiter and his Greek girl finally crossed the meadow, their silhouettes swelling, coming their way. Max and Harry crouched behind the shed. Katarina had rushed on ahead, skirting the road, checking for any tails. Their cigarette smoke arrived first, harsh and bitter, possibly Greek tobacco. They passed Max and Harry only ten yards away, footsteps patting along the compact trail, chatting in a mix of Greek and English. Then they were heading back down the road. Max and Harry followed at a distance, just close enough to spot their silhouettes in the dimming light.

They knew that streetlamps were up ahead. It would have to happen before that. Max and Harry picked up the pace, walking step-in-step for less noise, and the surrounding ravens helped.

Fifteen yards now. Houses, buildings, and streets were appearing again. Reiter had picked up the pace, his arm hooked around his girl's. Elbows jutting out, shoulders rocking, they fast-walked and turned down a dark intersecting street. Not the way they'd come.

Max and Harry glanced at each other. They turned, followed.

And saw nothing. No one. A couple houses were under construction here. They pivoted around, trying to look natural. They could expect Katarina to circle back.

"Give Kat a sec," Harry whispered. "Then we'll keep walking, slowly. She'll have our backs."

They strolled the dark new street, passing the shadows of unfinished and uncovered roofs, the timbers spiking into the sky.

A stack of stone blocks, shoulder high.

A figure stepped out from behind it.

Reiter.

Max and Harry halted.

"*Kuh-to tee?*" said Reiter.

ZGORZELEC
8:52 p.m.

Reiter aka Konstantinos "Stanley" Samaras had said it in broken Russian. Max and Harry had frozen.

"*Kim jesteś?*" Reiter repeated in Polish thick with American accent.

"Mr. Konstantinos Samaras," Harry said in English, "we're here to—"

"Who are you?"

"We're friends, Stanley," Harry said. "Don't be spooked."

"Says you. Jesus." Stanley's American English was high and tinny as if filtered through a phone receiver. "What am I supposed to think? It's pitch-dark out."

"There was no other way, I'm afraid. Our apologies."

Max stayed a foot behind Harry, playing the security man, to make things look safer.

"Where's the woman?" Stanley said. "There was a woman with you—"

"Please keep your voice down," Harry said.

Stanley's eyeglasses reflected moonlight like two shields. He sighed. "I saw you," he said. "You don't think I didn't see you? You've been shadowing me ever since I got off work."

"She's near," Harry said. "She's keeping watch. Where's your girl?"

Stanley squared his narrow shoulders, raised his chin. "I sent her on home. The back way. I didn't want her involved—"

"What did you tell her?"

"That you're my minders."

"Okay, good."

Stanley cocked his head at Max behind Harry's shoulder. Max leaned his head, smiled.

"Does he speak?" Stanley said.

"Why, of course," Max said in his best American accent. "Pleased to meet you. We've heard great things."

Stanley stared a moment. Then he smiled. A chuckle followed and he put a hand to his mouth as if catching food from spilling out. "Come on, who are you guys anyhow?"

"This isn't the best place to talk," Harry said.

"You mean here out in the open, or Poland proper?"

"Both."

"Right. Okay. Sure thing. What do you fellas have in mind?"

9:20 p.m. They had made it back to the half-basement safe house. Katarina had been waiting on the corner after surveilling their route back. Stanley Samaras had chuckled again on the way over and shook his head at them, but Harry reminded him to remain calm, however excited he may be. Max, for his part, was liking Reiter already. He thought Stanley might make a decent traveling partner on his extraction. Too few people chuckled at the surreal nature of a cruel world.

They sat in the dim open room. Stanley looked around as if he'd just had a blindfold removed, blinking at the beds like barracks and the greasy, tarnished metal kitchenette.

Harry gestured toward the table. "Please, take a load off."

"Gladly," Stanley said. "My feet are killing me."

He lowered himself onto a chair at the table as if it might break.

Max and Katarina stood back and let Harry deliver the good news. It was his show.

Harry knelt down to Stanley, who had turned the chair to the room and was grasping at the knees of his baggy pants.

"Mr . . . . Dr. Samaras, we're here to take you home."

Stanley nodded. He broke into another smile, but it twitched. He stared at the floor. He was so pale he glowed in the dim light.

"I have to take my pants off," he said.

"What?"

"In the evenings. I take my pants off, see, sit around in my short shorts. My *bampás* did the same. It takes the edge off. Helps me think."

"Knock yourself out." Harry stood back up, glancing over his shoulder at Max and Katarina.

Stanley removed his shoes and placed them together just so, then stepped out of his pants and hung them over the back of his chair. Then he sat, all white undershorts, knobby little white legs, and black socks complete with garters. He released a sigh.

"Pardon, ma'am," he said to Katarina, who waved away the very notion.

"There's nothing to think about," Harry said. "We're taking care of everything."

Stanley tried smiling again. But the corners of his mouth yanked downward.

"Hey, why the long face? We're here to take you out of here. To rescue you."

Harry was holding out his hands as if presenting Stanley with a new refrigerator. Max loved his brother, but he just wasn't cutting it as spokesman. Harry gave Max a sideways nod—his cue.

Max stepped up. He too knelt. He put on a hint of smile but pinched his eyes with concern. He spoke low, fatherly. Bampás. "Listen, Stanley. Can I call you Stanley?"

He nodded. "Sure, sure."

"I know that you must be afraid. But there's nothing to be afraid of. We are on a mission to get you home. You can have your old life again, your old job, or a new one, if you like. And baseball. And—"

Stanley burst out laughing, a high-pitched ring that bounced off the linoleum and pinged against the metal kitchenette. He stood. He paced the room, no pants and all.

"This is a joke, right?" he said finally.

"How do you figure?" Harry said.

"It's the test, comrades. Right, *tovarish*?"

"Hey, don't *tovarish* me, pal."

Max and Katarina shared a knowing glance, that of thespians acknowledging a colleague who had the chops. *Stanley was good*, Max thought. Of course he had to make double sure. Max would have done the same in his position. There was far too much at stake.

"That's good, oh, that's rich," Stanley was saying, truly grinning now, his teeth remarkably straight and white. "Where did you get such good English anyways?" he said to Harry, circling him. "Why, you sound just like my pals back home." Then he stepped up to Max and gave him a sympathetic frown. "Now, you, okay, you're good, but there's something off. Oh, don't be disappointed. It's all right. You're coming along swell, just swell." He held up a finger. "But you know, if I was to guess, seeing how I spent some time over on the German side of things, Austria, I'd bet that you might have been born a German. Right? *Ist das nicht wahr, Genosse?*"

Clearly, the nebbish was just a role. This scientist was a wily warrior. But what was his play?

"Better that you call me friend than comrade," Max replied in German.

"All right, swell, friend it is." Stanley shook his head smiling. He still had a finger up. "And a good evening to you, my dear," he said to Katarina, who was still standing over in the shadows by the door, keeping an eye on the street.

"Good evening, Dr. Samaras," she said.

"See! You three are good. You three can really play." Stanley found his seat again. He slapped his hands on his thighs with a crack. "Say, you got anything for a fella to drink around here? Let me tell you, I got lucky, just happened to spot you." He nodded at Max. "Saw that one first in a store window reflection—no offense, friend. So then I'm thinking, something isn't right here. This fellow has a fine air about him that just don't fit in sleepy old Zgorzelec. But I just put that in my pocket, because who knows? A fellow keeps an eye out. Supposing I'm wrong? But then I see you again, among my people, all these Greeks here, and of course you stick out. So I use my noodle. Start piecing things together."

Max had raised his eyebrows in appreciation. "You came into that laundry on purpose. For a better look. See how we'd react."

"That's right!" Stanley had his finger up again, and Max could nearly picture him in a white smock, brandishing a clipboard in his other hand, announcing to his research team that he'd landed on the big breakthrough. "Oh, now, listen, this was no fault of your own. You were good, just fine, fine. But this other fellow here, the one with the real American accent, now, he really knows how to move. A natural."

Stanley was now the kid going back over the street stickball game, play by play, and Max thought he heard Harry release a low moan.

"Oh, don't look so glum, pal," Stanley said to Harry. "You did great! It was only at the park that I was able to put the three of you back together again, and that took some doing, I can tell you. See, what I did was, I—"

"Enough!" Katarina shouted and marched past Max and Harry over to Stanley, leaving Harry to eye the street. She pulled up another chair and swung it around and sat on it backward, facing Stanley like the interrogator she had likely become.

Stanley recoiled, and the back of his chair tipped back and found the wall. His hands instinctively covered the crotch of his underpants.

Katarina kept glaring at him, her cheekbones like river stones in the dim downward light.

"*Shto?*" Stanley blurted in Russian. "I was only trying to help, I—"

"Explain yourself. Now. The truth, no more games."

"I had you figured for special minders, like you, uh, like they used to put on me at first. But then I wasn't so sure. The jaunt-to-the-park idea, I cooked it up to draw you in."

"What about the car?"

"What car?"

"A DKW sedan, two doors, black and red."

"I didn't see that! I was too busy tracking you three." The front legs of Stanley's chair hit the floor with a pop. He sat up. "Wait. Then who was that?"

"Maybe it was your actual minders. But they're better than that. You wouldn't see them. And if you did see them, you wouldn't know them."

"Oh."

"Now. Next. Who's the girl?"

"You don't know? That's my Dora."

"You met her here?" Katarina said, her voice softer now, and Stanley finally let his hands leave his crotch. "You can tell me. She's a refugee? A Greek Communist? Is that it?"

"That's right. Lost her whole family. Her newborn child, a fiancé. Poor thing. Starting a new life. They all are. Irony is, they're living in the houses of people the Russians and Poles booted out—the same Germans Dora and her clan were fighting when she was still a teenager. As partisans. Assassins." Stanley narrowed his eyes. "You understand that, I can tell."

Katarina nodded, gravely. "Go on."

"These Greek Communists, they sure buck some of the old country conventions, I can tell you. Thus me and her. Most Greeks would be picking a husband for her already."

"You're getting married?"

"I didn't say that! It's only been a month."

Katarina nodded, faintly, and Max imagined her in hot and dry Palestine, speaking to a child whose parents had died, who was about to start a new life. He shot a glance at Harry and saw him nod in gratitude, and pride. Max knew Harry wasn't going to break it to Stanley, not yet—that his Dora might just be the very minder he'd believed he did not require anymore.

"What if I told you," Katarina said, "that we really are who we say we are? We are working for the Americans. We are here to take you back to America."

Max wasn't sure what he'd expected. Jumping up and down. Crying for joy. A prayer, prostrate. But it wasn't what he saw. Stanley only stared back at her. He swallowed a gulp.

"Why, that's terrific," he said, and his voice cracked like crumpling paper.

ZGORZELEC
10:28 p.m.

The half-basement safe house lacked ventilation and was getting stuffy. Stanley Samaras had still needed more convincing. To prove they were the real thing, they had talked about American culture—radio shows, idioms, what little they knew about base-ball of course. Gallon of gas, twenty-seven cents; coffee, under a buck for a two-pound bag. Television, a new hit show starring *The Goldbergs* from radio. Perry Como, Frankie Laine, *South Pacific*. Max sang a few flubbed lines of "Good Rockin' Tonight." Katarina even showed him her forged Union of Persecutees of the Nazi Regime ID, worthless here without travel papers. They were putting it all on the line for him. They even considered telling him their real names. All the while, Stanley had sat immobile, as if listening to a scientific lecture. But he had clapped softly at the end. "Okay, okay, I believe you," he had told them. "Thank you, thank you. I had to be sure, see. You understand?" He had directed his smile at each of them with emphasis, as if punching buttons.

Katarina now sat alone with Stanley, at the table. He had wanted to know more details, the next move. She had told him to calm down first. She had made him put his pants back on.

Max and Harry stood in the shadows by the door. Max kept watch, peering out the small window. Once, a car approached with the same dark shape as the one in the park, but it kept going. Otherwise the street might as well have been an empty country lane, the few nearby windows just dim squares. Harry had taken to scowling at Stanley. He growled something.

"He's just scared," Max whispered. "He doesn't quite believe us. What's he supposed to think? Consider all he's been through. He's not you. Me even. He's a little forest animal."

"More like a fox," Harry said. "He needs a shock, is what he needs."

"No."

"Just keep an eye, please," Harry said and pushed off the wall and strode over to Stanley.

Stanley looked up, squinting. "Hello again, stranger. I still don't know your name—"

"Your wife has moved in with him," Harry said.

Stanley stared a moment. "Gee, you sure know how to persuade a guy."

"But she's not happy. I have it on authority that she longs for you, your wife. That she wants you back."

Stanley shot up, the chair banging against the wall. "That's a load of hogwash! She left me!"

"Look. We're here to take you back. Rescue you. So you can rescue that."

Stanley stared again. Harry stared back. He wasn't much taller than Stanley. But Stanley sat back down.

He stared at the faded linoleum a moment. He let out a long, wheezing sigh. He finally looked up. His eyes had turned glossy and soft.

"You just don't get it, do you? I do not want to go back, and I don't aim to. Not ever."

ZGORZELEC
10:57 p.m.

Harry had to sit down, feeling for a chair with his fingers like a man in the dark. Max followed his younger brother like a nurse making sure an elderly woman didn't fall. He found a seat next to Harry, patting his leg, Harry shooing him away.

Katarina glared at Stanley to explain or else.

Stanley stood before them, closed his eyes a moment, then opened his arms wide. "Look, fellas. Ma'am. I hate to break it to you, here, like this, and after all you've done, which I appreciate, I do. But I'm not naive. I was a walk-up."

Harry reared his head up as if he'd been slapped. His cheek even flushed red.

"A what?" Max said.

"Isn't that what you people call it?"

"It's called a walk-in," Harry grumbled.

"Yes. I walked in to them. The Russians. It was my idea."

Everyone stared. Just stared.

"Look, I know it's a shock," Stanley said. "Would anyone like some water?"

Max shook his head. Katarina and Harry just kept staring.

Stanley sighed. "Aw, heck."

"But that's not what you are," Katarina said eventually. "You're a defector."

"A traitor," Harry added. Max patted Harry's shoulder, Harry shook it off.

"Tell us about it," Katarina said and went to keep watch at the door window. They had forgotten all about it.

"It was in Vienna," Stanley said. "I figure I can tell you since you went to all this trouble." He told them the rest in a low, gentle voice, like a doctor telling them that someone had poisoned their dog and he didn't have an antidote. "We were sightseeing, the group and me. Scientists, assistants. I just slipped away from the pack, at a coffeehouse. Minders apparently didn't notice. Next stop, Soviet Embassy. It wasn't hard."

"So it was just like that." Harry snapped his fingers.

Stanley raised his chin. "I could have attempted it in Berlin—we were there, too—but I chose Vienna because of the Berlin Blockade. That made things tenser there. Blockade only ended last week, and the Berlin Airlift, but who knows—"

"Stop. Just, stop." Harry added a shake of his head. "You numbskull egghead, do you really think you did this all on your own?"

"Hey, come on. That's not fair. You know, you don't look so good. You want some water? Why don't I get you some water?"

Harry looked to Max. "Why don't you do the talking from now on? Before I wring his skinny neck."

Stanley blew air out one side of his mouth. He pivoted around and looked to Katarina, but she only stared back from the shadows by the door.

Max wondered what Aubrey Slaipe would have them do now. He opened his mouth to speak but sitting didn't feel quite right, so he stood and was sure to meet the eyes of all of them. He was taller than Stanley, so he stood back a little. Cleared his throat. "Well, then, it seems we're just going to have to come to some kind of agreement."

"I don't know how we can," Stanley said. "Because I'm not going back. You think it's about my wife. My kids even. I miss my boys, sure, and I would've brought them with me if I could have. But this is about more than that, see. Far more."

"Your work, you mean," Max said. "This facility here."

Stanley nodded. "That is the most immediate reason, yes."

Harry had sat up. He had stopped shaking his head.

Stanley looked to Max, who nodded for him to continue. Stanley paced in a circle, in and out of the shadows, and when he appeared again under the dim bulb his face was harder, tighter, his teeth showing.

"The American dream is a sham," he said, careful not to look at Harry. "I'm sorry to tell you this, but it is. You know how they treated my parents? They were just dirty immigrants. Why you think we always went to the Greek dry cleaner's, deli, diner? They were the only ones who would have us. In America it's supposed to be all men created equal but everyone thinks they're better than the poor guy right below them, unless you get real greedy, sure, and earn yourself a load of dough by hook or crook. Then you're a king. You do whatever you want. Then you're not an immigrant no more, no. But become a teacher? A doctor even? Scientist. Forget it." Stanley looked at Max. "You might be a naturalized American, I'm guessing, from your English." He glanced at Harry. "But you born ones, the fair-haired ones, they don't ever know how it is."

Harry wasn't a born one. He was naturalized. Harry knew how it was. It was why Harry had lost his German accent as a boy, so they wouldn't call him Hun and Heini. It was why Max, when he'd finally followed his family over later, in the 1930s, gave all he had to New York City as an actor but could only get roles playing the mustachioed WWI general in the spiky helmet or subsequently the heel-clicking Nazi. Most auditions wouldn't give him the time of day. Too many talented Jews were coming over as refugees and they certainly deserved the roles, spiked helmet and heel-clicking and all. But Stanley's people had not done anything wrong. They hadn't started wars. They were simply in need, nowhere else to go, tired, poor, yearning to breathe free. America had even invited them in, lifting her lamp to the golden door.

"I mean, why you think I'm Stanley and not Konstantinos?" Stanley added.

"Now you're Stanislav," Harry barked.

"So what of it? I want to help people," Stanley said. "America only wants you to make a buck. Don't believe the high talk, boys. The Russians want to prevent another war. They want to help people. And they have good reason, too, after what they've done and seen, real good reason. Now, look how they treat these Greeks here. They take them in! No questions asked. They feed them."

For now, Max thought. Nothing was for free.

No one spoke, so Stanley added, "All right, sure, some of these local Poles don't like it, but they didn't like the local Germans, either."

"Or the Jews," Harry said, beating Katarina to the punch. She nodded at him. "And neither do the Soviets. Just wait till you get a load of Joe Stalin."

"Where do you want me to start with America, huh? Should I start with the Indians, or should we move on to the railroads, the union busting, the sweatshops. Robber barons? I could write a book."

"Look who's Theodore Dreiser all of a sudden," Harry said.

"Maybe you shoulda written that book and saved us all this trouble."

Max held out a hand to the room. "All right, gentlemen, all right. Now, Stanley. You gave us your personal reason. And we understand. My brother—er, colleague—at the table over there can shake his head all he wants, but you are certainly entitled to state your reasons. Which brings us to the other one. The facility."

Stanley had folded his arms at his chest. His chin sat higher. His best impersonation of a locked safe.

Silence reigned. A dog might have barked, far in the distance.

Katarina nodded for Harry to come over. The two of them huddled by the door and whispered in the shadows. Meanwhile Max was left showing Stanley calming smiles and shrugs imploring patience, like some hotel manager waiting with a guest outside a room being made. Katarina whispered something else and Harry's eyes widened in frustration, Max saw, but then Harry finally nodded.

Katarina stepped out of the door shadows. "I have an idea. Stanley? Look at me. What if I brought Dora here? Would that help you agree—to something?"

Stanley's arms had lowered, and his chin. "It can't hurt. Dora never can."

"Now, you see?" Katarina smiled back, all loving and warm, all just for Stanley, as if about to start stroking his hair. "We are going to need food, anyway. I could pick up Dora on the way."

Stanley told Katarina how to find Dora in his building, and their secret knock and code word. Then he gave her his food order— *keftedes* if Dora had any; Dora made the best Greek meatballs.

"But it doesn't mean that I'm going with you all."

Katarina ignored Stanley's pledge. "There's one condition," she told him. "You must tell my two colleagues about your facility while I'm gone. All right? Yes. Good." Then she put her dark hood over her head and, thusly transformed into another Greek woman at night, slipped out the door.

And Max was left amazed at the brilliant wiles of a woman.

Max and Harry carried the table to the middle of the room, closer to the door so they could trade off watching the door window. They summoned Stanley over, which had the unfortunate effect of putting Stanley right under the bare light bulb above, like in an interrogation. Max proposed they turn off the light or at least cover it, but Stanley only shrugged. "It's all right, fellas. I'm used to harsh light in my work."

"Let's get to that," Harry said, taking a chair at the table while Max manned the door window. The street remained clear, and even fewer windows were lit in the distance.

Stanley held up hands, dropped them. "You want me to tell you about the facility. Of course I can't tell you. You know that. Even if I did want to go back with you."

"I'm not looking for details. Just some perspective. Help me understand."

Stanley closed his eyes a moment. He stared at the grainy tabletop. "It is my belief," he began as if giving a recorded statement, "that the Americans are developing germ weapons that could wipe out whole cities, continents even." He grimaced at them. "You understand the horror of these weapons? They are silent. No gas cloud. They make WWI gas look like a BB gun fight. Worse than any atom bomb. And I'm not even talking about what it does to civilians."

Max felt the skin crawl on the back of his neck.

Harry said, "Now, I don't think that's—"

"I do," Stanley said. "Because I know. You ever hear of Camp Detrick, in Maryland? No? Of course you haven't. There are precedents for this. Entomological."

"Entomological?"

"Using insects to carry pathogens, to attack. The Japanese did it in the thirties, to the Chinese. On a large scale. Their Unit 731 sprayed fleas and flies from airplanes, dropped bombs filled with more insects, disease. Horrific. Probably half a million Chinese died. The Nazis were studying that—Nazis, by the way, who the Americans have been smuggling in for their brains, using, by the way, the Nazis' ratlines. Oh, don't look at me like you don't know. Ratlines being the fugitive Nazis' escape routes. You have something called Operation Paperclip."

Harry winced, grinding his jaw. "Just stick to the point."

"Stew all you want, but you know they're just itching for a little war to test it out in," Stanley continued. "Or maybe it's bubonic plague you want? Or nerve agents? Tabun, sarin, soman. They're developing those, too. And meanwhile, the East Germans, right across the river there? They're saying the Americans are trying to wreck their potato crops, using potato beetles as carriers. Farmers have seen American planes dropping them."

"Propaganda," Harry blurted. "We might have Operation Paperclip, sure, and maybe I don't like it. Maybe I like ratlines even less. But the Russians have their own version. Their own Nazi doctors, scientists."

"*Dezinformatsiya*," Stanley protested. Disinformation.

Silence found the room. Max kept glancing out the window out of anxiety and couldn't help imagining this abandoned street populated by dead bodies inside intact houses, mouths still gaping open from their poisoning. It almost made a person wish for good old-fashioned rubble.

"Let us never forget," Harry told Stanley, "the Russians' standard operating procedure for everything from propaganda to crime to espionage to, I don't know, illicit love affairs: Always accuse the other side of exactly what you're doing and vehemently so."

"You really believe that, don't you?" Stanley looked to Max, who only stared back. "Well, supposing you're wrong?"

"Let me get this straight," Harry said. "You're working on the same thing, but for them?"

"What? No! I'm only working on the antidote."

Harry fought a laugh. "Says you! I thought you said you weren't naive."

Stanley raised his chin. "You may be the sword, but I am the shield."

"Let me lay it out for you. The Russians only need a shield, you see, if they're working on their own sword. That's how they protect their own troops, people. We believe the Soviet Union has deployed offensive biological weapons before. They used tularemia on Hitler's armies advancing on Stalingrad—their so-called rat weapon. Rats carried the infection, spreading it."

"What's tularemia?" Max said.

"Rabbit fever," Stanley snapped.

"Nasty stuff," Harry said. "Fever, ulcers, swelling lymph nodes. Death."

"Maybe they only want you to believe that," Stanley said. "But what of it? Supposing they did? It saved the war. You don't get it, do you? It makes plenty of sense for the Soviet Union to be wary, fearful. To defend themselves. You might call it paranoid, sure, but consider the facts. They lost tens of millions when we could have helped them much sooner. We waited until forty-four to attack the continent, on D-Day, all while they were dying for three years meanwhile. Three years. Millions. So many civilians, so many. I've seen the photos, so don't you tell me . . ." Stanley's chin quivered. His eyes glossed over. He pressed at the table as if to keep it from rising up and striking him in the face.

"All right, take it easy," Harry said.

Stanley lowered his head, his hair hanging over his eyes. His head reared up. "It's not just germ warfare. Not just that! There's new psychiatric drugs. Hallucinatory. Look at you two, you don't even know what I'm talking about." He pointed at his temple, twisting his finger. "Gets you right here, right inside the old noodle. All that remains to work out is the delivery means, see. As in warfare. How to affect people with it. Destroy their minds, silently. Happy now? That what you want?"

Harry held up a hand. "The Russians are doing this, or we are doing it?"

Stanley only laughed, but without seeing his face it sounded like a sob.

"You bring Dora here all you want," he said eventually. "But I'm not going."

"Just take it easy."

"And you better not harm her either. If you do I'll . . . I'll start screaming my guts out."

"I said take it easy. Calm down—"

"And don't try and drug me, slip me some newfangled Mickey, or her even, because it's not going to work!"

Harry slammed at the table. "Stop it, Stanley. Why would we do that?"

"Why? Because you can. I worked on those programs too. To muck up the mind. I told you. It's what the Russians are hoping to stop." He paused and straightened up, and he stuck out his narrow chest. "It is what I am working to stop."

ZGORZELEC
11:51 p.m.

Almost an hour had passed since Katarina left. Max took the table now, Harry at the door. Stanley grew more confident. He started smiling and laughing again. The bare light bulb glowing above their heads pushed out the rest of the room, the beds and kitchenette and tiled stove and faded linoleum, Harry and the door even. Stanley rambled. He brought up Broadway as if reading Max's actor mind. He raved about shows, *Oklahoma!* this, Lillian Hellman that, the Great White Way ad infinitum. He apparently loved it as much as baseball.

Max only rested his elbows on the table and let his face harden under the light, their one spotlight on this stage. *You want theater?* he thought. *Drama? Tragedy? I'll deliver the shock that Harry couldn't.*

He waited until Stanley ran out of words.

"What? What is it?" Stanley asked, his thick eyebrows drooping.

Max gave it another long beat. "I was an actor. It's true. I lived in New York City, in the shadows of Broadway. I gave it all I had, jumped right in. It spit me out."

"Oh," Stanley said. "I didn't know."

Max gave it another beat. Shifted his eyes to the ceiling, upper right, as if deep in thought, and then gave a hint of a sigh.

"Let me ask you something, Stanley. Did anyone ever talk to you about it?"

Stanley didn't answer. He cocked his head at Max.

"About here, I mean. Coming over. Look at me. No? A colleague? A friend?"

Stanley stared awhile. The rest of the room had left him too. It was only him, Max, and a pale sallow circle between them.

"You can tell me," Max said.

Stanley nodded but only kept staring. He must have stared for a good minute. His face opened up.

"I had a friend," he said finally. "A colleague, let's call him. He was on the Vienna trip. I confided in him."

"He talked you into it?"

"No, no, it was nothing like that."

"Then what was it?"

Stanley didn't answer. He clearly didn't want to reveal his accomplice's identity. He might have blanched a little. Max waited for Stanley, weighing how to reach him.

And a flask appeared, Harry's. Like the most professional waiter around, Harry had placed the flask inside the pale circle. Stanley lifted it. The lid was already off. He sipped, grimaced, took another sip. He slid it to the center of the table. Max sipped. Toasted Stanley.

"Go on," Max said. "It's all right."

"I didn't say he was a Russian or anything. I only said this was in Vienna."

"No. Sure, sure."

"Well. He, my colleague, he gave me a three-day pass, in a different name. So I could hole up in Vienna if I needed to."

"What about the minders? Your group of scientists had people watching over you, right?"

Stanley nodded. "There was a diversion. An auto accident, right outside our group in the coffeehouse. That was my chance. I knew it. My, er, colleague, he wasn't exactly any more practiced than me in these matters."

They never are, Max thought.

"But one thing he did say," Stanley said, "was just to wait for some kind of diversion. That would give me a chance to break off. We weren't that far from the Soviet Embassy, see."

"I see."

Stanley had hunched forward slightly, and his eyes darted back and forth, peering at the table as if it were a window he could see out. He didn't seem to like what he saw there.

"Take your time," Max said. "Would you like a cigarette?"

"No, never," Stanley said. "Have you seen what happens to lungs, exposed to foul air like that? I have. In my work, I have."

Stanley's eyes had glossed over, the shine before the wetness, and Max, too, felt a heat behind his eyes, and that moisture. He was one with Stanley. He was inside Stanley's character. He could have played him on this very stage.

"But, earlier," Stanley muttered.

"I'm sorry. I didn't quite catch that."

It took Stanley a moment. One corner of his mouth turned up in a sickly smile, and he had to shake his head to make it go away.

"Earlier, I had another colleague. Respected colleague. Almost a mentor to me, if you will."

Max nodded. Just waited.

"Oscar Kovak."

Max nodded again, gravely. "Oscar Kovak was a Communist, Stanley."

"I know, I know. Don't you think I know that? But he was just a thinker. An egghead like me."

"He's in custody now," Max said. "You couldn't have heard." Or at least the Russians wouldn't let you hear, was the implication.

Stanley said nothing for a while. He held out his hands as near fists, as if ready to yank on two ropes that would lower onto their stage. But they didn't.

Max had lied about the custody part. He had read about the theoretician and scientist Oscar Kovak, as he had been in the news back in America. The man was only suspected of being a Soviet go-between. There were trials coming, under the Smith Act.

Max and Stanley were blinking at each other as if each had just woken in a long-distance train compartment and didn't know where they were, what time, who was this fellow traveler?

Max knew the story all too well. A similar tragedy had befallen him in 1939. A nice Foreign Office man from the German Embassy talked Max into returning to his homeland. Since Max hadn't been able to make it as an actor in NYC, this discreet German man suggested, and later proposed, there was far more opportunity for "model" Germans back home now—meaning for those of pure blood. They all knew what that meant, Max even knew in the back of his head, and he wasn't ever going to pretend that he did not. He had taken the man's offer of passage in return for possible roles that had been stolen from those who'd been forced to emigrate or ended up in a camp, eventually. This was one reason he had deserted the war at the end of 1944. It was his way of standing up. He should have stood up long before. He supposed he had been standing up ever since.

The Russians had been working away at Stanley for such a long time. The realization made Max's stomach slosh around, like he was going to vomit.

A tear coursed down Stanley's face and Max's in turn. The same opposing side, his right, Max's left.

"But, but, that was so long ago," Stanley said finally. "Years ago." He said it to Max, to the dark room, and to Harry at the door.

Max wiped at his eye. "Stanley, look at me. Listen to me. We told you. My partner over there told you. It's the oldest play in the Russian book: Always claim the other side is doing exactly what you are doing."

He reached across the table, and he grabbed Stanley's hand. Stanley did not yank it away.

"They told me they were going to get my boys over here," Stanley said eventually, in a near whisper.

"I don't have to tell you the likelihood of that," Max said.

"No. No, I suppose not." Stanley finally pulled his hand away. He wiped at his eyes. "I just want to do good. I wanted to do the right thing, you know?"

"I do."

"You really do understand, don't you? Say, what's your name?"

"Max." Max raised a hand into the darkness around them, to calm Harry by the door.

"I know, I know—you can't tell me any more than that." Stanley sighed. He turned to the side slightly, staring into space. He finally nodded and said, "It doesn't matter about Oscar, about my mentor. Say they recruited me, tricked me even. We were friends. And we want to prevent this world from destroying itself. That's all we want."

But that was not what the powers that be ever wanted, not on any side. Max let the realization sink in for Stanley. He didn't respond. Stanley took a while. He was staring at the floor, hands dropped into his lap, shoulders slumping.

"That's all we want," he repeated.

"You can still stop this," Max said. "Sure, you can't stop history. You can't stop from failing. Your wife leaving you. There, I said it. But you can make something good from this."

Stanley kept staring at the floor, his face setting into a pale mask, skin permanently sagging. He was beyond crying. The shock. Yet an initial resolve was forming inside him, still in its graduated cylinder, but certain to crystallize. Max could tell. All it took was heat, the right elements, perhaps a measure of stirring. Max wasn't sure what this resolve might lead to, but it had to be better than inertia. He had learned that the hard way—inertia, indecision, idle hands even, call it what you will, it all led to ruin. He had to believe in that. He had to believe in Stanley.

"I believe you," Max said.

But Stanley only stared at the floor.

It was growing cold in the semibasement, yet they didn't dare light the tiled stove; besides, it looked as if it had last been lit when Napoleon passed through here.

Max turned to Harry and put a finger to his lips, like mother to father once baby was finally asleep: *Let the man work it out in his head.* And so Stanley did work it out. He had plenty to deal with—Max hadn't experienced such silence since he was stranded amid heavy snow in the Ardennes, between the shifting front lines gone quiet, between Christmas and New Year—"between the years," as his fellow Germans called it.

A soft knock at the door made Max start. They all straightened. But it was only their signal knock: two fast, one, two fast. Harry looked out, slowly opened the door, and two figures slipped through the cracked door like a strong draft. It brought the smell of roasted meat and faint perfume, a rustling of wax paper, the slightest panting.

Stanley had stood, peering into the shadows.

"Dora?" he said. "Is that you?"

ZGORZELEC
Night

"*Aftós eínai esý, agapité?*" Stanley said.

"*Málista*," Dora replied.

Max had stood, stepped back. Katarina pushed the door shut and Harry peered out.

The next elephant had entered the room. But Dora was more like a small wild cat alerted to the elephant's path. She pulled off her headscarf and stole glances at Max and Harry with big eyes as Stanley held her, whispering to her.

"She speaks English," Katarina said. *Because of the Greek Civil War*, Max thought. Because of British involvement. He could well imagine that Katarina, from her experiences in Palestine, had appealed to Dora by employing a common hate of the British.

Stanley whispered one more thing to Dora and she whipped around and glared at Max and Harry.

Her rounded features looked sturdier in the harsh downcast light, if not tougher, and her black hair looked even shorter, blending into the shadows. Her eyes all blackened. Max, in his ignorance of things Greek, couldn't help thinking of a Greek theater mask.

"What do you do to him?" she said. "He looks so terrible."

No one spoke. *We did not do anything he has not caused himself,* Max wanted to say. He instead gave her a slight bow and said, "Nothing whatsoever. We are simply discussing. Though we do face a certain challenge. Hello. You must be Dora."

She nodded, slowly, as if wary of even giving her name.

Katarina placed a bundle of waxed paper, a canteen, and a bottle of clear alcohol on the table and retreated to the door to relieve Harry, who stepped into the light. The four of them stood around the table—Max and Harry, Stanley and Dora.

"Why, there are only two seats," Max tried to joke. No one responded. "Please, you two take a seat," Harry said to Stanley and Dora.

"We are not hungry," Dora said. Stanley added a shake of his head.

"That's all right. Water?"

"No." They sat instead, and Dora kept her eyes on Max and especially Harry. Then she glanced at Stanley, pushed some wayward hair off his forehead, fixed his crooked collar, and sat up straight, suddenly the dutiful girlfriend. Max noticed she was missing a tooth, nearer the back. He wondered what other small misfortunes she knew. Sad compromises. They all added up.

"I'll only go," Stanley said, "if you bring Dora."

They had been expecting this yet it still came like a shock wave, echoing in the half basement like an axe chopping wood. But Dora looked most surprised. She recoiled in her seat, the chair actually skidding back, and she barked something at him rapidly. Stanley lifted a hand as if to touch her, but her look said, *Don't you dare.*

Stanley looked their way. "Could you, uh, give us a moment? She wasn't ready for this." Dora added a huff.

Max and Katarina joined Harry at the door while Stanley and Dora removed themselves to the farthest bed, sitting on the edge, discussing and arguing in rapid whispers.

Max gave Harry and Katarina a world-weary shrug. "A traveling circus."

"You got that right, brother."

He and Harry briefed Katarina. Stanley had been steered, had been . . . handled . . . whatever one wanted to call it. It had gone back years, originating with his most trusted confidant. Katarina nodded along, eyeing Dora and Stanley quarreling in hushed voices over at their bed.

"We tend to repeat the same mistakes," she said apropos of seemingly nothing. It unsettled Max—it was the same sort of detached statement that Aubrey Slaipe might offer, its profound relevance only revealed later.

"So we agree to Reiter's terms?" Max asked Harry.

Harry didn't answer. He'd gone quiet, still thinking. He knew they had to do it. Their first cause working together had been saving ethnic refugees just like Dora. Duty might be a mighty vessel, but morality was a fixed star. Yet something was keeping him back. He kept running a hand through his hair.

"Do I have to remind you, brother?" Max added.

"No, you don't. We'll have to. The Greek refugee angle might be enough for the CIA. If not, we get her a passport through Sabine Lieser."

Katarina meanwhile kept glancing over at the bed. "Hold on," she said.

Stanley and Dora had stood, holding hands as if ready to walk the aisle already.

"She's scared," Stanley announced. "She needs assurances."

Dora raised her chin and nodded, filled her chest with a deep breath.

"She'll get assurances," Harry said, then cleared his throat. "But there's something else I'll need too."

Oh, no, Max thought.

"I thought we had a deal," Stanley said.

Harry's shoulders raised. A shrug. "You know what I was thinking? You up the ante, I up the ante."

Stanley had no response at first. He squeezed Dora's hand.

Max opened his mouth to speak but Harry held up a hand to stop him. And Dora shook Stanley's hand loose. And Katarina blurted, "*Ach, Gott*. Here we go . . ."

"What kind of deal?" Stanley said.

"Maybe we should talk alone." Harry moved over to the table.

"We are alone. And we go now. With her." Stanley squeezed Dora's hand again, but she wouldn't look at him. "Before I change my mind."

"Now, just take it easy."

"Just tell me what you want."

"Tell him," Katarina blurted.

Dora shook off Stanley and sat back on the bed, staring at her lap. Stanley went over and whispered to her but she only showed him the top of her short-haired head. He stared at the ceiling and whispered to himself. Then he sighed and trudged over to the table as if climbing steep subway stairs into the chilling rain. He dropped into a chair and slumped, hanging his hands off his knees.

"I want you to go back to work," Harry said. "One last time."

"How can I?" Stanley said to Harry. "How?"

Harry had found his seat, to be eye level. This had to be man-to-man, objective, void of any cajoling, let alone intimidation. "It's after midnight, today's now Saturday. Do they operate on weekends?"

"The facility? Of course. But it's a leaner shift, lighter schedule."

"Do you go in?"

"Sometimes I do, sometimes I don't. Not usually."

"Later this morning you are. First thing."

Stanley drooped and seemed to shrink. Dora's eyes loomed from the dark bed, wider, whiter. Stanley seemed to sense them. He kept shrinking but couldn't lose them. Max exchanged a concerned glance with Katarina, who just watched with her arms folded.

"Stanley?" Harry said. "Listen. Look at me. Sentries? Security contingent?"

"Sure. All the same. Always. All Russians."

"What can you get?"

"Some. Papers, yes. But it's mostly up here." He pointed at his temple, which unfortunately looked more like a gun to his head.

"They pat you down?"

"No, not anymore; strike that—sometimes there are spot checks. My briefcase mostly, but . . ." Stanley sat up. "Supposing they do a body one, huh? Supposing they do pat me down?"

"We'll take our chances," Harry said.

The truth was that he was hedging his bet, Max thought. Harry was mixing duty and morals, navigating that mighty vessel using the one shining fixed star. Max admired his mettle. But God help them. And now Max wondered, with a cruel rumble in his belly, if they deserved their new bounty. He couldn't help recalling what Stanley had said, what the man believed. Even more frightening than any weapon either side was currently developing was the erosion of truth, of his faith, Max felt. Without it, how could a person know what to fight for?

"What about Dora?" Stanley said.

"We keep her. Here."

As collateral, he meant. Dora muttered something in Greek from the bed.

"Where does she normally sleep?" Harry said.

"She has her room, in my same building, but she's usually with me."

"Good. No one will miss her, not early in the morning. You following me? You go in first thing, get what you can, come back. We won't be here. We'll be ready to go nearby." Harry glanced at Katarina, who nodded; Max nodded. "I'll tell you where," Harry added. "Get what you can from your place, if you like, but only take what you can carry light, and nothing that gives you away."

"How do I do it?" Stanley said, his voice firming up now.

"You have a small camera, a Minox, something of that sort?"

"No, nothing doing. I have no access to tools like that."

"Then you carry it out."

There was no time to teach Stanley a writing code, let alone use it. And they had no good concealment device. Stanley released a sigh through his teeth. "So, papers? I'll see what I can do. Sometimes doors, drawers get left open. I can't promise."

"Fine. We can open a seam in your jacket, resew it. If that doesn't look feasible, just wrap them around your calf, your upper arms. I trust they have rubber bands, string? Maybe don't take your briefcase in. If you do, leave it mostly empty, to decoy them in case of a spot search. Your choice. You know how things work inside."

Stanley nodded. "Yes, all right. I could make some notes on my regular notepad. It's all scientist shorthand, anyways, and no one's the wiser."

"Good. Don't take more than an hour or so."

198

"Jesus." Stanley lowered his head to the table again, within an inch of it, as if about to bang his forehead, again and again.

He turned to look at Dora, but she only stared back, her eyes wet, and she looked smaller now, more fragile, just the frightened orphan girl she likely still was inside.

ZGORZELEC
Saturday, May 28
2:00 a.m.

They finally ate, in silence, the room filling with aromas of pepper and garlic, mint and thyme, basil, onion. Dora's *keftedes* were slightly fatty but flavorful and the fresh flatbread fluffy and moist. Max ate from his watch at the door window. This should have been a feast, a celebration. It was more like the hour before a deadly night patrol. They picked at the meatballs and tore at the bread while ignoring the tzatziki, sipped at the water to get the food down, and didn't touch the bottle of a clear Greek alcohol. Dora apologized for the inexcusable lack of feta cheese. She ate over at the bed, facing the wall. Stanley soon joined her.

Max joined Harry at the table when Katarina relieved him. "Kat's mad at me," Harry told him. Harry allowed himself a drink of the clear alcohol, which smelled of anise. He poured Max one. "She says we're risking too much. The thing that gets me is, she always knows better."

"She has a right to be mad."

Harry hung his head.

Max patted him on the arm. "But I expect nothing less. We have to try, don't we?"

"Always, Max. Always."

5:00 a.m. The sun had just risen. Saturday morning. They had attempted to sleep. Max sat on the edge of his bed, groggy. Katarina was still on watch at the door. She hadn't woken Harry for his shift, Max realized. She sat in a chair with one shoulder against the door. Stanley snored, lightly. Beds creaked. Dora rose eventually, wandered into the toilet installed in a closet— a true WC. Max lay back, stared at the ceiling, trying not to think too much. Soon Harry found his way to his bed and crouched next to him like the platoon sergeant before that night patrol.

"You sleep?" Max whispered to him.

Harry didn't answer. "You?"

"Sure."

He felt Harry smile in the near dark. "Listen, I been thinking—"

"You don't have to say anything."

"If anything should happen to me, make sure they get out. All right? All of them."

"We should be saying this to your former girlfriend over there," Max said. "She's the one with the true mettle—"

"Just say it."

"All right. Yes. I will make sure."

Harry patted Max on the stomach. "You know something? Sometimes you sell yourself short."

7:00 a.m. They had all risen, eaten, washed up, and had on them what they could carry in bags and packs, just enough to make them look like hardy refugees resolved to make their way across a continent after enduring all manners of hell. Refugees came and went and would for years. Germans, too, had been kicked out of Poland and the East by the trainloads, the millions, generations. Impersonation was all they had, should they be stopped. Katarina and Max still had their Persecutees of the Nazi Regime booklets. Dora had her refugee papers, now questionable. Harry, lacking travel papers, had ditched his identification. He and Stanley had nothing.

Earlier, Max, Harry, and Katarina had huddled by the door for their final briefing. For the rendezvous spot they had chosen one of the houses under construction, where Stanley had first intercepted them. They simply had to trust the location, that no one would be working there early on a Saturday morning. Then they had today and Sunday, tops, before people started noticing Reiter and a Greek refugee girl missing.

Now they all stood at the door like sleepy early-morning workers waiting for subway car doors to open, though in cruel truth they were rookie paratroopers about to leap for the first time from a gaping-wide airplane doorway thousands of feet up.

Katarina would go alone and track Stanley coming to and from the facility. They would just have to trust Reiter. They had done all they could. They had demonstrated to him that his cause was compromised if not rotten, then bought insurance by holding Dora.

Harry placed a hand on Stanley's shoulder. "Are you ready?"

"Yeah," he said.

"Are you sure?" Max added.

"Sure I'm sure."

"He is ready," Dora said, and looked him in the eyes to fortify him. But once Stanley stared out the door and took a deep breath, Max saw how her eyes darted, and her hands clawed at her sides.

* * *

8:30 a.m. The sun had risen above the unfinished frames of roofs, now looming like so many giant rib cages. Max, Harry, and Dora sat inside the stone-block outer walls of a partially built home at the crest of a slight rise. This gave them plenty of cover and surveillance options; a camouflaged pillbox couldn't have done much better. Random stacks of building materials provided more cover in case they needed to flee. The maze also gave anyone ample opportunity to sneak up on them or flank them, Max thought, then banished the idea. For safety's sake, he had told Stanley to simply walk down the middle of this street once he returned—unless he was being followed. In that case, they could only hope Katarina would manage to intercept him, shake their pursuers, and deliver him back here.

Harry observed the street, and Max watched the tree line behind the property. Dora huddled between them, surrounded by their few bags, staring at the bare planks under their feet as if able to peer through to the cellar. She looked to Max, and he smiled back. She forced out a smile but tugged on her headscarf. Max kept smiling. He hummed an old favorite, "Mack the Knife," almost twenty years old now. Dora leaned her head sideways in a girlish if not flirtatious manner. Sure, his humming a tune was buffoonish, but if it amused a girl in danger? Who cared.

"Can it," Harry said. "It's too quiet out there."

A warm breeze was flushing the morning chill from inside their cold stone box, bringing in odors of gypsum, untreated wood, and possibly strong glue. Nearby signs in Polish and Russian touted the benefits of Soviet housing, but there were also the trespassing signs—surely an offense if not a state crime. And suddenly the smells to Max become those of ashes, and sharp splinters, and poisons.

"He will come," Dora told him in her wooden English, "he will come," obviously seeing the concern in his eyes. She added a pat on his wrist and it made him smile again.

Harry held up a hand for silence. Someone was coming? Max scanned the tree line and spotted nothing among the skinny birch trunks.

Then they saw him. His shadow preceded him, a long, warped version of Reiter, his worn little hat like a massive conquistador helmet.

Then he passed under the rising sun and through his own shadow and it was just Stanley. He had his briefcase under one arm. His gait seemed a little stiffer, but Max remembered he might have paper wrapped around his limbs. Dora moved to stand but Max placed a hand on her shoulders.

As Stanley passed their building site, Harry clucked his tongue. As instructed, Stanley knelt down as if tying his shoe, scanned the perimeter in every direction, then stood and strolled inside their stone-block hideout.

Dora hugged him, both of them squatting down. Harry and Max kept watch. This wasn't over yet.

"Where's Kat?" Harry said as he scanned the street.

"She'll be along," Stanley said.

"Did you see her?"

"No. But I felt like she was there." Stanley added a nod at Dora to confirm it, and she nodded back, the corners of her eyes swelling with tears.

8:45 a.m. Fifteen minutes later, and Katarina still had not returned. The construction site remained as quiet as ever. Stanley and Dora were clutching their bags, their eyes bulging at each other, taking turns comforting each other in whispers. Harry had gone quiet. He was thinking things out, Max knew, what-ifs, final options.

"We have to consider the possibility," Max whispered to Harry.

"We can't leave without her," Harry said.

"There might be construction today. Some anyway. We don't know their schedule."

Harry nodded, but didn't budge.

Max waited a couple minutes. "She might have left, Harry. She's already helped so much. She might even have another mission, one she could not tell us about—"

"She wouldn't," Harry snapped. "Not without good reason anyway."

9:00 a.m. They had decided. They had to go. If someone was holding Katarina, even she would divulge their rendezvous spot eventually.

Harry took one last look, as did Max.

Stanley and Dora leaned into the bare stone wall as if ready to burst right through it.

"All right, we go," Harry said.

They entered the unfinished street and began walking east, away from town, along one side of the road, Harry in front, Max in back, Max telling himself they really did resemble just another harmless group of refugees making their way across Central Europe.

They descended the rise of the street. Before them lay a meadow, a connecting country road, and wooded countryside. Katarina knew their rough direction for the first day. She was a good tracker. Max wanted to remind Harry of that, but his brother's now confident gait confirmed that Harry was sure of it too.

Max sensed something and peered around for any movement, shadow, sound. He nearly ran into Stanley's back. All three had frozen before Max.

"Keep walking, act normal," Harry urged from the corner of his mouth.

Now Max saw. A car was coming up from the connecting road and had turned their way. A sedan. It looked like the same black-red DKW as the evening before. No one spoke. It might just be a coincidence. They kept walking. Max even feigned conversation like an extra in a street scene and forced out a smile for good measure.

The car had the same plates. It approached, slowed, and turned. It stopped diagonally, blocking the road.

Now they stopped, huddled like the refugees they appeared to be.

The sun reflected off the car again, blocking their view of the two occupants. Then the driver's-side window lowered halfway, and a hand waved them over.

They stood about twenty yards away.

"Come on." Harry stepped forward, and they followed. He stopped about ten yards from the sedan. Stanley and Dora stood behind him, using him for a shield. Max moved on instinct, mechanically. He rushed up to front all of them. He had the most believable papers. He was Emil Wiesenberg, a Victim of the Nazi Regime.

The passenger-side door opened. A man stepped out from the shadow of the car. He moved around the hood and removed his hat.

"Shit," Harry said.

Max shuddered. His stomach seemed to drop to between his ankles.

Hartmut Dietz stood before them.

"Hello, gentlemen," he said.

No one spoke. Max's first thought was that Stanley had sold them out, as was Harry's, since they both glared at Stanley.

But Stanley only shook his head at them, violently so, his face blanching rapidly.

Dietz leaned a hip against the hood and raised one leg, like an American gangster. All that was missing was the tommy gun. Then he raised a pistol from his pocket, a stubby little Mauser HSc, just enough to show them.

He added a hint of a bow. "There is no way around me," he said.

Stanley was still shaking his head. Dora stared in horror, her eyes stuck wide open, darting between Stanley and Dietz. Stanley coughed, gagged. Then he vomited on the spot, a hot gush catching the sun.

ZGORZELEC
9:15 a.m.

Dietz had Max, Harry, Stanley, and Dora line up at the car like children for a delousing shot while his driver, a stocky type with a hamburgered nose and a sour odor Max tried not to identify, silently patted down each of them. Dietz's graying thin hair glowed like silver floss in the sun, and he had rings under his eyes.

"You work too hard," Harry said.

Dietz blew air out one side of his mouth.

A white heat had filled Max's chest and head and he considered jumping the driver and seizing the gun that he was sure to have. But where was it? And what about Dietz? Would Harry anticipate it? They needed a plan first.

Then Harry gave Max that glance that said, *Keep your cool; let's see how this plays out.*

Then Max remembered that this was Poland, that Dietz was an East German now.

"I just should've killed you," he growled at Dietz. "For Irina."

Dietz ignored him. He helped frisk Stanley and Dora, who had frozen as if just told they were standing in a live minefield. He rushed it, saying nothing to them.

His henchman took a step back, and Max used the opportunity to glance around the tree line. He couldn't spot any other men with Dietz but he couldn't be sure.

"Our cozy sedan will not fit us all, I'm afraid, so I will walk you. Move . . ."

Dietz walked the four of them back up the street as his henchman rolled the sedan slowly along behind them, practically killing the engine twice as he did. Max kept exchanging glances with Harry. Max had expected Soviet jeeps to come speeding up and more men to emerge from the woods. But Dietz was discreet, his henchman practically shy.

They passed the half-built house, descended the other side of the rise. All four were exchanging anxious glances now. Still no Katarina?

The fact that Stanley had not disclosed Katarina to Dietz said something for his intentions. But it could also mean . . . Max felt a twinge between his ribs and had to swallow hard. He started to see blood and the waxen face of the dead and squinted his eyes shut to the thought. He couldn't look at Harry.

Minutes later, they turned onto the road to their safe house. Max had imagined locals peering out of distant windows in fear, but all seemed quiet. Where were the comrade henchmen in overcoats, the Black Maria with no windows? And why would the Soviets allow an East German like Dietz across the border, no matter his position?

"Keep together, don't stray," Dietz barked, his voice increasingly strained.

Dora was sobbing and Stanley whispered to her in Greek.

As they passed the half-basement safe house, Dietz said, "Stop."

The sedan rolled on and kept going. And going. It picked up speed.

Dietz showed them the Mauser from his pocket. "Well, don't just stand there in the street. Go inside."

"Go inside where?" Harry said, stalling.

"Where do you think, Captain Kaspar? Back to your safe house."

The car had turned at the next corner, and its rumble faded away.

Harry gestured at Stanley and Dora to open the half-basement door.

"Halt! Wait."

Katarina was walking up the street to them, casually, as if on a morning stroll. Max's heart sank a moment. But then it flushed with something like hope. He even nudged Harry in excitement, but Harry only shook his head.

"She's back," Dietz said.

"Who?" Harry said. "Who's she? I don't know—"

"You take me for an idiot? Your colleague, confidante, agent, whatever she is. She was tailing our Herr Samaras here the whole way."

Harry waved hands at Katarina. "Go, run for it!" he blurted.

But Katarina only slowed, pivoted to scan their surroundings, and then faced Dietz.

"Well?" she said to Dietz. "Are you going inside, or not?"

The six of them shuffled inside the safe house. The door was open, they'd left the key on the table. Harry, Max, and Katarina stood around the table while Stanley and Dora found their seats on their bed.

Dietz kept between the door and room. "I can't say this was not a surprise," he said. "Well done, Max. You made it much further than I would've guessed."

Max ignored him.

"But who are you?" Dietz said to Katarina.

"I should ask the same of you," she said.

Dietz smiled. "Oh?"

"I've been watching you the whole time," Katarina said, her voice gaining a harder edge. "You are on your own."

"There's that car," Max said. "There could be more of them."

"It's long gone," Katarina said. "And there's not. He's operating solo. An East German." She added a sharp laugh.

Max and Harry exchanged glances. Should they jump Dietz?

"The Russians let Dietz travel to Communist Prague," Harry said. "He could call in the cavalry." He widened his eyes at Katarina as if to say, *Go, I'll distract, you make a break for it.*

Katarina only shook her head. "I'd bet that thug of his was hired. Probably came with the car. That about right, Herr Dietz?"

Dietz took a step back. He trained the Mauser on them and switched on the dim light bulb. "Sit. All of you!"

Max, Harry, and Katarina sat at the table. The light streaming in through the door window combined with the dim glow of the bare bulb to cast Dietz in a jarring mix of angles and shadow and gleam. His black Mauser shined on the edges and the barrel was well worn. Max recognized it now—it had been Harry's own, back in Munich. Dietz had taken it from them when he escaped to the East. Max's gut roiled, his blood boiled. He scowled at Dietz strutting around the room now, checking things out. His dear Irina was dead because of Dietz.

"You still have my paratrooper's knife, too?" Harry grumbled at Dietz.

Dietz forced a smile. "Sadly, no. I had to sell it, along with my dear Sauer 38."

The other gun he had on them that cold Munich day. His former police service pistol.

"Life was none too easy in the East, at first," Dietz said.

"Spare us the sob story," Max said. "What is this, Dietz?"

Dietz took a deep breath.

"You're trading us in for bigger better things?" Harry said. "That it? Impress your Russian masters?"

"No. You are." Dietz lowered the Mauser. Took another deep breath. He strode over to the table, placed Harry's old gun on the table, added a magazine from his back pocket, and gave a little bow.

"I am coming with you," he said. "To the West."

ZGORZELEC
9:56 a.m.

Dietz, after saying it, looked like he had a case of diarrhea. His movements were halting, jerky. He felt his way over to the nearest bed, lowered himself onto the edge, and sat. He sighed like a balloon being let completely out of air.

"Say that again to my face," Harry said. "Because I don't think I'm hearing so good."

"You're going to get me out," Dietz said.

"I thought you wanted to be a double," Max said. "The big man."

"Not anymore. You had your chance. I told you."

Harry grimaced at Max and Max could only sneer back, at the sickness of this world. Katarina just observed. Stanley and Dora looked as shocked as ever—they leaned into each other, propping each other up.

"To the West? You mean the West that you fled," Harry said, "because you had a past that wasn't going to pass denazification. A past you deceived for and even had people killed to cover up."

"I did not kill Irina." Dietz looked to Max. "I told you that. I will tell your people that. Anyone. The Americans. It was an accident. My hired hand did it."

"Tell it to the wife and kids you left," Max said.

Dietz caught Stanley's attentive gaze and looked away, from all of them.

They sat in silence. Harry eventually produced the bottle of clear Greek alcohol. Ouzo. Dora found them glasses from the kitchenette cupboard and set them on the table, her hands shaking more than they ever had. Harry poured and gave Max a glass first because he could tell Max was seething. The stuff burned down Max's throat like anise seeds still baking from an oven, but it would suffice. Because Dietz had plenty of explaining to do. Because that Mauser pistol was still sitting out in the middle of the table.

"Start talking," Harry told Dietz.

"Before we kill you right here," Max added.

Katarina just stared at Dietz.

Dietz looked at the faded linoleum floor between his knees. "I never wanted to emigrate to the East—call it fleeing, defecting, whatever you will. I never wanted to leave my wife, Lila, my dear children. But you forced me into it, you and your brother there. Lila will never come over here. I wish to find them, to contact them."

Stanley perked up at the revelations, as did Dora. Max ignored them. He and Harry were too busy grinding their jaws, scowling.

Dietz began speaking mechanically, as if reciting a confession. "I have certain information to offer the Americans. I have knowledge of the Soviet apparatus, from the inside. I'm in the ruling East German SED, naturally, and I work for the East German K5, attached to the Soviet MGB, MVD. They were grooming me for a post in a new East German secret police: the Ministry for State Security. And then there's my wartime intelligence, from the Russian Front, which I understand the

Americans are increasingly interested in. I can be of great use. Harry, you have heard of the Gehlen Organization? It's your own intelligence agency, run by none other than former Major General Reinhard Gehlen, head of Wehrmacht military intelligence on the Eastern Front. Oh, don't look at me like that, Harry. You should be glad. I could have found a way to return on my own, surely. But I came to you. I offer myself to you. I am taking a chance, I know, but I have much to offer—more than I can tell you. Do not frown. You can still take Dr. Samaras back. You still win the game. And you bring me as your big extra prize." Dietz tried forcing a smile, but it only looked like a small dog bearing fangs, his tapered teeth enhancing the effect.

"Some game," Harry snapped.

"I play chess," Dietz said. "I had an endgame. My plan was to return all along, ever since I fled. The road out was the same way in—that road was you. I thought going double was a way back. The opportunity had presented itself. I don't believe in luck, gentlemen. I believe in preparation. Think of your endgame, Harry. You can salvage your operation. The CIA can."

"I'm not salvaging a damn thing," Harry said. "And stop calling me Harry."

Self-seekers like Dietz never stopped, Max thought. They were fierce storms leaving all destroyed in their wake, leaving innocent survivors to clean up, mourn, and be forever plagued with a vengeance that in turn threatened to turn them into tempests doomed forever. And yet, Dietz believed he had his reasons, his justifications. He had only been trying to get by in a cruel time. He had been only serving his country. He had been shielding his family from harm. He had sought salvation in a welcoming regime. He was traversing a churning river, leaping onto stones that tumbled away as soon as he stepped on them, then the next, and the next. Max winced at his own empathy—if he didn't stop, Dietz was going to end up the Bishop of Munich.

"I'm sorry, Max," Dietz said to him.

"Stop using our names!" Max shouted and pounded on the table. A boiling rush seared the inside of his skull. His heart be damned. Empathy could go to hell.

"Take it easy," he heard Harry say.

But Max already had the Mauser, clenching it, waving it. He kicked out his chair and shot up and lunged at Dietz on the bed. Dietz fell back, his head lashing back off the other edge, nearly hitting the floor. Max grabbed him by his hair, pulled his head up, smacked him on the jaw with the pistol butt.

Dietz's mouth opened in a silent scream and Max shoved the Mauser in.

"Irina!" Max shouted. "Irina . . ."

Hands grabbed at his shoulders. Harry, Katarina.

He pulled back. Stepped off Dietz.

Dietz had let him attack. Harry had already emptied the Mauser's magazine, Max knew that. His eyes ran hot but tears wouldn't bleed out. His heart was back now, tight with sorrow, grief. Panting, he wandered back to the table and set the pistol in the exact spot it had been. He straightened his clothes. He picked up his chair. He dropped onto it.

Some time passed, minutes maybe. The light seemed to dim, then lighten. Harry and Katarina made their way back to him at the table.

"I'm sorry," Max muttered to her. "I was never like this . . . before. Harry knows."

"Neither was I," she said. "But it's all right, dear. We'll be back."

That brightened him. He tried a chuckle. It made him snort.

"Get it all out," Harry told him.

"No, I'm doing better."

* * *

Dietz had not said another word. He had sat at the table and pushed his hair back out of his face. His jaw looked red but the skin hadn't split.

Stanley and Dora stared in silence from their bed as Max, Harry, and Katarina circled around Dietz, blocking Stanley and Dora's view in case someone was a good lip-reader. They spoke in German to make sure.

"So you crossed the border of Communist Poland on your own," Harry said to Dietz. "You don't have travel papers."

"That is correct. No, I do not."

"You really are not going back."

"No, I told you this. Prague was my chance. A special case. Because I had a past with you. It didn't work. I tried telling you my plans then, when they were questioning you. But I could never get you alone long enough. But I did keep you on track, didn't I, Harry?"

All looked to Harry.

"All right, all right, yes. In Prague, Dietz did confirm to me that the Soviets had moved Stanley to Soviet East Germany. Bautzen. But it was old news, as it turned out."

"Prague was always a risk," Dietz said. "After their big coup, those Czech Communists are even more hard-nosed than the Soviets. Still, I should have run then and there. Like you did! You threw off both the Soviets and your own people, or at least made it appear so. The Russians think maybe you lost your mind! That was smart of you, Harry, a little reckless, but—"

"Spit it out," Harry said.

"Yes, all right. I had a long-term plan. I convinced them to release you in Prague, that you were just a cowboy, didn't know what you were after. Yes, it was I. I want you to know this. You shouldn't thank me. I am making amends. But I also expected something in return." Dietz sighed. "So now I have my own plan B."

"A con is more your style," Harry said.

Harry could be right, Max feared. Dietz might only be plying the oldest trick in the book. Hitler knew it, Goebbels. The biggest lie: Never accept blame; concentrate on one enemy at a time and blame him for everything that goes wrong . . . people will believe a big lie sooner than a little one; and if you repeat it frequently enough people will sooner or later believe it . . .

Dietz was holding out his hands to them as if about to have his palms read. Practically a beggar. "Why would I lie to you now? Like this?"

"Because your Russian animal trainers tell you to. Because you're looking to get a leg up."

Dietz stared a moment. He sat up straight and gestured at Stanley aka code name Reiter. "Look at him. He doesn't even wish to return. He loves the Socialist way. He is the scientist on the big great banners." Dietz spoke up. "Aren't you, Herr Samaras?"

Stanley didn't reply. Dora stared back in apparent horror, grasping at Stanley's shoulders.

"Leave the man alone," Max said.

Dietz ignored him. He turned to Harry. "Oh, you thought he was the poor, innocent American, held against his will. Of course you Americans assume that, because you think your-selves exceptional. But, as you well know—being born German yourself—this idea of judging one's self exceptional, it only gets you into grave trouble in the end. As we Germans now know. All of you, you too . . . Miss? Frau?" Dietz gestured at Katarina for her name, but she only stared back with her arms crossed, as she had been the whole time, observing Dietz with the same curiosity as one would a rare insect. He pointed at Stanley. "But your Dr. Samaras over there, he's the new Soviet man now. He's their current trophy, along with that secret facility of theirs. Did you know that he's the head scientist there?"

All eyes turned to Stanley.

"I'd tell you he's lying," Stanley said, "but who would believe me?"

"He didn't tell you that part, did he?" Dietz said. "So. He might bolt the first chance he gets, with or without his girl. Probably with. She loves it too. Communism did so much for her. It brought her to warm, lovely, and inviting Poland from cold, gray, unforgiving Greece. Who knows? He might even become a double once he gets back. I assume he has some secrets on his person—that must be why you sent him back to the facility, Harry. Yes? But what are they? He tells you he's back on the American team. This could be. Or, he's not. She. With an orphan, a stray, who knows what you're bringing home? Then your big prize is a Trojan horse. Look at him. He's probably thinking about it right now. I'm sure it has crossed young Dora's mind."

Max glanced over and found Stanley and Dora sitting with their heads bowed, as if listening to prayer in a pew. Were they concentrating to hear? Could they even hear? Were they scheming? He looked to Harry. Harry, too, had his head bowed, but it was from reasoning, weighing pros and cons, his jaw shifting slightly like he did when concentrating. This was still his show. His mission. Again Max entertained the thought of killing Dietz somehow, perhaps on the escape route, but his heart was not in it now. The man had at least caused his dear Irina to be killed, but he had also spared him and Harry when he could have done them in easily.

For a moment, he felt like he was floating, one with the glow of the light bulb. There had been enough killing, he decided. Let the Americans deal with Dietz. The man would get what he deserved in the end. If he himself killed Dietz, he would only get what he deserved—lifelong remorse for more killing would be getting off lightly.

Katarina was nodding at him, as if hearing his thoughts. He found her oddly quiet, even for her. He had never seen her eyes so hard and focused and dim.

Harry's head raised finally. He stared at Dietz for what must have been a minute. Dietz held the stare, but his eyelids drooped in something like sorrow, remorse even.

"Very well," Harry said.

Dietz slapped his hands in triumph.

"Don't gloat," Harry said. "It's unbecoming."

Stanley and Dora stared back with wide eyes.

"We wait," Harry said. "We leave once it gets dark." He turned to Dietz. "What did you tell your people?"

"About my absence? Nothing. I had the weekend off. But I'm always around. Someone probably already noticed me missing."

"How did you cross over?" Harry said.

"Probably very much like you—on a dinghy, during the night."

Harry didn't confirm it. He was too busy thinking, his eyes racing around. Their traveling circus had just gained another animal.

"I have a route," Dietz said.

Harry snorted at him. "Were you ever going to reveal this information, or just keep it in your pocket the whole time?"

Dietz held out his palms again.

"Do you have an escape route or not?" Max added.

"You first, my dear captain," Dietz said to Harry.

"This isn't a game, you two," Katarina blurted.

"There's too many people," was all Harry said.

No one spoke for a moment.

Dietz kept his eyes on Harry. Eventually, he took a deep breath and leaned forward, his forearms resting on his knees. "You can tell them, Harry. It's all right."

Harry glared at him.

"Tell him what?" Max said.

Harry ignored him.

Dietz pressed a hand to his chest. "I know it pains you to tell them, but must I? Must I spit it out, as you say?"

"No," Harry said. "No, you don't."

"Isn't that why you met with a certain Catholic contact in Görlitz?" Dietz said. "It was the whole reason you went there, wasn't it? That was your only way over. You knew the facility and likely Dr. Samaras were on the other side of the Neisse, here in Communist Poland, across such an inaccessible border. Am I right so far?"

"I used a ratline," Harry blurted. "All right? A goddamned Nazi escape route."

"Is that what you Americans call it, a ratline? Amusing. Very well."

"I only used the contact to get us across the border," Harry groaned to no one in particular.

Max's heart ached, straining to pump. He knew what Harry was thinking, what must have been plaguing him all along. A rat was a rat was a rat, he would say.

"You use it the whole way?" Dietz chirped, as if wanting to toy with Harry.

"No!"

"Harry," Katarina said, "you don't need to—"

"I want to! Get it all out. I was worried the Russians were going to move Reiter to the Soviet Union, to their other facilities. So I needed to move fast. For that I needed to make a clean break. Appear like a loose cannon. In Prague? Okay, my escape, yes, that was through a ratline contact. Dresden, Bautzen, those were real helper agents, and they were taking quite a chance. But I had no choice with Görlitz. I used another ratline contact."

"Nor do you have a choice now," Dietz said. He looked around the room. "My route is the same as yours. We head south. It's all mapped out. Arranged. Others have used it, Nazis from the Baltics to Croatia and many points in between. Call it a ratline if you must, but it will work."

"Is that why we saw those two nuns in the park?" Katarina said to Dietz.

"They weren't helping him," Harry said. "They were there because of me. To confirm the goods. And they're probably not even nuns."

He had raised his chin in defiance, but Max could see the anguish in his brother's eyes.

"We use ratlines," Harry added. "I never wanted to. All right? I'm not proud of it."

"To smuggle out Nazis, that right?" Dietz said. "For your rockets, your new bombs, your biological warfare, the US Army Chemical Corps. Surely you know of Dr. Walter Schreiber, for one, former general in the Wehrmacht Medical Service? Also an expert in biological agents, as it happens. Well, the smart doctor is suddenly in the West now . . ." Dietz let the words trail off.

Harry stood. "Forget it. Let's just get a move on."

Katarina had a hand up. Her expression had remained blank, unfazed. "There's still one problem," she said. "What about Dora?"

Dora started. She shot up, shook Stanley's hand free. Stomped into the middle of the room with her fists balled, panting, mouth hanging open.

Stanley stood, his hands outstretched. "Dear? What is it, dear?"

Dora kept her back to him. She frowned at Harry, Max, Katarina.

"Leave me here," she said. "Take him. I don't want to go. I will not go."

Stanley's arms lowered, and his face took on a pale jade color as if he might vomit again. Dora's mouth hung open, practically drooling, her teeth bared. She was terrified, and she was angry at being made terrified. Stanley saw it even with her back to him. He took a step toward her, arms back out as if she might fall and he had to catch her.

Harry and Katarina exchanged glances. They all knew the score now. Dora had been a Soviet plant, the honeypot minder. It was another of the oldest tricks. Deploy the orphan. She had been playing along, giving nothing away, hoping for a solution. At first she must have figured Dietz was working for the Soviets, not some suspect East German acting solo. Now Katarina was calling her bluff.

Dora turned to Stanley.

"*Kai su, Dora?*" Stanley said, his voice straining. Max understood it: *Et tu, Dora?*

"I'm sorry, Konstantinos," she said.

Dietz stood. "*Posmotri na menya,*" he said to Dora in Russian, and she looked at him. From the way Stanley cocked his head, not even he knew that she knew Russian.

"You can leave," Dietz said. "No one is making you come with us. Not even I." He glanced at Max. He turned to Harry. "Is that all right, Captain? She'll only be a liability."

Harry nodded.

Katarina was already blocking the door. Max read her mind. What if Dora went straight to the Soviets? There was only one way of making sure she wouldn't.

"Let her go," Harry said. "She won't tell."

Katarina stared down at Dora before her.

Dora had her hands clasped at her waist as if ready to curtsy. "I won't tell," she said. "Never."

Katarina kept staring. "Go home," she said finally. "You were there the whole time. You went to Stanley's, and he was gone."

Dora nodded, repeatedly, working it all out in her head.

Katarina didn't have to spell it out for her: If the Soviets found out from her that she'd lost control of Stanley while in her company, the consequences could be dire. A Gulag. Siberia. Worse. It was better like this. If she was good enough to fool Stanley, she was good enough to swindle the Soviets. She would survive to swindle anew.

"I'm so sorry," Dora said to the room. Then she turned to the door, marched toward it, and flung it open, vanishing into the light of the still-new day.

"No!" Stanley screamed. "No!"

Max rushed over and slapped a hand to his mouth, lowering him to the floor as he cried into Max's hand.

THE RATLINE

They rode in the truck in silence. Max, Harry, Katarina, and Stanley Samaras. It was too loud and jolting to speak, the drive-train droning and knocking under the wooden planks of a truck bed caked with what looked like dried mud but might have been manure, judging from the pungent smell. Dietz rode up front with the driver.

It had been so easy. After they had calmed Stanley down, which quickly became a case of threatening him that they had to bolt before it was too late, they had huddled at the table so Dietz and Harry could share the few details that they knew of the ratline. Both confirmed that the code word was *Wendelin* when precisely prompted by a ratline contact. Meanwhile Stanley lay on his bed, waiting like a man prepared for surgery. "It's already too late," was the only thing he said. And then they had left, just walked outside and down the street and continued southeast out of Zgorzelec through a valley and a meadow, following a stream. They had waited inside a barn while Dietz talked to the man inside the farmhouse. Harry had let him do the talking. He was the Nazi rat, after all.

Now they jostled along in the truck through what used to be Silesia, still southeasterly, skirting the northern border of

Czechoslovakia according to Dietz's concise account. Tarp covered the truck bed, and crates and barrels blocked any view out the back, as they were supposed to be hidden, after all, but they could peer out the side of the tarp canvas, which all of them except Stanley did regularly at first until the greenery and open farmland and depressing country junctions began repeating themselves. The driver had kindly placed sausage, bread, and water in the back along with sacks of grain for them to lean and lie on. Stanley lay on one with his face buried into the crook between the sack and the cab end of the bed. He might have slept. He might have cried. His resolve had dissipated, replaced by a lukewarm jelly. Max had known men like Stanley during his short times on two fronts. The will to survive simply left them. No one had even seen them killed. They had simply vanished. Vaporized. Max told himself this was a good thing, at least for their journey. Stanley was compliant now, uncaring, did whatever they told him. Harry assured Max that Stanley would be all right once he returned, that America would take him back with open arms and show him just how wrong he had been about them—and about the Soviet Union.

At one point the driver turned into a dim clearing and stopped to change the license plates. Later they stopped for the driver to relieve himself along the road. Dietz stood outside next to the tarp over the cab. "When do we reach the border?" Max asked through a break in the fabric.

"We already passed it," Dietz said. "Secret forest road. We're well into Czechoslovakia, in fact, right on schedule."

Stanley didn't so much as grunt, or turn their way, or even need to relieve himself. He certainly did not eat. Max nearly considered checking his pulse. They drove until the sun lowered to the horizon. Outside the town of Olomouc, they pulled up to an inn. The truck rolled around back and entered a shed with a back-loading door opening to a waterway. This was the Morava River. Another man helped them into a canal boat as the truck pulled away. It was all very efficient. They sat around a table in the cramped main cabin. The windows were open and the river trickled by, buzzed by insects. The captain only stared at them, then went back into his wheelhouse, obviously not thrilled about the extra passengers. A boy of about sixteen helped him, explaining that the boat had a secret compartment below if needed, that they were not to show themselves out on deck, that the curtains were to remain closed but they could peek out. He produced a bottle of whiskey that Dietz stood on the table. He set out four glasses and filled one for Stanley. Stanley just stared at it.

They pushed off and floated along as the sun went down, the river delivering a slight chill through the windows. The boy turned on a couple dim lamps, shut the windows, pulled the curtains, and left them alone. Soon a bitter tang of diesel oil permeated the cabin, which turned Max's stomach. He tried to focus on something good. Dietz was now with the captain in the wheelhouse and out of their hair. The whiskey was nice. The faint lights of country river windows drifted by, and smoke settled on the water from a chimney, and once or twice he thought he saw silhouettes of a deer or a wolf watching them pass. He was reminded of a Karl May story, then of Tom Sawyer and Huck Finn on the Mississippi River.

They were heading due south on the Morava. Harry and Katarina sat close, taking up one corner. Max wished there were a way to leave them to another lovely reunion, but even the mattresses crammed below were too indiscreet for lovemaking unless the boat were a bordello.

Stanley snatched up the whiskey and drank it in one gulp, poured another, gulped.

Max moved the bottle away.

Stanley was sweating. He glared at him, at Harry. His now bloodless eyes widened as if he'd just woken up, and they scanned the various doors and cabinets of the cabin. Max imagined him seeking a weapon, any weapon, and then he started muttering to himself.

"I'll kill that Dietz, see, that's what I'll do. Do the world a favor. The Soviets forced her into it, she didn't wanna. Forced her into it . . ." His words trailed off, back into disbelief.

Max put a gentle hand on his shoulder but Stanley shook it off, his other shoulder banging against the window.

"Take it easy," Harry said.

"You take it easy."

"Be quiet," Katarina snapped.

Silence found them. There was only the drone of the engine and dark river on all sides, under them, darker and darker. The dim lamps gave the surrounding wood of the cabin, table, and nook an amber glow, like a brass prison cell.

Stanley started sobbing. He stared through a crack in the curtains, out into the night. He eventually sniffed away his tears and sucked it up. He peered at them in the dim light. "Listen. He will sell us out. You all know it. We gotta do something. You do—"

Smack. Katarina had slapped him, moving fast and agilely, barely rocking the table. "I said, be quiet," she growled, and Stanley slumped down, his head nearly under the table.

"I'm sorry," he said after a while. "I'm so sorry."

"I know," she said.

Dietz joined them in the already confined cabin. He pulled up the one chair and planted himself across from the four of them in the window-surrounded nook. He smelled like harsh tobacco and grain alcohol schnapps, neither of which went well with diesel. All did their best to ignore him. Max played the weary traveler and laid his head back, closing his eyes.

He soon heard Dietz drumming fingers on the tabletop, followed by an awkward silence in which Dietz was likely trying to make eye contact with someone, anyone.

"Well, quite the little reunion we are having," Dietz said eventually, chuckling, and Max got a whiff of that schnapps filtered through a man who hadn't brushed his teeth for a while.

"Yes, wasn't the war something?" Katarina said.

"I only mean, you and Harry clearly know each other. From before, was it? Hour zero?"

Stunde Null. The surrender. The early days of the occupation.

"Thereabouts," Harry said.

Dietz slapped his knees. "I knew it," he chirped.

Max had one eye open now.

"There is something else about you," Dietz said.

"Oh?" Katarina said.

"You look familiar."

"Everyone looks familiar after shots of schnapps and the lights down low," she said.

"That's it. This voice." The table edge pressed into their stomachs as Dietz leaned forward for a better look.

"What's your name?" he said, grinning, his teeth shining like caramel in the light.

"You know I can't tell you that."

"Ah, come on. It's on the tip of my tongue."

Both Max's eyes opened. Katarina was staring back at Dietz, baring her own teeth, all white pickets.

"You were in that one film, you know." Dietz snapped fingers. "The count's young lover. You sang. Or was it the cavalry officer?"

Stanley had sat back up. Harry kept his eyes on Katarina, and Max saw he had a hand on her leg to steady her under the table.

"*The Mistress of Tannenberg*," Katarina said finally, like a lawyer offering a plea in court.

"That's it! You're Katarina Buchholz."

Katarina nodded, a hint of a bow.

"*Ach*, I should have known. Harry here once served in Heimgau, his first posting. You're from that area, are you not? More Bavarian than I even."

Katarina had put on a smile now. She poured whiskey all around.

"Well, well. In the presence of a real star," Dietz said. "So how does this involve you?"

Katarina nodded at Max, a hat tip. "We actors, we're always looking for a good role to make our own. Can't help it. It's in our blood."

Dietz lit her a Russian cigarette. She took it and inhaled greedily before shooting it back out as a billow into his face. He breathed it in. He drank.

"You working for the Americans?" he said.

She ignored the question. She downed her whiskey in one gulp. "Your turn. Let's talk about your past."

"I already told you—"

"You sure are in a hurry to get out, aren't you?"

Dietz only stared, his smile fading. She dropped her grin. Smoke cleared.

"Maybe there's another purge coming?" she continued. "Maybe your SED party membership isn't going to save you anymore?"

Harry nodded. "We've gotten word of more purges coming, possibly several, East German as well as Soviet."

"Maybe even that minder of yours in Prague couldn't protect you anymore," Max added.

"What is this, an interrogation?" Dietz looked to Harry and tried putting a smile back on, but his jaw kept rejecting it. He cleared his throat. "I already told Max. I was vetted by the Soviets. Completed my rehabilitation, my training. Which is far more stringent than anything undertaken by the West, I can assure you."

"Maybe," Katarina said. "But you can't change the past."

The face-off between Katarina and Dietz had shut down the reunion. Max, Stanley, and Katarina slept below, fitfully, their mattresses merging, the air stale and the noxious odor of diesel relentless. Dietz kept clear of Katarina and resorted to speaking only to Harry. He slept up in the cabin. Harry joined him reluctantly but felt a duty to keep an eye on him. In the morning, the captain's boy fed them from the tiny galley, hard rolls, lumpy butter, sour instant coffee.

That morning and day, Sunday, May 29, they continued down the Morava River, drifting past meadows and tree-lined shores and many lazy bends in the river. Canals and locks proved free of peril, and towns were often set back from the banks, painting the horizon with red roofs and spires. They saw soldiers on the banks once or twice and faced a couple controls and checks, but the captain took care of it all. He even waved at a passing patrol boat. Only once did they have to stay hidden in the secret compartment below. They heard bootsteps on board but also laughing and then they were drifting onward again. It was one well-greased ratline. The sun was out and the water sparkled and Max would've liked to lounge out on the narrow deck. He imagined himself with champagne and a jaunty captain's hat and chuckled at the absurdness of it.

One look at Stanley was enough to kill the laugh. He ate little and stayed below, staring at the ship's hull in the near dark.

In the afternoon, Dietz huddled with the captain in the wheelhouse. Their jaws were set and their nods grave and the boy stood listening with his head lowered. Max pulled the curtains shut tighter.

The Morava passed a tributary from Austria, the Thaya, and soon formed the border with the Soviet Zone of Austria. They saw soldiers, riverbank barriers, and viewing platforms, and Max stopped peeking out through the curtains.

He sat belowdecks and watched Stanley. The man lay immovable on a mattress, staring up with his eyes open, a zombie. It was all too reminiscent of the shell shock Max had seen too many times, and he feared Stanley would never be the same. Or, he wondered, was Stanley contemplating the shell shock to come—the horrors that were to strike all those civilians, all those woman and children and elderly, soon to be decimated by the new weapons he would help create in service of a system he had rejected?

The Morava emptied into the mighty Danube River as they passed ancient Devin Castle, its ruins extending from high cliffs like a scene in a Romantic-era painting. Steering left into the Danube, they soon saw Bratislava Castle looming on the left and then they were passing through the Slovakian city, under bridges, passing barges, all of it a blur of stolen glances. Max peered out and saw the gray greens of a patrol boat and yanked the curtains shut. They hid in the secret compartment. Again they heard bootsteps on board but no laughing this time. They were crossing another border, the captain showing papers. The boat chugged on and they eventually dared to reenter the cabin. They traveled around a bend, the riverbanks flattening, widening on either side.

"That's Hungary on our right now," Katarina said, "the Communists took over for good last week," whispering for no reason but resolve, and Dietz nodded at her, the first time the two might have acknowledged each other all day. After Dietz looked away, Max saw Katarina studying him, from the corner of her eye.

They would be landing soon.

THE RATLINE
Monday, May 30
2:49 a.m.

Max awoke. In the dark. His heart beat too fast and the sweat ran off him, soaking the pillow below, the covers above. On a bed. He'd been having one of his disturbing near nightmares from the Russian Front: he lay paralyzed on his back in the mud at night as the shelling struck all around, his ragtag unit rushing by, fleeing, and refugees, and horses. He kept trying to move but could only make it inches, the obstacles increasing, combining, the mud even sticking to him.

He looked around the dark room, letting his breathing and eyes adjust, piecing reality back together. They were in someone's country house on the outskirts of Gyor, Hungary. Their river boat had turned right, into the Mosoni tributary, and chugged toward the city. The captain and his son dropped them off before that, on a nondescript, welcomingly inconspicuous sandy bank. It was the start of the next phase of the ratline—heading southwest along the border of Hungary neighboring the Soviet Zone of Austria, then over the border into the Slovenian lands of what was now the Socialist Federal Republic of Yugoslavia—currently no great friend to Stalin despite the name. From there they'd continue southwesterly, skirting Ljubljana, and head for the coast.

At a junction on the outskirts of Gyor, Dietz had met a contact in a toy shop who told him to lie low for the night while the rest of the route was confirmed. They were to leave before the sun came up, on foot and on schedule. "We'll be on our own for now," Dietz had told them. "At least for a day."

It was good news, but Katarina had only nodded with her lips pursed. She kept eyeing Dietz, Max had noticed. It had bothered him. Despite his hate for Dietz, he wanted them all to get along. For the good of the goal. For his commitment to save Harry. For Harry's duty to Stanley and to the America that needed Stanley and would likely convince him of his errors in the end. America had a way of doing that. What was it someone had said? Men and nations behave wisely once they've exhausted all other resources. That was America. That had to be Stanley.

Max so wanted to believe it. He even felt an immense warmth, inside him, despite his pillow and covers having cooled. He usually worried at this hour of the night, like all did, hoping they wouldn't become night terrors. In his mental gymnastics to avoid that, he should have turned to resolve, and thus should have been hoping for Dietz to be damned to hell once he helped get them to safety. But now he felt something else again. It wasn't forgiveness, necessarily, but it was something like understanding. The man had done what he had to do. Hadn't they all? Weren't they doing so now?

The country house was modest but comfortable, with faint aromas of thyme and fresh berries. Dietz's corner bedroom even had a fireplace. Harry and Katarina were sharing the one upstairs attic room, complete with romantic dormers, while Max and Stanley had a room facing a garden with a view through quaint French doors. It was closed off by thick curtains now. Stanley was sleeping in his single bed, snoring slightly. Max could only imagine what nightmares he had, what night terrors. The man had deteriorated so much since Dora had openly betrayed him.

Max was now too awake. He considered a glass of water. He wondered if the tile oven needed stoking, to give them a little extra heat when they all rose to hit the road, still groggy, grumpy. He thought of Katarina again. He'd had the first watch that night, sitting in the living room in a worn old leather chair, situated just so with a view both out the front windows and through the kitchen to the back garden. She had relieved his watch. He had told her good night and she the same to him, but then she had pulled him back, by his sleeve.

"Thank you," she had whispered to him.

"You're welcome, my dear. Good night."

"No. I don't mean for taking watch. I mean for all of it. For going after Harry."

Max felt a flush in his cheeks. "I was only doing what I must."

"Which is so much more than so many. You're a kindhearted man, more so than Harry, perhaps." She added a soft chuckle. "You could have been a teacher, a comforting priest."

He didn't know what to say. He held a hand to his heart. "Thank you," he repeated, but his voice strained this time.

"You take good care of your brother, no matter what happens. He's too upstanding for this world."

"Amen," Max had said, and she had smiled one last time, and she had rubbed at his shoulder as he left into the darkness, back up to his room.

Max had thought about that as he fell asleep. She had been the one who filled him with something good to wake up to in the middle of the night, he realized. She had turned his looming night terrors on their head, and whoever had accomplished such a feat in all the history of man?

Now he pulled on his shirt and socks and, stopping in the doorway to make sure Stanley was still snoring, padded down the dark hallway as quiet as could be, using the area rugs to avoid creaking the floorboards.

It was 3:00 a.m. Harry had the shift after Katarina, starting now. The two of them might still be out there together. Max entered the living room to give his brother an encouraging pat on the back, get him water if he needed some.

The leather chair was empty. Max stopped in his tracks, pivoting around, eyes scanning the contours of furniture, cupboards, mounted antlers, and through to the kitchen. Nothing, no one, no sound. He pulled his shirt closed. His pulse had quickened, just enough to focus. He felt the chair's dry hide. Still slightly warm. He felt a light draft—the front door was cracked open. He rushed over to it, and as soon as he did a shadow filled the void. He reared back.

Harry. He did the same. "Shit, you scared me."

"What's the matter?"

"Keep watch here, I'm going back out."

"Why?"

"Just do it," Harry whispered hard, but it was less a hiss than a plea.

Max watched and listened. He saw nothing outside. The house remained so quiet he wanted to scream.

Then he thought he heard a faint dripping sound and imagined a faucet, somewhere in the dark. But it wasn't the kitchen.

Harry returned panting. He pulled Max over to the leather chair and dropped into it.

"She's . . . gone," Harry said.

"She what? Wait. Why did you go outside?"

"Because she knew my shift was starting. She would have waited outside until then, which is just like her. Keeping watch on me all while getting away with it."

"Getting away with what?"

Harry took a deep breath. His head rotated up at Max mechanically, his eyes widening, a carnival automaton built to scare.

Max knew. He nodded.

Harry took Max by the arm and walked him to the corner of the house. Halfway there, Max could sense it. A metallic smell. His heart beat so fast now it was like a small distressed dog, scraping to get out of his chest. That faint dripping was no faucet, and it grew louder.

Harry pushed open the door to Dietz's room, carefully, nodding for Max to enter as if Max had never seen a doorway before. Max drifted inside, letting his eyes adjust to the slightly darker room. The dripping resounded here. Blood. It dripped onto a pillow set under the bed to muffle it. A dark patch on the bed, and below it. But where was his face? All Max could see in this dark was white. It was a sheet, pulled up over his head. Max looked to Harry, who nodded again, and Max pulled away the sheet.

Dietz's throat had been slit. The dead man stared up at Max, white eyes protruding, his mouth gaping slightly, and Max remembered finding his Irina like his, and his heart wrenched, and for a second he imagined Dietz saying that he was sorry.

"There's a note," Harry said.

THE RATLINE

Nazi War Criminal

Never Forget

פושע מלחמה נאצי

לעולם אל תשכח

read the note, in English and Hebrew. It was pinned to Dietz's chest, crisp white letterhead that Katarina must have found in the den, written with a black fountain pen.

Max just stared. All the white, the paper, the sheet and bedding, and Dietz's blood-drained, waxen face—all had a slightly blue cast from the moonlight seeping in around the curtains. He wanted to feel something, he supposed, fear even, but all he detected was a slight chill and a little hunger. None of this turned his stomach. He had seen it so much before.

"She left me a note, too," Harry said, his voice straining.

Max escorted him out just as Harry had led him into here. They stopped at the dry old leather chair in the living room, to keep watch together, but neither took the chair.

Harry paraphrased Katarina's note. At some point during her journey with them, possibly in Karlovy Vary, possibly in

Dresden, she had gotten new intelligence from her handlers that Hartmut Dietz had an even worse wartime record than anyone knew. New records had been found. In the East, behind the lines, Hartmut Dietz had led evictions of Jews for "deportation" to camps and had promptly directed the SS to their valuable belongings left behind, from which he had surely gotten a cut of the take. The sickest middleman there ever was. Katarina had decided to pursue him in a manner that would not disrupt Harry's or Max's efforts, waiting until the coast was relatively clear. But she was also ashamed for leading a dual agenda. "Never mix business with lovers," she wrote. Harry took a deep breath and recited, "'We have our own causes, me and you. History and future conspire against us. Tell Max that I'm sorry and not to hate me. I did it for his Irina as much as for anyone.'"

Max had lowered into the chair, his hands clawed, palms up. Heat filled his neck and his chin quivered. "She was always protecting us," he muttered.

Harry patted him on the shoulder.

Max tried to smile. "Well, an actress with her talents? She always was known for her lovely exits."

They continued keeping watch. A silence set in. After a while, Harry's eyes welled up. He wiped at his face.

"You found her, didn't you?" Max said. "She was still outside."

Harry nodded. "Just like I thought."

Max knew the rest. They were able to say goodbye.

"And of course she knew that I'd go outside looking for her," Harry said. "And you know something, Max? I wouldn't put it past her to come back and check on our progress. Make sure we make it, though we might not even know it, she's that good."

"Indeed," Max said and gave her a little bow in the dark.

Before them the windows loomed a little less dark, like fine square blue gems offered up to them.

"Now," Harry said. "On this ratline, no one should know who Dietz was, is, or what he is supposed to look like. That's not how they work. It's all cells. So we should be okay. We know the password, what to say."

"What if we simply made our own way? On foot. We've done it before, me and you."

"I don't know. I'd say that's even riskier with Reiter along."

"Sad but true," Max said. "We need to keep a good eye on him."

"Agreed. He might even need a little talking to . . ."

They heard a creak, and faint wheezing. Stanley himself stood at the opening to the hall, staring at them.

"Serves the bastard right," Stanley said, his voice straining.

Max stood.

Harry bounded over and grasped at Stanley's lapels and pinned him against the wall. Stanley released a squeak, as if drained of air. He didn't fight it.

"Did you tell anyone?" Harry barked. "Did you?"

Max rushed over. "Harry, come now—"

"Look at me, Stanley. Look! In Zgorzelec. At the facility?"

Max stopped. Harry was right. They had to know.

Stanley tried speaking again but could only get out another squeak.

"Did you or didn't you? Are we safe?!"

Stanley wheezed, his mouth gaping.

"You're choking him." Max pulled Harry off Stanley, Harry letting him.

Stanley gaped at them, gasping, panting, keeping his back pressed against the wall. "No, I did not," he said. "Because I trusted you, see. And I trusted Dora. But why should that mean any of us are safe? Ever? Why?"

THE RATLINE
8:00 a.m.

Full daylight. Three of them left—Max, Harry, Stanley. They rode a local train, heading southwest, the farmland fields and minor towns of western Hungary rolling by. Back at the country house, they had used a handcart to dump Dietz's body, wrapped in canvas tarp and weighted with stones, into the Rába River that ran along the home's property. They didn't bother cleaning up the blood. Let the bastards enjoy more unclaimed death. "Let the CIA figure out a different ratline," Harry had told Max.

The train had picked up speed, the clicking becoming a droning in their compartment, and Max breathed easier. He saw Harry do the same across from him and Stanley. No one knew who they were, what they looked like, how many. They needed the ratline one last time, to cross the border into Yugoslavia. Three men was easier, certainly. But they also had to trust that Stanley would keep it together. Harry had taken his secret papers off him and Max had taken a quick glance—it all looked like shorthand indeed. Stanley hadn't fought that, either. The whole morning he had remained compliant, and lumbering, as if groggy. Now he slept next to Max, sometimes snorting himself awake, sometimes murmuring and whimpering in his sleep, his head sometimes resting on Max's shoulder, and Max let it stay there because it usually calmed Stanley. Max and Harry would've shared a good laugh if it weren't so pitiful. Max's heart wrenched thinking of all that the man had strove for and lost. He couldn't help imagining a guinea pig in one of Stanley's own labs, on a wheel, believing, knowing, it was getting somewhere. Having no idea of its true purpose, exploited in its short life and death.

Fields rushed by, browns and greens and yellows. Max realized that they, too, were still on a cruel wheel, their escape not yet over. Dietz could have had them disposed of at any point along the ratline, once among his fellow comrades, his fellow henchmen, so Katarina might have even saved their lives. And Dietz might even have been a double, living the biggest lie. Max closed his eyes a moment and imagined Katarina on this very train, watching over them as she always had, and it let him gain some precious calm and rest. He wasn't sure he believed in God, but he could always put his faith in an angel.

11:37 a.m. The scrapyard loomed like a tank blown apart on the front line, charred, rusting, all jagged lines and shadows. Who knew if anyone still remained inside. Had they been burned to a crisp, their black hands still clenching hatches? Or were others now using it for cover and lying in wait to fire?

They had navigated the streets of Szombathely after getting off the train and had reached the location Dietz had confirmed to Harry. Harry gathered them close like the huddle for an American football game and gave them an equally American pep talk. "Remember, boys, look sharp. Give nothing away. We play this right, it should be a piece of cake. We have the code name. Ready?"

Harry patted them on their shoulders. They passed through an open gate, hearing the rattling of a chain and a dog growling, but they could not see an animal or an owner. Max smelled metal and grease and now heard the gurgle of a motor, somewhere beyond. The grounds were muddy despite the dry weather. A heap of scrap rose to their left and a wooden outbuilding stood to the right, the siding dark and stained with tar.

They approached the plain door of the building, five yards away. The windows had curtains and Max thought he might have seen someone move.

The play was for Harry to do the talking, Max to look suspect, and Stanley to keep his mouth shut at all costs—if he had to, he was to ramble in Greek.

The front gate shut behind them, metal squealing, pulled by a man in coveralls. They stepped onto the covered porch. They eyed the perimeter again and could see men rise from the scraps and from behind barrels, maybe six, seven. Max thought he smelled burning oil now. Was it from that gurgling motor? The truck they were to take to the border?

They had all tensed up, even Stanley, his little fists balled and trembling.

The door to the building swung open, a man emerged. Max had expected a dueling scar, an eye patch, perhaps a dent in his head from combat or escaping a Russian prison camp. But the man was young and his skin immaculate, his facial features no worse than the fine lines of a young and rising actor. He could've just as well been a former Hungarian SS man. Sure enough, he spoke in accented German.

"Can I help you?" he said.

"I'm looking for the local priest," Harry said, initiating the code word phrase.

"What is his name?" the man replied.

"Wendelin," Harry said. The code word.

The man nodded. But he withdrew, back into the building.

From the dark inside they heard whispers, exchanged glances. A click sounded, suspiciously too much like the safety of a gun.

The man returned. "Where is Dietz?" he said.

Harry just stared, stunned. No one expected this. Harry had told them that no one used names on a ratline and Dietz had confirmed it. They hadn't even discussed the prospect.

Max's heart thumped. Was this Dietz's one final sick trick?

Their pause was too long and yet the long beat was warranted, he then realized, because it fit the character. Calling out a name would make anyone wary.

So Max straightened his shoulders. He pushed by Harry.

"I am Hartmut Dietz," he reported, brusquely and with a hint of Dietz's Munich accent, his arms ramrod straight to his side. He was prepared to click his heels and give the Hitler salute if this forlorn fascist Adonis demanded it.

The man straightened. He gave a slight bow, mechanically but respectfully, more like a courtier of old than some former SS man.

"Never," Max barked at him, "ever, use names again. Is that clear?"

"Yes, sir!"

"Fine. Now cut out this nonsense and send us on our way. We have transport, yes? No, yes? Speak up!"

THE RATLINE
2:35 p.m.

Their Hungarian ratline fascist minions drove them farther southwest toward the border of northernmost Yugoslavia in a pristine small coach that might have once been a tour bus. The three of them had the whole ride to themselves apart from the driver, who said nothing, seemed to hear nothing. Max, Harry, and the still despondent Stanley rode in the very back, each with their own row, Max warmed by the fine leather getting all the sun in the windows.

Harry was beaming at Max. "Such a fine actor. You still got it, Maxie."

"I could have gotten us killed," Max said.

A pause followed. He and Harry burst into a rolling chuckle.

Meanwhile Stanley rested his forehead to his window and gazed out at the vast open land, and Max hoped it made him think of home somehow, of the American Midwest at least. This was their deliverance. These borderlands had bred all manner of underground networks, stretching back through the war and the contentious Kingdom of Yugoslavia and to the Austro-Hungarian Empire and on back forever, it seemed, smugglers and assassins, irredentists and saviors. The allegiances changed, yet these underground routes had always involved cells, each successive contact and link unknowing. Whether it was Yugoslav smugglers or Nazi sympathizers, good or bad, they simply had to trust the mistrust of centuries.

A little under two hours after leaving Szombathely, their tour bus entered woods as vast as the open land. The driver parked at a trailhead, tipped his hat to them. They took the trail, met a man, gave the Wendelin code word again, and the man walked them over the border into Yugoslavia. At this point, less experienced and sorrow-hardened men might have worried that Dietz's fellow travelers were only sending them into the woods to put bullets into the backs of their heads. Such was the way of Gestapo, SS, and any such rats, really. Stanley didn't even look anxious. He simply trudged along with his shoulders slumped, staring at the ground before him like a worn-out infantryman in dire need of rear-line rest, and again Max didn't like the look. Too many of those footsloggers developed a death wish if allowed to fester too long.

The border of the Soviet Zone of Austria had loomed just a few miles north, like a weight about to be dropped from the sky any moment. Now it was the British Zone north of them. That might have been one recourse, but Harry had another. They continued walking southwest along a country road and Harry, at point, stopped, turned to them and announced:

"That's it. We're free of the ratline for good."

They were miles into the Slovene lands of Yugoslavia, and Harry felt confident they would find a way through, even if caught, since Yugoslav leader Tito was feuding with his fellow Communist, Stalin, and was always happy to welcome friends who were not yet enemies. They walked another hour. Soon, though, the Slovene lands would begin to rise into green hills and forbidding mountains. So they walked into the next town, found the station, and caught a train to Ljubljana using, fittingly, the Yugoslav money that the Hungarian ratline men had given them.

Stanley hardly spoke the whole time, except for one thing. Apropos of nothing, he said: "You know what I miss. What I'm going to miss. You guys overlooked it. It's not the baseball. Not Broadway. It's the corner diner."

TRIESTE
Tuesday, May 31
12:01 a.m.

Max smelled saltwater but could not see it, nor was he close enough to hear the sea apart from an occasional distant horn. He stood at the open window of their corner suite living room, the fine sheer curtain caressing his ear. He looked out at the horizon and saw only a mass of black, dotted with random lights the sizes of pins, and wondered if they were fishing boats, pleasure craft, or patrol ships. He figured the latter and for once it let him breathe easier. This port city was the namesake of the Free Territory of Trieste. Like Berlin, like Vienna, the Free Territory was still under international control, the United Nations Security Council this time. Closer to their window he made out a broad, boardwalklike square, and then rooftop after slanted rooftop, ever closer together as the hill rose up to their grand building, all red shingles and ornate stonework, all vestiges of faded Habsburg Empire and defeated Italian fever dreams. The streetlights revealed narrow, cobbled lanes at certain junctions and steep slopes, all wedged in between the old buildings like the deep crevices of a steep and dangerous ravine.

They had made it, Max had to remind himself. Once they had entered Ljubljana earlier that day, they had been lucky enough to catch another train for the Adriatic Sea. They reached the border a few hours after dark, not quite midnight. Harry already knew the Free Territory from previous operations. Zone A, the northern sector that included the port city, was guarded by a combined force of US and British military. As their train reached the border for Zone A, Harry had politely asked a British corporal if he might speak to the American liaison desk, and within an hour he had settled Max and Stanley in one last safe house—this overblown suite in this declining yet still proud hotel in Old Town just up the hill from the harbor.

Max turned to the living room and breathed it in, inhaling the admittedly overly sweet aroma of the carnations seeming to swell from a crystal vase on the marble-topped credenza. The suite bedroom he shared with Stanley even had two canopy beds. And yet he could not sleep.

He now smelled the peppery reek of burnt motor oil, not sure if it had wafted in off the water or from deep down in those crevices below, and he pushed the window shut, careful not to catch the fragile curtains in the window frame or lock. He sighed. He should have been feeling elation. They should be out on those streets, drinking prosecco, toasting to their feats, but this quarter was dead at this hour. This suite of theirs should have been delightful, but the furniture was heavy and too shiny and dark, reminding Max less of dead empires than simply a funeral parlor. Those carnations the color of blood did not help, nor did the dim light. He had only allowed himself to turn on one beaded lamp, as he didn't want to wake Stanley finally sleeping in their suite bedroom, not even with a hint of light through his door.

After the US desk gave them entry to the Free Territory,

Harry had announced to Stanley that he would like him to rest for the night, to let him recover. It might have been the first time all day that Stanley had looked them in the eye. He had added a nod, a disturbingly put-on smile. "I do need to get my wits about me," he had said. "Thanks, fellas."

Harry had left Max and Stanley here at the hotel. "I have to go brief the CIA desk here," he had told Max. "Stay close to our troubled scientist." Harry's concern, Max knew, had less to do with delivering a package in good condition than with unease about Stanley's state of mind. Deep down, his brother still wished Stanley could be convinced that the America Harry himself had embraced was still capable of good in the world.

So Max had stayed close. He had even made sure that he and Stanley shared one of the two suite bedrooms. He had been going to wait up for Harry, but who knew how long the CIA would keep his brother. He turned off the beaded lamp. A final chill followed him from the shut window, and he pulled the belt of his snug, fleece-lined silk hotel robe tighter and dug his toes into the matching slippers.

He slipped inside the dark bedroom and expected to hear Stanley's telltale snore. He let his eyes adjust, could make out a lump under Stanley's covers. But it didn't look right. His heart raced. He checked the window but it was closed and lacked a balcony, too small and high for escape . . . Unless? Max, sweating now, pushed the window open and popped his head out. Vertigo hit him from the height, forcing him to pull back. They were five stories up. He directed his head out once again, cautiously, and scanned the street below to confirm all was clear.

He faced the room. Clicked a light on. Stanley's lump was just his pillow. He paced the room, feeling at paneling, and opened the wardrobe.

"Damn."

The back wall pushed through, a concealed door. *Those damnably baroque Habsburgs*, he thought. The secret door opened to a narrow servants' stairway and up to an attic hallway, then onto the roof.

"Your brother forced me up here," Stanley said. "Sure, not with so many words, but he forced me, practically pushed me off. And you? You went along with it."

Stanley sat out on the steep slant of the centuries-old mansard roof. The only thing holding him there was the small dormer he straddled, his legs hanging off either side. He looked like a boy on a rocking horse, and the juxtaposition would have provided a barrel of laughs on stage or possibly anywhere that wasn't five tall stories above.

Max's gut twitched from a sudden need to retch, to vomit. He straightened up and the panic eased.

"Just . . . wait. Don't move. Please."

Stanley didn't answer, only turned his head to gaze back out again. Max was facing him from the side. The stairs had delivered him onto a modest rooftop patio with a stone balustrade. He pivoted slowly in place, calmer now, but with his arms out as if he were the one balancing on the roof. He peered around in the dark. How had Stanley gotten up there? The wall holding the stairway door also had a sturdy iron pipe running up onto the upper mansard roof. Stanley must have scaled it. Max could only shake his head in the dark. He had to hand it to Stanley. Maybe his expert climb even involved some of that science once offering so much promise but now seeming to doom the world faster than they could dream and think up more of it.

They should have seen this coming, especially after Dora. He should have. It was his duty. He was the heart of the operation.

"I found that secret door," Stanley said to the sky, "and it was so strange, so fantastical, that it just seemed like it was meant to be. You know?"

"No, I don't."

Max took one step his way. Stanley should have had a splendid view of the Gulf of Trieste from up here, but at this dark hour all he got were the same dim and fractured views that Max had just seen from their suite—the streetlamp glows choking in the narrow crevices of the lanes far below, a maze of other roofs slightly lower, and beyond, across the Adriatic Sea, just a solid mass of dark nothingness on until the horizon. Max stood no more than ten feet from Stanley. The balustrade was at arm's length and he touched the rough, practically crumbling stone. He wasn't about to look down. He already felt like the roof patio was moving, an earthquake only he felt. Stanley loomed in silhouette, nearly fused with the dark.

"You're right," he told Stanley. "We should have listened to you better. I should have pushed Harry more."

"Is that his name?" Stanley snorted a laugh. "I wasn't so sure."

"Yes, and mine is Max. I told you."

Max took another step closer, toward Stanley, toward the balustrade. He imagined himself reaching out to Stanley. A narrow gutter extended along the base of the roof. It might prove better than Stanley climbing back up. But the bulky red shingles looked as old and crumbling as the balustrade. Maybe Harry would return and find them up here, he thought. All he had to do was stall. But then a distant light found Stanley's pale face, and Max saw Stanley was scowling at him, a glaring half-moon.

"I wasn't coming to save you," Max said. "I was trying to save my brother. Harry. That's right. He's my brother."

"You did it," Stanley said. "Congrats."

"That's not what I am saying. I'm talking about you. There are things that can still mean something. This world is horrible.

I know." Max pressed both hands to his heart, and it wasn't affected. It was the only way to take the heat off his eyes. "I've seen it firsthand. Competing nations, rival empires? The connivers? The warmongers and the greedy and the cowardly powerful? They can all go to hell."

Stanley nodded. He shifted in his dormer saddle and shingles rustled and cracked around him. It made Stanley stiffen.

Max used the opportunity to take another step forward. He now stood where the balustrade met the wall and roof. If he leaned Stanley's way, he could probably touch his arm or foot if he stretched.

"There are people to live for," he said.

"Supposing I don't want to cooperate. Then what, you think they're just going to let me go, your Americans? Hand me a nice little college appointment in the Midwest somewhere?"

"I do not see why not. Look at me. I now own a little club in Munich."

Stanley laughed. "Oh, that's rich."

"It's true."

"You know what's also true? They let Nazi scientists choose too."

"Touché, Stanley."

A long silence followed. Max, searching for another option, peered at the dormer window under Stanley's crotch but only saw solid wood—the window had been boarded up. He then caught a glimpse of the narrow alley far below and moved away from the edge in a crouch.

"Gravity," Stanley said. "It looks so great on a chalkboard."

Max nodded, finding his feet again, raising his head back into the open air.

"The Americans need to obtain what I have," Stanley said. "What I know. But it's up here." He pointed at his temple. "They will get the information out of me one way or the other. The Soviets were good. Sleight of hand counts for plenty when you don't have outright leverage. My fellow Americans might be better, though. They might even convince me of it for good. Convince me I'm saving the world."

"No," Max said. "You can't believe that, that they—"

"I know it! I told you. They're working on the drugs for such things right now. I was. I . . ." Stanley let the words trail off, and he tugged at the imaginary horn of his imaginary saddle.

"Harry won't let that happen to you." Aubrey Slaipe wouldn't.

"You know what I realized, after Dora?" Stanley said. "I don't think that either of them should have what I know. Neither the Americans, nor the Soviets. Neither deserves it. Neither has come close to proving it. No. I do not wish to live in a future that I helped destroy."

"Please . . ."

"But, you should, Max. You're a good fellow. You know the future can be good. I only know it can be bad. Because of me."

Max leaned out to Stanley, one hand clutching a shingle, the other grasping the balustrade. His chin hovered over the plunging chasm and he didn't care. He could see individual cobblestones, an ancient gutter, grates. He fixed his gaze back on Stanley, who gaped back at him now as if Max were the one about to leap.

"Don't jump, Stanley."

"The Americans will make up some story," Stanley said, his voice hard. "The Soviets, too. Don't you ever believe them."

"Stanley . . ."

"If you can ever get a message to my boys, tell them that I loved them. And that I had tried, I really had."

"No. I won't do it. I won't. You will. Come on . . ."

Max stretched out his arm.

Stanley took a deep breath. Seconds passed. He rocked back and forth, and he pushed off the dormer like a kid on a playground slide without a word or shout of freedom. He caught a shingle then the gutter on the way, which tumbled him around, and, as if defying gravity itself, the wind carried his weight for a moment before he plunged.

MUNICH
Wednesday, June 1
9:00 a.m.

"American Tourist Killed in Soviet Captivity," read the headline in the *New York Herald Tribune* that morning. According to the story, Konstantinos "Stanley" Samaras, a "low-level" US research scientist on vacation in Vienna, was imprisoned by Soviet authorities after he unwittingly strayed into an off-limits area of the Soviet Sector. Mr. Samaras, most recently of Washington, DC, was killed by Soviet guards in an unfortunate altercation that followed. The implication was that Stanley had stood up for himself and for American freedom. The article was short, lower corner of the front page. It carried no quotes, no sources, and might as well have been a press release. They didn't even mention that he had a PhD.

Max had just picked up the paper from the international kiosk in Schwabing on the way to the Kuckoo Nightclub. Now he had to prop himself against the bar inside the empty club. The story drained him, making him feel like he hadn't slept at all even though he'd been out cold for hours from the exhaustion.

When Stanley had leapt to his death in Trieste, Max had rushed down all the stairs of their hotel and through the empty front lobby. No one had noticed him in his robe and slippers, it was so late. Getting his bearings, he had found Stanley on a dark side street. Just bones and flesh. Fortunately, for everyone but Stanley, his face was against the cobblestone. Max had expected others to come rushing out, lights to come on around him, a dog barking, but it was only him and Stanley again. He'd probably made little sound on impact, the walls were so high and close together and void of windows. So Max sat with Stanley a while. Talked to him. Might have even assured him he had done the right thing, under the circumstances. He eventually pulled himself up and wandered back into the lobby, where a bellboy gaped at him and all the blood on his hotel robe and slippers. Max kindly requested that the bellboy first bring him a blanket and then call the American Legation and ask for a Signor Harry Kaspar, who was staying at this very hotel. Max draped the blanket over Stanley and waited for Harry while he rushed over from the CIA desk at the American Legation. And then, after he finally was able to pry Harry's feet from that side street, he stayed up with Harry in their suite even though Harry had nothing to say. Max had opened the windows and they could hear the faint swishes of someone splashing water over the cobblestones. And Harry had cried, openly, for the first time Max could remember.

There had been too much shock and no time to talk from then on. Harry got an early call in their suite, and the next thing they knew they were riding back to Munich in a C-47 cargo plane, inside which there had still been nothing to say among the deafening drone, the rattling of straps and cables, the clanking of metal crates. Upon landing that evening in Munich they had been pulled their separate ways, Max into a taxi home,

Harry into a long, black unmarked sedan that might as well have had "CIA" stenciled on the sides.

Max was to meet Harry here at 10 a.m. He'd been hoping Harry could have met him last night at his old billet near the English Garden, the boardinghouse now run by his former housekeeper Gerlinde, but alas. Harry had had plenty of questions to answer in Trieste and the Americans would have more questions for him here before he could find anything like normalcy.

Normalcy. A cozy routine. Max tried giving it names in his head but they weren't filling his heart with much warmth yet, despite the everyday scene all around him. He pushed the *Tribune* down the bar but it was impeded by a dirty glass, no, two. He took a look around and sighed. The place was filthy. It must have been another wild night. Things always went to hell as soon as he left for a few days. Had it really been over two weeks? He didn't feel much like counting out the days. He wandered around the Kuckoo, his Kuckoo, wincing at the bitter reek of undumped ashtrays and the sour stench of stale beer in glasses and who knew what on the floor. Pretty soon he had pulled off his suit jacket and rolled up his sleeves and was slowly, deliberately placing glasses onto a tray and wiping things down, and it gave him something like peace of mind. What was a little mess, anyway? He found the broom and swept, and swept, in no particular pattern, and ended up finding a faux diamond bracelet on the floor. He looked forward to seeing its owner beam when she returned for it, and for the first time in probably days he smiled to himself all alone. He went down to the cellar to put it in the safe and found all his money inside, just as Aubrey Slaipe had promised. Of course the Munich CIA desk had known the combination.

He wondered if his lovely waitress Eva was still sleeping upstairs. That sweet voice. Those dimples. She just might make it as a singer. The first thing he would do after Harry left? He'd take a few dollars from that safe, head upstairs, knock on Eva's door, and invite her out to a wonderful meal.

9:55 a.m. Harry pushed through the door at five till, just as Max knew he would, always early. Max was sitting at the far end of the now gleaming bar top, a ledger and a small pot of coffee before him, his suit jacket hanging neatly off the high-backed barstool. Harry sat with him, and Max poured him a cup from the two he had set out.

"Thanks. And good morning," Harry said. "Get any sleep?"

"Trying. You?"

Harry only chuckled. He spotted the *Tribune* and snorted and Max didn't need to ask.

"Publicity men come up with an angle faster than we can even feed them a line," Max said. He never called it "propaganda" around Harry.

Harry stared at the bar a moment, his coffee raised halfway to his mouth as if wanting to speak but knowing he should not. Max glanced at the ledger. It had been a hell of night indeed, best ever. Eyebrow raising. Maybe his staff had even celebrated after, thus the mess, and he couldn't blame them for that. And yet he felt little excitement, despite having come so far since 1946. He should have felt inspiration for the night to come here in the bar, Wednesdays always being busy, and he might even perform a few numbers himself, maybe a duet with Eva. But all he could think about was the mission and undertaking another one to counteract the failures of the last, and who in the hell could he help that didn't end up getting hurt? The numbers and lines of his ledger blurred from it.

"Wait till you get a load of the Soviet line," Harry said. "*Pravda, Neues Deutschland*, both reporting that a low-level police official named Hartmut Dietz committed suicide after failing his rehabilitation. Usual propaganda. Dietz was from the West and a former Nazi, so good riddance."

"Good lord, that was fast."

Harry shrugged. "They like to get ahead of the story. Probably had one prepared. Those purges we talked about are already underway, I'm hearing."

Harry could have just as well been talking about the Stanley Samaras story. Max almost told him so. He poured Harry more coffee instead. He pretended to analyze the ledger. He knew that he'd never be able to get Stanley's message to his kids. The Americans would never allow it, not Harry, Slaipe, none of them. It would remain Classified for eternity.

"Well, what are we doing here?" Max said. "You called this meeting."

Harry slowly turned to him, his head on a swivel. "You know why."

"I suppose so, yes."

"Mr. Slaipe likes to go over certain things just between us, like '46. You remember. He'll be here any minute."

They sat in a silence. Sipping coffee. Max pushed aside the ledger. He couldn't make heads or tails of it anyway.

"How's business?" Harry said.

"Good. It's good." Max held up hands as if to say, *Who woulda thought?*

Harry looked around the room. "Squeaky clean, too. Spiffy."

"Thanks." They sat in more silence. Max was always surprised how little they had to talk about when it wasn't a mission. "Have you written to *Mutti* und *Vati*?" he said finally.

"I will. You?"

"I intend to, yes—"

"Kat was right about Dietz," Harry said. "What she did."

Max nodded, but he wasn't so sure anymore, despite Irina. Dietz had let Dora live, after all. Maybe imprisonment was better. He added a snort. "You remember something that Stanley said? He told us that he was going to miss going to the diner. Future tense. He was never going back. I didn't pick up on it."

Harry patted his lower arm. "It's a new type of war we are in, brother."

"I'll say. They used to talk about wars to end wars. Now it's just about ending each other."

"You got me there. Listen, I can tell you one thing: there was nothing good on those papers Reiter brought with him. That's the early word from our analyzers. Just random notes, everyday equations."

"No, I expect there wouldn't have been. He and his mind were not going anywhere."

"Keep this under your hat," Harry added after a few beats, lowering his voice. "Word is there have been certain experiments, in their early stages, between both sides. What had Stanley called them? Psychiatric drugs. Hallucinatory. So he might have been right all around."

Max's heart sunk. He could practically feel it balanced on his knees under the bar counter. "He also said they were working out the delivery method, how to affect people worse. Destroy their minds. So I imagine that grim leap of faith he took off that roof was always looking better to him than having his own work turned on him. Turned on all of us."

Harry only grunted. He seemed to have shrunk at the bar, like a man on a bender gambling all he had, all day and night, and here he was betting the last of it. "I tried doubling down," he said, as if reading Max's thoughts. "But you know something? I only got burned."

"I caused Stanley's death," Max said. "If I never would've been so stubborn as to come after you, he wouldn't be dead. Dietz wouldn't have found us with his plan. None of it."

"No, I was the one," Harry said. "If I hadn't made Reiter go after those papers, Dietz would never have caught up with us. He'd be in a Gulag or he'd have taken that goddamn ratline to, who knows, South America? America. I hate to think it. No, Max. I screwed it. I misread the endgame. Reiter's as well as Dietz's. And where would I have been without you? I'd probably be dead, or in Bautzen. And I never would've seen Kat again."

Max couldn't help nodding to that last part.

"So we're even," Harry said.

They laughed. But their smiles faded.

"All that really counts is helping people," Max said. "Somehow. All the rest makes a smart guy like Stanley jump."

They heard a precise knock on the front door to the Kuckoo Nightclub. Max and Harry jumped off their barstools, stood up straight, and Max shouted, "Come in." The door swung open and an athletic young man in a blue suit and crew cut entered and couldn't have been more American if he were wearing one of their colorful leather football helmets. "*Gut-en Morg-en*," he said in equally accented German and planted himself with his back to the door. "Is anyone else on premises, gentlemen?"

"Just us chickens," Max said.

Harry glared at him. "No, Arthur."

The crew cut named Arthur nodded and pivoted back out the door.

"They're using more security now," Harry said to Max out the side of his mouth.

The door swung open again and Aubrey Slaipe strode in, smiling, surprisingly, and holding his hat as if ready to twirl it, except he was using his artificial hand.

"Long time, gents," he said and directed them to a table as if he owned the place. He passed on coffee. He sat facing them, his smile now faded, replaced by reddish stretch marks and creases on pinkish skin as if he'd slept too hard.

"If only Frau Katarina Buchholz could be here too. She's a formidable one. Listen, I'm all for what she does. It's their due. Those Israelis, they sure know what they're doing. I don't know where they get their info, whether from us or someone else, but they can have it."

Max and Harry nodded along.

Slaipe leaned forward. He glanced toward the door. "Between us? Our All-American Superman out there is not just my body-guard—they're keeping a keen eye on me. When I was young and something like impressionable, if not approachable, college and slightly beyond, I was a red-card-carrying member. That's right, don't look so shocked. Communist Party, Wobblies, the whole kit and caboodle."

Max fell silent. Harry might have snorted.

"But I'm all vetted and clean," Slaipe said and smoothed out his pant leg as if to prove it.

"For now," Harry said. "Anyone can use that against you. There's the House Un-American Activities Committee, there's—"

"Indeed. And I suspect they might try. America, on the home front at least, isn't as confident as it seems as the new world power."

With that, their debriefing commenced. It was not long. Max barely listened, answering on cue. He wondered if they all were not just tools like Stanley in the new Cold War. There was even the blackmail required for *Kompromat*—Max's WWII under-cover mission for the SS, and Harry's commandeering a plunder train for vigilante justice. Not to mention Aubrey Slaipe's distant past now. It could always be used against them, by either side.

And then Slaipe was standing finally, slipping his hat back on, and Max and Harry walked him to the door.

"There's something that's still not clear to me," Max said.

Slaipe stopped. "Oh?"

"Did you know that Harry was going to go strike out on his own?"

Slaipe glanced at Harry. He clucked his tongue. "You saw the look on my face after Harry bolted. I don't ever want to feel that way again."

"But perhaps that was only for show?" Max said.

"Max knows a performance when he sees one," Harry said. "Can I just tell him, Mr. Slaipe?"

Slaipe removed his hat. "Be my guest."

"We ginned up the prisoner swap so I could keep going, to look like I was out of the fold by choice. Out of control. Reiter was too important. Mr. Slaipe here knew about it and, yes, I know what you're thinking. We used ratline contacts. I'm still not proud of it. Happy now?"

They started for the door again.

"Wait," Max said. "That's not all. You, the CIA, would love someone like Dietz to be your man in the new state of East Germany, one of them anyway. To stay there. What if I had agreed to his terms, relayed the message? Over there, would he now be a double agent, mole, whatever it's called."

Slaipe fought a smile. "You're perceptive as ever, Max. But Dietz didn't want to play along in the end, did he? Things were getting too hot for him. So he made his own move. So we shall never know. Amen."

Harry lowered his head as if praying—that or just relieved he didn't have to play a part in Dietz becoming a CIA treasure.

Slaipe led them to the door and finally put on his hat.

"Well done," he told them. "None of this was your fault, and in some quarters, it's even being claimed as a victory. Files closed."

"I just hope my name's not on that file," Max said.

"Consider it done." Slaipe gave him a long stare, and then the both of them. "Be careful, you two. At some point, you do something so much, you become what you're doing instead of what you're trying to become. Take it from me, the pot calling the kettle black."

And Slaipe disappeared back into the surprisingly gray early summer morning.

Max and Harry stood there a moment.

"I didn't want you to have to deal with Dietz," Harry said. "It's not just his past with us. Who knows what he could've pulled."

"I know. It's all right."

"Talk about a snafu," Harry said.

"Speak for yourself," Max said. "All I ever wanted was to get your ear back on."

Harry smiled and touched his ear to make sure. "Well done, like the man said."

"Champagne?" Max said. "Finally?"

Two minutes later they were back at the bar, glasses out, cork popped. It was only postwar *Sekt* but not bad for German stuff. They didn't sit. Any good toast demanded they stand.

Max held up his glass, bubbling away. "At least we have each other," he said.

"Nuts to that," Harry said, raising his glass, and Max already knew the toast. "At least the world has her."

Katarina.

AFTERWORD

This story is fiction but, as in my other novels, certain persons and events are based in truth and found in the historical record. The early CIA, only just created from the National Security Act of 1947, was at first a small organization with a poor track record. Its efforts to place intelligence networks behind the Iron Curtain failed miserably from Yugoslavia to Latvia, its agents usually discovered immediately. Thus Harry's and Aubrey Slaipe's worries about missions constantly failing and lives lost, their concerns in turn fueling Harry's decision to go rogue. His target, the scientist Stanley Samaras, is notional but based on a variety of scientists who were voicing doubts about the rapid advancement of modern weaponry through science. Real-life examples include: the influential yet pro-Soviet American bacteriologist Theodor Rosebury, whose revealing journal articles likely prompted the Soviets to increase their germ warfare efforts; US atomic researcher George Koval, who was born in the US to Russian immigrants but, after spying for the Soviet atomic bomb project, left on a European vacation in 1948 and fled to the Soviet Union; American biological warfare expert Frank Olson, who leapt to his death from a Manhattan hotel in 1953 under suspicious circumstances after sharing with colleagues his deep concerns about their germ warfare projects.

In the early Cold War, the US biological weapons program was centered around Camp Detrick in Maryland. The Soviets had their own research centers and facilities, but most are believed to have resided deep inside the Soviet Union itself—the facility I place in Soviet Poland is purely fictional, to keep Stanley Samaras within reach of Harry. The specter of such weaponry, while banned by treaties, remains as horrific as ever.

Regarding Poland: The Soviets actually did resettle Communist Greek refugees from the Greek Civil War in Zgorzelec, along the new postwar border of East Germany. Many of these Greeks later returned to their homeland or were deported, but the vestiges and descendants of those Greek refugees live on in Poland today.

The fledgling East German intelligence agencies Hartmut Dietz worked for, such as K5, did exist at the time, small and limited in scope, strictly controlled by the Soviet Military Administration in Germany. The notorious Stasi we all know today had its roots in this period, after a series of purges of the type that would spook a questionable operator like Dietz into fleeing west. Another real-life organization in my story was the VVN, or *Vereinigung der Verfolgten des Naziregimes*—the Union of Persecutees of the Nazi Regime, which Katarina uses as her cover.

The Jewish Avengers were an actual group, also known as Nakam or Gmul. They started in secret inside a British unit called the Jewish Brigade right after the war, their British cover allowing them to hunt and assassinate known Nazi war criminals. After the immediate postwar period, however, such groups returned home to participate in the founding of the State of Israel and the wars to come. The notion of the Israelis using a gentile assassin (or more) to fill the role unnoticed is not known to history but seemed the perfect mission for

Katarina given her background and need to atone for her native Germany.

The so-called ratlines existed as well. They helped Nazi fugitives escape to South America and elsewhere, often passing through fascist Spain or the Vatican with the help of sympathetic Catholics. Sadly, the Americans eventually got involved just as Harry loathes in this story. It all came down to another of those lethal and sometimes shameful competitions created by the Cold War: US intelligence, as part of Operation Paperclip, used the nefarious escape routes to bring over important Nazi scientists and military experts before the Soviets snatched them up. My specific route behind the Iron Curtain is fictional. But for a survivor like Dietz, maneuvering to make the most of his value, offering himself to the American-run Gehlen Organization composed of former Nazi intelligence officers, the ratline that he and Harry are fated to share is right up his alley.

I'd like to thank a few people who helped make this story all it can be. My agent, Peter Riva, never gave up on it, and Mara Anastas at Open Road Integrated Media gave it a new life along with the Kaspar Brother series and other novels. I'm grateful to Emma Chapnick, Laurie McGee, Sidney Rioux, and the whole team at Open Road. Freelance editor Scott Pack and beta readers Lauren Lanier and Carie Ageneau provided valuable editorial feedback. And my wife, René, as always, was there to support me every step of the way.

Lines of Deception is the fourth book in the Kaspar Brothers series. The story of Max Kaspar forced into a suicidal mission during WWII is told in *The Losing Role*, while Harry Kaspar's deadly postwar rite of passage follows in *Liberated*. Max and Harry reunite in 1946 Munich and tangle with the Soviets in *Lost Kin*.

ABOUT THE AUTHOR

Steve Anderson is the author of the Kaspar Brothers novels: *The Losing Role*, *Liberated*, and *Lost Kin*. *Under False Flags* is the prequel to his novel *The Preserve*. Anderson was a Fulbright Fellow in Germany and is a literary translator of bestselling German fiction as well as a freelance editor. He lives in Portland, Oregon.

stephenfanderson.com
stephenfanderson.com/mailing-list